Beloved Bookroom Mysteries by Dorothy St. James

The Broken Spine
A Perfect Bind

A
Perfect
Bind

Dorothy St. James

Berkley Prime Crime
New York

BERKLEY PRIME CRIME
Published by Berkley
An imprint of Penguin Random House LLC
penguinrandomhouse.com

BERKLEY and the BERKLEY & B colophon are registered trademarks and
BERKLEY PRIME CRIME is a trademark of Penguin Random House LLC.

Library of Congress Cataloging-in-Publication Data

Names: St. James, Dorothy, author.
Title: A perfect bind / Dorothy St. James.
Description: First Edition. | New York: Berkley Prime Crime, 2021. |
Series: Beloved bookroom mysteries; 2
Identifiers: LCCN 2021012444 (print) | LCCN 2021012445 (ebook) |
ISBN 9780593098608 (hardcover) | ISBN 9780593098622 (ebook)
Subjects: GSAFD: Mystery fiction.
Classification: LCC PS3619.T245 P47 2021 (print) |
LCC PS3619.T245 (ebook) | DDC 813/.6—dc23
LC record available at https://lccn.loc.gov/2021012444
LC ebook record available at https://lccn.loc.gov/2021012445

Printed in the United States of America
1   3   5   7   9   10   8   6   4   2

Book design by Alison Cnockaert

For the everyday heroes:
The store clerks, the janitors, the medical professionals,
the cooks, the dishwashers, factory workers,
the librarians,
and all those who came to work despite the pandemic
and kept the world going.
Thank you.

A SHORT LIST OF KICK-ASS
LIBRARIANS THROUGH THE AGES

by Tori Green, Owner of Perks Café in Cypress, South Carolina

Dorothy Porter: In the 1930s, the librarian of Howard University's Moorland Foundation created her own classification system in response to the Dewey decimal system's institutionalized racism. Her system organized collections to highlight the role of African Americans in all subject areas.

Zoia Horn: In 1970, this U.S. librarian was sent to jail because she refused to testify against library patrons who had gathered to plan antiwar protests.

Alia Muhammad Baker: In 2003, during the Iraq War, the head librarian in the Al Basrah Central Library in Basra, Iraq, broke the rules and removed thirty thousand books from the besieged library. She stored the books (many historic and irreplaceable) in her home and in homes of neighbors. The library was destroyed before all the books were saved.

Chapter One

As a rule, librarians hate secrets. Our entire lives revolve around providing free and open access to information. Good information. Correct information. We abhor lies. We rip the covers off cover-ups.

So what was I, Trudell Becket, dedicated assistant librarian, doing tending a secret as carefully as a gardener tends her most fragile flowers? Or as devotedly as a cat lover might care for a certain stray tabby who had taken up residence in her cottage?

It's for the books, I reminded myself as I hurried down Main Street with a heavy tote bag hanging from each shoulder. One bag was filled with the books I'd loaned out to neighbors here in the Town of Cypress. And the other? Well, never mind about that one. Like anything important, secrets take work.

The warm September sun formed dappled patterns on the sidewalk as it shone through the century-old cypress trees lining the street. I paused for a moment in front of the town's centerpiece—the public library.

This stately building was one of fourteen public libraries built at the turn of the twentieth century in South Carolina by Andrew Carnegie. Designed to resemble a classic Roman temple, its polished stone exterior and grand arching windows had served as my personal palace of dreams after my parents' divorce. The books it contained inside had saved my life.

I jogged up the full flight of grand steps, past a row of granite columns, and through the library's front entrance. The foyer, with impressive marble walls and terrazzo flooring, had a ceiling gilded with faded gold paint.

I rushed through the first floor without pausing to brew the first pot of coffee or chat with the rest of the staff signing in at the front desk.

This secret I'd been tending for the past month was the cause of my haste. Every morning I dreaded what I might find in the basement.

The library's back stairs led down into a raised basement. Down here no embellishments decorated the walls. My sensible shoes squeaked against the plain concrete floor as I passed a warren of storage rooms and a metal back door that opened into a small parking lot and alleyway.

I hurried on, turned a corner, and—

Not again.

I wanted to stomp my foot, but such a violent motion would upset the little stowaway tucked in my second tote bag, the one hanging from my right shoulder. Dewey Decimal, a skinny tabby cat, stuck his paw out of the bag and swatted my elbow.

"It happened again," I told him.

This was the third time.

Dewey lifted his head. He gazed at me with his big green eyes in a thoughtful manner as if he understood.

After closing, someone had broken into the library. The past two times this had happened, none of the other librarians had noticed that an intruder had entered the building. The pricey computer equipment, 3D printers, and sewing machines upstairs were all untouched. Instead, the villain had crept down to the basement and to the heavy double doors that led into what used to be a WWII-era bomb shelter. They then picked the old lock and had wreaked their mischief here.

The old bomb shelter was no longer simply a forgotten relic from the past. Last month my book-loving friends and I had transformed the space into a bookroom. A *secret* bookroom. A vibrant bookroom. A place where the books lining the shelves could serve as a lifeline for others in the community who needed them as dearly as I once had.

As I walked through the old bomb shelter's partially opened doors I shuddered.

Like before, books had been tossed off their shelves. This time the mystery section had been attacked. The adventures of Miss Marple, Koko and Yum Yum, and Amelia Peabody lay scattered across the floor. Covers had been bent. Pages crumbled. Shelving units torn from the walls.

I closed my eyes and drew in a long, slow breath.

Who would do this?

How could someone do something so very evil?

I couldn't report the break-in. I couldn't ask the police to investigate. I couldn't even tell the head librarian what was happening. To report it would mean revealing the bookroom's existence.

My friends and I had created this space after the town manager had modernized the library upstairs. The renovations had included removing all the printed books in order to create a bookless library. *A library without books?* The very idea of it still made absolutely no sense.

But that is what had happened to our library. The shelves of hardbacks had been replaced by tablets, computers, e-readers, and a café. The town manager had ordered this done because he'd wanted to use the hyper-modern library as a way to impress the high-tech industries he planned to lure to our little town.

In a desperate act of rebellion, I'd saved hundreds of the books before they could be taken to the landfill. By creating this space, I'd broken the rules. I'd put my job at risk. And because I'd taken the books from the library, I may have even broken the law.

The legality of what I'd done wasn't something I had researched too closely. (I really didn't want to know.) Keeping this bookroom going was my passion, my reason for getting up in the morning.

Now, inexplicably, someone was stealing into our sanctuary and tossing around those same books I'd vowed to protect as if they were worthless. Why? If this break-in was anything like the past two, my friends and I would soon discover nothing had been taken.

With a sigh, I closed the vault doors.

I then carefully lowered the second tote bag to the floor and let Dewey out of the bag. The skinny tabby cat, crouched low, walked cautiously around the room. He sniffed one of the books lying open on the floor and arched his back. His black-and-brown-striped fur fluffed up. "Hiss," he said.

"I'm unhappy about the mess too." I started to gather the books, putting the ones that hadn't been damaged in one pile and the ones with bent and crumpled pages in another. The binding from Agatha Christie's second Miss Marple mystery novel, *The Body in the Library*, had been completely ripped apart.

"Monsters," I whispered as I cradled the broken hardback and tried not to cry. "What kind of beast would do such a thing?" I asked Dewey, who was tilting his head from one side to the other while staring curiously at the wall where shelves had been ripped down.

"It's the poltergeist," a gravelly voice answered.

Startled, I crouched down to Dewey's level and stared into his wise green eyes. Did the cat just talk to me? I shook my head. That was ridiculous, simply ridiculous. Cats didn't talk.

Besides, the voice had come from behind me. I stood up and turned around to find a man in his late seventies dressed in tweed pants, matching tweed vest, and brown bow tie standing in the doorway. His silver hair needed to be combed. His wire-rimmed glasses slid down his nose. He pushed them back up with a chubby, callused finger.

"Mr. Crawford," I said. "You startled me."

Hubert Crawford was one of our regular patrons. He was also president of the local museum board. He took his position as caretaker of history seriously. He dressed in vintage suits as if he lived in the early twentieth century, drove a 1950 Chevy that left a trail of thick smoke as it coughed its way down the streets, and refused to touch a computer.

Dewey sidled up to him and, purring loudly, rubbed against the man's leg. Hubert reached down and scratched my cat behind his ears. "Land's sake, has anyone ever told you that your cat's stripes form what looks like a skull on his head?"

Pretty much everyone who had ever met Dewey told me they saw the skull. Far too often for my liking, if truth be told.

I gave Hubert the same answer I gave everyone. "I suppose if I squinted I might be able to imagine seeing something like a skull in his markings. If I may ask, how did you get in here?" The library didn't open until ten.

I took a step back. Was Hubert Crawford the vandal hurting the books? Had he returned to the scene of the crime? Was I in danger?

Instead of doing anything remotely sinister, he nudged his glasses up the bridge of his nose again. "I walked in through the front doors," he said. He pointed to the institutional clock above the door. The clock's hands pointed to ten minutes after ten.

Oh no! I'd spent too much time down here. I should have been setting up in the main library. The other librarians, especially the sharp-eyed head librarian, Lida Farnsworth, must have noticed my absence by now.

"If you'll excuse me, I need to get upstairs," I said as I carefully set the ruined copy of *The Body in the Library* on a nearby table.

Hubert didn't budge from where he was standing, blocking the doors. "I was wondering how long it would take for it to make its presence known," he said as if he hadn't noticed how I was trying to squeeze past him. "I had suspected something like this would happen."

"You did?" That stopped me.

"I knew *the thing* wouldn't like that you turned this basement into a bookroom and made it a place where people hang out. It has never liked people, you know."

A thing? Not a person?

I shook my head. I had no idea what he was talking about.

"The thing. The thing. The poltergeist, girl." He huffed. "Haven't you done your research? The poltergeist is coming in here and flinging the books around."

"Poltergeist?" Was he serious?

He nodded, which only caused his glasses to slide down his nose again. "My maw-maw used to talk about it. She worked here as a girl, back in the early twenties. Nineteen-twenties, that is." He launched into a lengthy lecture about what the town was like back then, listing who was mayor at the time and what shops lined Main Street.

"Your maw-maw? You mean your grandmother?" I prompted, hoping to get him back to what she'd seen. "What did she say?"

"Oh yes. Maw-maw was my father's mother. Dreadful stories she used to tell us youngsters. They gave me nightmares something fierce. My mother thought those nightmares meant I was being attacked by a demon. She'd say all kinds of prayers over me and made me sleep with a window open and a Bible under my pillow, which—let me tell you— only scared me more. But back in those days it was a commonly held belief that demons came for youngsters like that. In fact—"

"What stories did your maw-maw tell you?" I asked, trying to get him back on track.

"Oh . . ." He nudged his glasses up his nose yet again. "Maw-maw used to recount strange happenings at the library. She would hear odd noises coming from the basement. The full-time librarians had warned her to never come down here. They told her it wasn't safe. They told her about the poltergeist who ruled over this area of the library, an angry force from beyond the veil. A demon perhaps, the same kind my mother feared was haunting my dreams. I never personally saw evidence that a poltergeist existed, not until you opened up this place." He rapped a knuckle against the metal door he was still blocking.

"With all due respect to your grandmother, this isn't the work of a ghost." I started to try to slide behind him again. "If you'll excuse me, I need to check in upstairs before someone comes down here searching for me."

"Of course. Of course. There was some sort of hubbub upstairs as I was coming in. Overheard someone complaining about a class the library is offering because it involved devil worship."

"I have no idea what that could be about. We aren't offering any classes like that." Mrs. Farnsworth would never stand for it.

He shrugged and finally stepped out of my way. But as he did, his brow furrowed. "We'll need to research the troubles happening down here some more. See if we can't figure out what caused the poltergeist in the first place. Perhaps that knowledge will help us figure out how to stop it from destroying this place."

"You do that," I said, humoring him. The damage that kept happening to the secret bookroom was the work of a very real vandal, not some made-up phantom.

But who could do such a hateful thing *to books*?

And why?

That was something I was determined to find out.

Chapter Two

Goodness gracious, Tru! There you are," Flossie Finnegan-Baker exclaimed in a voice that was both whispery and frantic. If she hadn't called out to me, I probably would have collided with her. I'd been so wrapped up in thinking about why someone would be wreaking havoc in the basement as I hurried up the stairs and out into the first floor that I hadn't been paying attention to my surroundings. As it was, I had to do a little sideways dance to catch my balance and keep from landing on my friend's lap.

She abruptly halted her wheelchair's mad dash toward me. Her gaze darted toward the front desk. "Mrs. Farnsworth is complaining up a blue streak how you hadn't showed up for work. Hearing that nearly made my heart stop. I was worried something bad had happened."

"Something bad *did* happen," I cried a little too loudly.

Lida Farnsworth's sharp gaze snapped in my direction.

The head librarian was a stickler for keeping the library as silent as possible. "People need the opportunity to hear themselves think," she liked to remind us. "Heaven knows there's not many places where that can happen. They even have televisions at the bank blaring out the news. Can you imagine?"

"*Something did happen*," I repeated, this time in a whisper.

"Not again. Is it—?"

Before Flossie could finish her question, I held up my hand. "I had better go talk with Mrs. Farnsworth. If she thought I wasn't here, it must mean I forgot to sign in. Again."

"Tru, you really need to be more careful. If you keep making these mistakes, she'll start questioning why you're spending so much time in the basement," Flossie cautioned as we made our way toward the front desk. "And if she suspects something funny is going on in her library, you know she'll start poking around. And we can't have that."

"No, we cannot." Flossie was right. I needed to do a better job pretending nothing was wrong.

Even though Flossie was nearly eighty years old—and had graduated high school in the same class as the stern Mrs. Farnsworth— she appeared to be decades younger than the head librarian. Maybe her youthful appearance came from the humor that nearly always sparkled in her eyes. Or maybe it was from her loose, free-spirited hippie, tie-dyed clothes. Today she was dressed in various shades of red.

Despite our forty-year age difference, she was one of my dearest friends and most ardent supporters of the secret bookroom.

"How did Mrs. Farnsworth seem, besides in high dudgeon because she thought I had failed to show up this morning, I mean?" I asked.

"She was scowling." Flossie shuddered.

I winced. While Mrs. Farnsworth was rarely happy, making her *un*happy was akin to sticking a fork in an electric socket. It's something you should never do.

"Don't worry. I covered for you. I told her I thought you were in the bathroom," Flossie said with a satisfied nod.

"Please, tell me you're joking." Please. Please. *Please.*

"Well, it was the first excuse that came to mind," Flossie confessed. "Why?"

"You used that one to explain my disappearance the last time someone had vandalized the bookroom." For days afterward, Mrs. Farnsworth had followed me around while providing all sorts of dietary advice on how to keep regular. Apparently, regularity was a topic near and dear to the head librarian's heart. She talked with me about ways to promote gut health for *hours*. "We seriously need to come up with something else—anything else—to tell her for the next time this happens."

"Do you think it'll happen again?" Flossie sounded alarmed.

"I have no reason not to think it. If only we knew why it was happening in the first place, perhaps we could take steps to prevent future break-ins."

"Was anything taken this time?" she asked.

"Not that I could tell. But there was damage. Like before, the shelves had been pulled off the walls. And several of the books have been harmed." Some of my favorite books.

Flossie made a noise in her throat that sounded like a growl.

"This time it happened in the mystery section." It was a section of the library where many of my oldest and most beloved fictional best friends lived.

Her growl deepened. "We need to figure out how to put a stop to this."

"If you ask me, whoever has been messing with our books should be defaced," I whispered, and then quickly added, "Is that terrible of me?"

"Honey, of course not. I was thinking the same thing," she whispered back. "And worse."

With fierce support like that, how could I not love Flossie?

I wanted to brainstorm with her about shoring up security in the basement, but I spotted the library's new IT tech, Anne Lowery, marching toward us.

"There's no coffee in the break room," Anne complained before she even reached us.

This morning her inky-black hair sported several pretty rainbow streaks. But there was nothing resembling a happy rainbow in her surly expression.

"The café sells coffee." I nodded to the small café that had replaced the children's section during the renovation.

"But you make coffee. Every morning," she grumbled. "You and Mrs. Farnsworth are as irritatingly reliable as clocks. But, this morning, there was no coffee."

"I had something else I needed to attend to this morning." I sighed. "I'll brew a pot after I talk with Mrs. Farnsworth."

"Hours late." She huffed several more times. "Figures. Nothing goes right in this backwoods place." Anne had relocated to Cypress from Silicon Valley. To say she'd been experiencing culture shock would be an understatement.

"What's really bothering you this morning, dear?" Flossie asked, which I thought odd. Anne was always going on and on about how she couldn't buy this or couldn't find that in town. She was like one of those vintage audio vinyl records my father liked to collect, one of the broken ones that was always stuck on a groove. Complain. *Skip.* Complain. *Skip.* Complain.

"First, I find out that that shifty mechanic couldn't be bothered to open his garage this morning to explain to me why he's not done fixing my car's radiator. You know the first time he 'fixed' it, he installed a used radiator that didn't last a week? And then Reverend Goodloe sent his wife to the library this morning to tell Mrs. Farnsworth that the class I'm offering this month was an abomination and had to be stopped." Anne followed beside me, clumping unhappily in her leather boots.

Was that the hubbub Hubert had been talking about? "You're not offering classes on devil worshipping, are you?" I had to ask.

"Not you too!" she said too loudly.

Mrs. Farnsworth's gaze snapped in our direction again.

"That crazy Reverend Goodloe came in first to complain. And then that lazy mechanic, the same one who messed up my car, also claims to be Goodloe's right-hand man. He came in the next day. And now the reverend's wife is here," Anne muttered. "All of them are saying I'm corrupting the good people of this town, which is nonsense."

The reverend's wife, Mrs. Hennie Goodloe, dressed in a stark black dress that resembled a nun's habit, was standing next to Mrs. Farnsworth, angrily tapping the toe of her highly polished Mary Janes.

"I suppose you're going to take that woman's side." Anne huffed several times. "Everything I do around here is destroying the fabric of Cypress's society, isn't that what you've been telling everyone?" She huffed again. "It's a tai chi class, by the way. I'm certified to teach it."

I'd heard of tai chi. "Isn't that like slow karate?"

"No, dear. It's a kind of tea," Flossie said, and winked at me. Her eyes sparkled with mischief. "They sell it in the café over there. Are you going to teach us how to make it at home?"

"That's chai tea," Anne corrected. She started to say something else, but Flossie blustered on.

"Yes. That's the stuff. I prefer to drink Coke, mind you, but I'll sign up for your class. I've always wondered about the spices they put into chai tea. The rich flavors remind me of my travels to India. Such an aromatic country. Did you know Masala chai originally didn't contain black tea? That ingredient was added to the chai recipe in the 1800s after the British started tea plantations in India."

Anne's ears had taken on a red hue. "I'm not teaching a class about tea," she said from between clenched teeth.

"Can't imagine why Mrs. Farnsworth would stop you," Flossie said. "That drink has nothing to do with worshipping the devil. And people around here do love their tea. Did you know that sweet tea was invented in the nearby town of Summerville? They even have a festival that—"

"I don't understand why everyone is so ignorant in this backwater town. It's not as if you people don't have access to the Internet." Anne's voice sounded strained.

I put a hand on Flossie's shoulder. "My friend is teasing you, Anne. Aren't you, Flossie?"

"I am teasing. So sorry, dear. It's the devil in me that makes me do it. Oh, but you're not teaching about devils, are you?" Flossie said with a gurgling laugh. "I do know a fair bit about tai chi. I've taken classes from a renowned Lao Shi in China. He was very accommodating of my limitations." She tapped the arm of her wheelchair.

Anne sniffed. It was her way of accepting an apology. "It doesn't matter. Those religious Goodloes are on a mission to make sure I won't get a chance to teach the course. No class. No car. No coffee. It's enough to make me want to kill someone."

The former town manager had hired Anne to oversee the library's modernization process. Anne's goals had been in direct conflict with mine from the outset. She had cheered the town manager's efforts to dispose of the printed books, while I had done everything possible— *short of murder*—to stop that madness.

She'd won. The books were gone, save for the ones I had squirreled away in the basement's secret bookroom. The library no longer looked anything like the once-sacred temple of learning that had served the community for over a hundred years. It was now filled with sofas, meeting rooms, computers, and electronic equipment I was only beginning to learn how to use.

"I am sorry about the Goodloes. They can be . . . rigid in their beliefs," I said, hoping to make her feel a little bit better. Pastor Goodloe had started his own church when he had disagreed with Reverend Percy. He had claimed Percy was too liberal and that the man was leading the flock astray. I didn't know the entire story. Mama Eddy always took me to the church on the other side of the downtown park.

Anyhow, starting splinter churches after a philosophical or personal clash was a common pastime in Cypress. There were at least a dozen other churches around town that were founded after a disagreement between parishioners.

"Anne, I am sorry about the coffee. I shouldn't have been in such a rush." If I'd followed my regular morning routine of signing in and brewing the coffee, neither Anne nor Mrs. Farnsworth would have noticed my absence.

"I suppose you were you doing something"—Anne pointed to the floor—"down there?"

"Maybe." I stopped and took a hard look at my younger coworker. Shortly after I'd opened the secret bookroom, Anne had nearly discovered what I'd done. While I don't think she had ever been inside the room, she knew I was sneaking my kitty into the library and leaving him in the old bomb shelter. She liked to hold that knowledge over me like the sword of Damocles held aloft by a single horsehair, ready to come crashing down on me at any moment.

Had Anne broken into the bookroom? Was she the one damaging the books because she considered them hopelessly old-fashioned?

She flashed a glance over at Mrs. Farnsworth. A sly grin spread across the younger woman's face.

"Meow," she said as she made a motion as if her hand were a cat's claw.

Mrs. Farnsworth looked our way and frowned.

"I already said I'd make the coffee," I whispered.

"One of these days Mrs. Farnsworth will realize how much time you're spending in the basement with that cat of yours instead of doing your job, and she'll fire you." Anne wrinkled her nose and looked as if she was honestly concerned. "When that happens, you'll have no one to blame but yourself."

"You're right, Anne. I do need to be more careful."

"I was just telling her the same thing," Flossie chimed in.

Anne sucked in a sharp breath. Her shoulders tightened.

"We're agreeing with you. I have been careless." I'd been recklessly spending more and more time in the bookroom lately. Although my friends took turns volunteering in the basement, assisting patrons and checking out the printed books, I couldn't seem to help myself. In my mind, libraries were about the books. I hated to stay away from them.

"Mrs. Farnsworth," I said as I hurried over to her. "I am so sorry that I forgot to sign in this morning. I was—"

Mrs. Farnsworth cut me off. "Not to worry. Not to worry. Flossie explained." She patted her flat belly sagely. "It's an affliction that can strike any one of us. Have you been using the fiber supplements I recommended?" Mrs. Farnsworth then turned to Hennie Goodloe. "Ms. Becket has been suffering from terrible digestive issues these past couple of weeks."

"The poor dear," Hennie said. "I'll pray for your recovery. As for the other business, Mrs. Farnsworth, I expect that, for the good of your patrons, you'll do the right thing."

"I always do the right thing," Mrs. Farnsworth shot back.

Hennie gave a sharp nod of satisfaction and marched toward the exit, her thick-soled shoes clapping loudly on the terrazzo floor.

"The nerve of that woman to lecture me on morals." Mrs. Farnsworth looked like she could kill someone. The expression seemed to be a common one at the library this morning.

When she turned to me, it took all my willpower not to shrink back from her. "You really should take your bowel health seriously, Ms. Becket."

"Especially at your age," Anne added with a chuckle. She'd joined us as soon as Hennie had left the building.

"I'm not that much older than you," I reminded Anne, who seemed to think I was born during the age of prehistoric man.

"At any age." Mrs. Farnsworth shot the younger woman such a sharp look that Anne actually paled.

Dorothy St. James

"She's right, you know," Mrs. Edith Frampton, a retired school-teacher, said as she hurried over to us.

We all wished the tall, silver-haired Edith a good morning. Before she had a chance to answer us, I stepped forward and asked her if I could help her find anything, in an effort to get away from Mrs. Farnsworth and her bowel health lectures.

"I've been working on my apple pie recipe," Edith said as she brushed at some flour stuck to her cotton shirt. The fabric's pattern was an explosion of tiny apples of all shades of reds and greens. "There's still something missing from my pie. This year is my year to win. I can feel it in my bones. Does the library have any resources that will help put me over the edge with flavor?"

The Fall Festival was coming up in a few weeks.

"Now, Edith." Mrs. Farnsworth tapped her toe as she spoke softly. "You know our policy is to stay out of the way when it comes to apple pies." Every year, the bakers in town turned downright vicious as they all attempted to win the apple-pie-baking contest. After a real hair-tugging fight over an old recipe book broke out near the 640s in the nonfiction section a few years ago, Mrs. Farnsworth had instituted the policy that librarians were not, under any circumstance, to get involved with pie research.

"But the books . . ." Edith gestured to the open floor plan. "They're no longer here. What do I do?"

"The books are all still here, and countless more," Anne said. "You can access them from the terminal. I can show you."

Before Anne could run off with Edith, Mrs. Farnsworth spoke up. "Edith can figure it out on her own."

"But I don't know how to—" Edith protested.

"You can figure it out," Mrs. Farnsworth said sternly.

Frowning, Edith shuffled toward the bank of computers.

"Ms. Lowery," Mrs. Farnsworth said with a frown, "you're new here, so you don't know the trouble we've had in the past. The Fall

Festival brings out the worst in our patrons. It is our policy not to assist anyone with their apple pie recipe in any way. Do you understand me?"

"But—" Anne protested.

"Do you understand me?" the head librarian repeated.

"Yes, ma'am."

"Good. Now, back to what I was saying before we were interrupted. It's never too early to be heeding my advice. You need to add fiber to your diet as well, Ms. Lowery. Is your"—she cleared her throat—"you know, what is it like?"

"I . . . um . . . I . . ." Anne stammered.

She wasn't the only one who felt embarrassed by the conversation. My cheeks felt like they were about to catch fire. I didn't want to discuss my bathroom habits with my boss. I'd already had enough of that discussion the past couple of weeks to last a lifetime.

"Speak up," Mrs. Farnsworth said with an encouraging nod. "Both of you."

I looked around. Anne had crossed her arms over her chest and hunched her shoulders. Flossie mouthed, *I'm sorry*, and Mrs. Farnsworth nodded again, clearly expecting one of us to say something. Nothing was going to save us from having this conversation. "I . . . It's . . ." I stammered while Anne did the same.

At that very humiliating moment, Doris Heywood came running toward us. She wore a pair of cute cat-eye tortoiseshell glasses. Prescription eyeglasses had been one of her first small-business ventures. Last year, she was selling hair-care products. The year before that, she was selling a foul-smelling powder that was supposed to make you lose weight no matter how much you continued to eat. And now she was selling essential oils.

The younger woman's blond hair, twisted into a bun that sat on top of her head, bounced with every step. She was professionally dressed in a dark green wrap dress and matching stiletto heels that clacked loudly on the terrazzo floor.

"I haven't had time to look at your pamphlet," Mrs. Farnsworth said even before Doris reached us. "And even if I had, I don't see how sniffing some herbs will do anything for my arthritis."

"It's all very scientific. If you'd simply let me give you a demonstration. But . . . but . . . but . . ." Doris seemed to have run out of air. All the color had drained from her usually pink cheeks. She looked at each of us. Tears flooded her eyes.

"Are you okay?" Flossie asked Doris.

"Do you need to sit down?" I started to roll the front desk chair over to her.

She shook her head and then opened and closed her mouth several times before shrieking, "There's a body!"

Mrs. Farnsworth immediately shushed her. "Shhh!"

"A what?" Anne yelped, a little too loudly for the library.

"Shhh!" Mrs. Farnsworth shushed her.

"*A what?*" Flossie whispered.

I shook my head, because there had to be something wrong with my hearing. Handling all of those mystery novels this morning must have somehow damaged my ears, because what I think I heard her say sounded too much like the beginning of an Agatha Christie novel. Certainly, Doris couldn't be saying what I thought she was saying.

"Take a couple of deep breaths." I put my hand on her arm. "Now, what are you trying to tell us?"

She did as I'd instructed and took several deep breaths. The ragged wheezing she produced made her sound as if she was winding herself up.

"I—I just saw it. There's a body." Doris put her face directly in front of mine and shouted, "There's a body behind the library!"

Chapter Three

———·———

This is ridiculous. It's as ridiculous as believing the snake oil that girl has been trying to sell me could cure anything," Mrs. Farnsworth muttered as she led the way through the library to investigate.

"Oh no. You're mistaken. It's not snake oil. The oils I offer are extracted from the purest substances," Doris was quick to correct. Her bright voice trembled. "Essential oils are pressed from a variety—"

"Did you know that the original snake oil, imported from China in the 1800s, was actually quite effective in treating bursitis and arthritis?" Flossie interjected.

"I have read something about that," Mrs. Farnsworth said. "But in today's etymology, snake oil is synonymous with quackery, charlatanism, deception, and fraud. And what I'm saying is that we're going to find that no-good Owen Maynard out there sleeping off his latest bender, not a dead body."

Owen Maynard has been a thorn in Mrs. Farnsworth's side for as long as I've worked for the library, which is a little over thirteen years. The town's only car mechanic would occasionally have an argument with his wife, run off to the Lakeside Tap, and get drunker than a robin with a belly full of juniper berries. Owen had always been smart enough to not drive all the way home. Instead, he would take his truck down the block to the library and park in the small alleyway behind our building to sleep it off.

I dreaded it whenever Mrs. Farnsworth would find him back there. Encountering him in that state could put her in a black mood for days. I suspect it was the unrepentant grin he'd give her whenever she chased him off library property that made her so very angry. Unlike everyone else in Cypress, Owen wasn't the least bit cowed by her.

We took the service elevator down to the basement. Flossie and I exchanged nervous glances as we passed the bookroom. Thankfully, the doors remained closed.

As Mrs. Farnsworth had anticipated, we found what looked like Owen's rusty red truck in the alleyway. At least a quarter of the population of Cypress had fishing trucks that looked just like his. The truck had been parked at such a crooked angle that we could barely open the back door.

"That man is a menace," Mrs. Farnsworth grumbled as she marched toward the passenger's side. "I swear I'm going to call the cops on him this time."

"*That's . . . that's the body.*" Doris pointed a shaking finger toward the truck.

The driver's black curly hair was pressed against the driver's-side window.

"Not a body," Mrs. Farnsworth said with disgust. "A drunkard."

She hammered on the window.

He didn't move.

"Um . . . Mrs. Farnsworth," I said as I squeezed between the truck and the library wall to reach the front of the truck.

"Wake up!" She hammered even harder on the window.

"Please, Mrs. Farnsworth. Stop. No matter how hard you knock, you're not going to rouse him." From where I was standing, I could see that his face and shirt were both stained red.

There would be no waking Owen Maynard. The man was dead.

Mrs. Farnsworth remained next to the truck's passenger-side door, glaring at the window. She hadn't moved. Not as Flossie dialed 911. Not as young Doris sobbed loudly. Not as three police cars pulled up behind the truck. She stood with her arms crossed over her chest, her lips tightly pinched together.

"Mrs. Farnsworth." Police Chief Jack Fisher spoke as gently as I'd ever heard him speak. "We need to get to the body."

She jerked her head in his direction as if startled to see that we were no longer alone in the alleyway. "I don't have time for this," she said, stepping away.

"What happened here?" the lanky police chief asked.

"Isn't it obvious?" Mrs. Farnsworth snapped. "I don't have time for this," she repeated.

Chief Fisher turned to Anne, who shook her head and scowled. His gaze passed over me as if I didn't exist and landed on Doris, who was now sobbing into a handkerchief.

He grimaced.

"I—I found him," Doris finally said with a sniffle.

Fisher pushed his camouflage-patterned ball cap so it sat higher on his head and scratched his forehead. "You just happened to walk by and notice the truck parked back here?" he asked Doris, who was still sniffling into her linen handkerchief.

"I was bringing essential oil samples for Mrs. Farnsworth to try." She sniffled a few more times before leaning in closer to the police chief. "She suffers from the arthritis. My daddy has it, and he swears the eucalyptus oils I'm selling have cured him. I wanted to share that information with Mrs. Farnsworth and let her rub a little on her hands. I'm sure that once she's tried it, she'll become a lifelong customer."

Even though Mrs. Farnsworth had moved away from the truck to stand near the library's back door with the rest of us, there was nothing wrong with her hearing. She snorted. "She wasted her time bringing that stuff to me. If I want medical advice, I'll go visit a doctor."

"I'm glad she came. She saved one of us from the shock of finding Owen," I pointed out. "And thank goodness school is in session or a child might have been the one to make that ghastly discovery."

"Why did he have to go and park behind the library? I told him that the next time I found him out here, I'd make sure the police picked him up," Mrs. Farnsworth said as we watched the police officers string yellow crime-scene tape around Owen's truck. "Well, they're picking him up, all right."

"This is a popular parking place at night," Flossie said gently.

"I don't care what people do at night. It's just that they have no right to do it *here*. No one should be putting their rattletrap truck behind *my* library. There are 'No Parking' signs everywhere."

"No one needs me to stay here, right?" Anne said. Her voice sounded weak, shaky. "I don't know anything about these people. And shouldn't someone be inside? The library is still open. Shouldn't I go inside?"

I looked at Anne. She appeared pale and maybe even a little green. She hadn't gone to the front of the truck. She hadn't seen Owen as he'd stared at nothing. So why was she so upset?

That's when I remembered. She'd complained just this morning how Owen had neglected to fix her car, plus the man had been working with Pastor Goodloe to sabotage her tai chi classes. Didn't she say not more than ten minutes ago how she was angry enough to kill someone? Did she find Owen in his truck on her way in to work? Did she bash in his head for interfering with her plans?

No, that felt too . . . too . . . easy.

Besides, I interfered with Anne's plans on a daily basis, and I was still alive.

"You have a good head on your shoulders, my dear. Always thinking about the library. Yes, you should go inside." Mrs. Farnsworth slid a glance in my direction. Clearly, her praising Anne was also meant as a rebuke of my recent behavior.

Not that she was wrong to point out my shortcomings. I had been spending too much time in the basement and not enough time upstairs doing my job.

Mrs. Farnsworth managed to open the back door without banging it into Owen's truck. "I'll go with you. If the police need us to answer their questions, Tru can tell them where they can find us."

"I'm not sure the police chief would agree—" I started to protest.

"What has happened here has nothing to do with us. And, I shouldn't have to remind you—but clearly you've forgotten—we have a library to run." Mrs. Farnsworth's rich voice seemed to bounce off the alleyway's walls. All police activity stopped. The officers turned to stare at her. "I don't have time for this," she said even louder.

"It's all right," Fisher drawled. "I'll come looking for y'all once the state lab boys get here."

Mrs. Farnsworth made a sharp nod of approval before sweeping inside. "Did you see the empty liquor bottle on the seat next to him?" she asked Anne, who followed on her heels. She clicked her tongue. "Shameful."

I started to head inside as well. But Flossie snagged hold of my sweater's sleeve and held me back.

"Wait a minute." She nodded at the police chief. He was leading Doris over to a female officer. "I want to see something."

My friend had produced a notebook from the colorful tote bag hanging from her wheelchair and started to jot down notes.

Flossie was a successful novelist. So successful, in fact, that with the royalties from her latest book, she'd purchased a shiny new red Corvette that had been converted by a custom car company to accommodate her wheelchair.

Based on the research Flossie conducted at the library, I suspected she wrote thrillers. But I wasn't sure. No matter how hard I pressed (or how hard anyone else pressed, for that matter), she refused to reveal her pen name or the titles of any of her books. "Oh, you've read them," is all she'd ever say.

I leaned forward and tried to read the notes she was busily writing in that notebook of hers, but she'd written them in shorthand. I could read shorthand. My mother had made sure I learned all the secretarial skills as a teen, since a good secretarial position would land me a wealthy husband. But Flossie's shorthand was a sloppy mess.

"I don't know how you decipher those notes of yours," I complained.

"I use my own code." She gave me a sly glance. "Ah, finally. I wonder what took him so long to get here."

"Who?" I asked, even though I knew exactly who she was talking about. Detective Jace Bailey was one of the lead investigators the last time there had been an untimely death in the library.

Jace glanced in our direction before heading over to have a word with the police chief.

In high school, I'd tutored him in English. I'd also nursed an elephant-sized teenage crush on the boy. The school geek and the captain of the football team? Such a match might work in an after-school television special. In real life, the crush ended with me humiliating myself.

Jace had worked as a detective on the NYPD. But he'd recently left New York in disgrace and was back in Cypress with a burning need to prove himself.

"Detective," Flossie said in a singsong voice while nudging me in the side when he'd finished with the police chief and was finally walking over toward us.

"I didn't find him," I blurted. As soon as I'd said it, I realized how silly it sounded. I wanted to kick myself.

Jace shook his head and smiled at me. "And good morning to you too."

I could act cool and calm around practically everyone. But not Jace.

The reason he made me jittery wasn't because I still harbored a schoolgirl crush on him. Despite what my friends thought, I wasn't pining away for his affections. I was jittery because he knew I was keeping a secret from him.

Whenever he was around, all I could think about was that I needed to hide the secret bookroom from someone so skilled at uncovering secrets. As an officer of the law, he'd feel obligated to report what we were doing. And if that happened, town hall would shut it all down.

"Sad business, that." Flossie pointed her pen at the truck. "Do the police have any theories about what might have happened?"

"Now, you know I can't tell you that," he replied. He leaned against the library wall. "Has anything out of the ordinary happened at the library we should know about?"

I bit my lower lip and looked at Flossie.

This keeping-secrets business hurt like a burr in my heel. What if the break-ins and Owen's murder were somehow related? Wouldn't that be something I needed to tell Jace?

"Well?" His eyebrows rose.

"I . . ." What could I say? Did I confess all?

"Didn't think it was a difficult question." The way he was looking at me made my heart thump that much harder.

"It's not a difficult question," Flossie agreed. "And yet, at the same time, nothing has been ordinary at the library lately. The books are gone. It's like coming to a computer café. Cold spaces. Unfriendly. I avoid places like those like I try to avoid the flu. Except that one time when I was traveling through Tibet." She closed her eyes and smiled. "Never saw a prettier sight than that cybercafé situated on the top of the mountain. Cyber Sam's, I think it was called."

"You don't mean Everest?" Jace sounded as if he wasn't sure he believed her or not.

Flossie's eyes popped back open. "Are you kidding me? Everest would have been too much work, even for me." She tapped the arm of her wheelchair. "But there were plenty of mountains that our four-wheeler could reach. And after a month without civilization, a cyber-café is a welcome sight indeed."

"I suppose it would be," Jace said, his brows furrowing.

"They also sold Cokes. Nirvana." She sighed. "All I'd been able to find for weeks was yak's milk and tea. I drank yak's milk. For weeks. Can you imagine?"

"For someone who has never left South Carolina," I admitted, "it sounds quite exciting."

While wondering what yak's milk might taste like, I silently applauded Flossie for distracting Jace. And she wasn't done. "My Truman would have agreed with you," she said. "He enjoyed drinking the yak's milk so much he wanted to bring a supply home with us. He claimed it tasted like wildflowers. The man, God rest his soul, must have had something wrong with his taste buds. He tended to eat and drink all sorts of nasty things and wax eloquently about them. Drove me batty."

"What else did he like to eat and drink?" I asked, trying to keep her talking.

What were the chances that a murder would happen on the same night that the bookroom had been ransacked? The two incidents had to be related. Didn't they?

"Tru, is something troubling you?" Jace asked. Drat that detective. He was too good at his job.

"Actually,"—it'd be wrong to keep this information from the police—"there is—"

Ow!

Flossie elbowed me in the ribs. Hard.

"Um . . . nothing." I rubbed my side. "There's nothing bothering me."

"Are you sure?" Jace moved toward me.

"Don't look now. Betty is on her way over," I said, never in my life so happy to see our local reporter.

"Terrible, terrible thing," Betty Crawley said as she approached. "And at the library, no less. Would you like to give a statement, Trudy? Would you care to say something to assure the public that the library is a safe place to visit?"

She thrust a recorder at my face.

I pushed it aside. "You need to talk with Mrs. Farnsworth. And my name is Trudell. Trudell Becket. Not Trudy."

"Oh, right. Becket's girl." That's what she said nearly every time she saw me. Perhaps she thought that if she could get me riled enough over her constantly getting my name wrong, I might say something outrageous. She was always on the lookout for sensational quotes to put in her news articles.

Jace, bless him, ushered Betty to the entrance of the alleyway. While he did that, Flossie and I made our escape into the library.

"You don't think what happened out there is somehow related to what happened in here?" I pointed to the bookroom's double doors. "Because if there's any chance that the two are related, you know I'm going to have to tell the police about it."

Flossie tapped her pen against her bottom lip several times before answering. "I don't see how there could be any connection between the two crimes." She rolled toward the bookroom. "You heard Anne just this morning. People don't like car mechanics. They overcharge. They don't fix the car properly. Clearly, they go around making enemies all over the place."

"I don't think that's true," I said. I held the bookroom's door open for Flossie to go through.

Dewey greeted us with loud purrs and friendly head butts against our legs. Flossie reached down and scratched the scamp behind his ears. "I don't suppose you know who is causing all this trouble," she said to him.

He looked up at her as if he understood her. After a moment, he meowed.

"Ah, really?" She nodded as she replied.

He meowed again.

"Oh? Is that so? Gracious, wouldn't life be so much easier if animals could speak English?" Flossie looked up at me. "They notice so much more than we can ever imagine. If only they could tell us their secrets."

As she rolled toward the circulation desk, Dewey took a running leap and landed on her lap.

"Good morning, Hubert." Flossie sounded cheery. I don't know how she did it. She acted as if we hadn't just found a murdered man on the other side of the back door as she happily stroked Dewey under his chin. "What are you researching today?"

"Poltergeists," he answered with a big grin. He loved it whenever anyone took an interest in his work.

"Really? That's quite different from your regular topics of inquiry," Flossie commented as she sorted through the book slips that had been pulled from their books' pockets yesterday after she'd left for the day. "The last time we talked, weren't you studying the movements of the Swamp Fox for an article you're writing for a state magazine? What made you move to the supernatural?"

"He suspects a poltergeist is the cause of the trouble down here," I said before I started to gather a few more mystery novels from the floor.

"Indeed?" Flossie said with great interest.

Hubert's expression brightened as he recounted the same theory he had told me. When he was done, he asked, "Is it okay to go out into the hallway? I would like to buy a coffee from the café. I had started to leave a little while ago but heard such a commotion in the hall I decided it would be wiser to wait."

"Yes. Yes. It should be safe to go now," Flossie said. She had rolled over to the manual typewriter, where she started to type a new card for the card catalog. "Very wise of you to wait, though. There was a murder in the alleyway. I'm sure it has nothing to do with the library," she was quick to add.

"Indeed?" Hubert's brows shot up. "Anyone I know?"

"It was the mechanic Owen Maynard. Looks like someone hit him over the head with one of his liquor bottles."

Hubert nodded, but didn't say anything. For a talker like Hubert, that was noteworthy.

I started to worry, again, that I needed to tell the police about the vandals breaking into our bookroom. Perhaps Owen saw them breaking into the library and had been permanently silenced.

"I don't mean to be a nag, Tru dear, but shouldn't you be working upstairs?" Flossie said.

My friend was right, of course.

I hurried upstairs to get to work on a new children's healthy cooking program that was scheduled to start next month. But no matter how hard I concentrated on ways to make broccoli, carrots, and beans fun, I couldn't shake the worry that by keeping my silence about the break-ins I might be unwittingly helping someone get away with murder.

Chapter Four

On my lunch break, I carried a tote bag filled with books across the street to the Sunshine Diner, where Tori Green, my best friend since kindergarten, was waiting for me. She'd texted a half hour ago, suggesting I meet her there.

Why she wanted to eat here perplexed me. She owned the local coffee shop, Perks, which was just a block down the road. The Sunshine Diner, with their free coffee refills and endless supply of gossip, was her business's biggest competitor.

After entering the busy diner, I wondered if I had somehow misunderstood her text. She wasn't sitting at any of the tables. I wandered deeper into the restaurant, searching for her, when my neighbor Cora Parker—who was one of the town's biggest gossips—tugged on my elbow.

"I heard what happened behind the library. So shocking." She clicked her tongue. Her artificial blond bangs had so much hair spray in them that they looked as if they were reaching up for the ceiling. "And to think Owen had just taken over as vice president of the museum board last month after Fenwick Harrington's untimely demise."

"You don't mean Owen Maynard, do you?" I didn't know Owen had been a member of the museum board, much less the vice president. Unlike many of the other board members, whom I knew well, Owen had never stopped by the library to do research for the museum. And he'd never been let in on the secret that there was a bookroom in the library's basement.

Only dedicated readers of print books who could be trusted with the secret have been invited to browse our shelves. While this policy made good sense—if the wrong person found out about the library, it would be a disaster—I hated depriving the gossipier residents of getting to enjoy the print collection in our library. That was why I'd started carrying around my tote bag. I loaned out books to people like Cora Parker, who couldn't stop herself from talking and talking and talking.

True to form, she continued to gossip about Owen and the museum board. "That group is going to have a difficult time getting anyone else to volunteer for that position. It sure will. If I were a member, I'd be sitting on my hands at the next meeting. I hate to imagine what will happen when they all get together. All sorts of sniping and finger-pointing, most like."

I nodded absently. Her gossip rarely held much interest for me—for one thing, she seldom told me something I didn't know. Although Mrs. Farnsworth claimed that our library patrons came to us in pursuit of higher knowledge, gossip was a huge draw for some of the residents who flocked to the place. It was a great spot to learn about what was going on in town. And yet, Owen's connection to the museum was one piece of information no one had mentioned this morning.

Why had Hubert kept silent about his connection to the murder victim? If Owen had been the vice president of the museum board, an organization that was the center of Hubert's life, I would have expected him to have provided some kind of reaction when he'd heard about who had been murdered. Whether anyone wanted him to or not, Hubert provided the smallest details about any topic that was remotely important to him. And nothing was more important to him than Cypress's local museum.

Why would he clam up now?

"Do you know if the other members of the museum board had any problems with Owen?" I asked, wondering if that could be the reason for Hubert's silence.

Cora's eyes widened. "Oh! Are you doing another one of your investigations? I bet you are, you clever girl. Do you think one of the museum board members killed poor Owen?" Her loud voice caused all the conversations in the diner to come to dead silence.

"No," I lied.

Of course, that was exactly what I was wondering. If the museum board's involvement wasn't a concern, surely Hubert would have mentioned that Owen was a member. I looked around the diner and saw that everyone's eyes were on us.

"No. That's not what I'm saying," I said loud enough for all those prying ears to hear. "The police are investigating. I'm sure they already have a handle on what happened in the alleyway last night. We were simply having a neighborly conversation."

"I don't know," Cora said. She tapped her finger in a quick beat on the tabletop. As she tapped, she started to speculate on the other members of the museum board. If we'd been alone, I might have let her ramble on. But with everyone in the diner listening in on our conversation, all I wanted her to do was to stop talking. I didn't need word to get back to Mama Eddy that I'd taken on another investigation. My mother believed activities such as playing detective were below our family stature. According to her, I came from a family that paid others to do such embarrassing *and dangerous* things for us. She hadn't yet forgiven me for putting my life in jeopardy the last time I took on a murder investigation.

"I heard you've been having trouble getting your apple pies to turn out," I said to Cora, still talking loud enough for half the customers to hear.

That bit of news got Cora to snap her mouth shut in record time. Women in Cypress took great pride in their cooking. Recipes passed down from generation to generation were considered more valuable than the family silver. And Cora's mother had been revered as one of Cypress's queens of the kitchen. The fact that Cora struggled with her apple pies must have been a source of great embarrassment for her, especially with the local Fall Festival coming up in just a few weeks.

I reached into my tote bag and handed her a thick recipe book sporting a photograph of a juicy red apple on the cover. "This book is considered to be the authority on baking with apples. My aunt Sal absolutely swears by it."

That last part was another lie. (Gracious, those lies of mine were piling up today.) Never in my aunt Sal's life had she ever read a recipe book. And it showed. The woman had once nearly burned her house to the ground while boiling water for tea. Yet her apple pies were something of a legend around these parts.

"This is the cookbook your aunt uses?" Cora snatched the book from me and started flipping through its pages.

One of Cypress's biggest unsolved mysteries was how Aunt Sal, the town's worst cook, managed to win the festival's apple-pie-baking competition year after year for the past ten years, taking over the top spot only after Cora's mother had passed.

All of the town's other bakers worked for months perfecting their family's treasured recipes in the hopes that this would be the year one of them would finally out-bake Aunt Sal's famous apple pie.

"Please give the book back to me in a couple of days, okay? I'm sure others will be interested in using it."

Cora hugged the book to her chest. "Thank you. I'll take good care of *this* book. Thank you. Thank you, ever so much."

Still not seeing my friend Tori at any of the tables or in any of the booths, I started to leave the diner. That's when I heard a strange hiss.

Or perhaps it was more like a *pssst.*

I followed the leaky-air sound to the diner's back corner. A lone person occupied the booth there. She held a magazine up high, covering her entire face.

"Tori?" Hiding her face wasn't typical behavior for my normally super-outgoing friend. "Are we spying on the enemy?"

She shushed me, sounding alarmingly like Mrs. Farnsworth. "I don't want him to see me," she whispered as she peeked over the top of the magazine to peer at someone behind me.

"Who?" I asked.

"Don't look!" she snapped when I started to turn around. That's when I noticed the magazine she was hiding behind.

"*Brides Today?*" I asked, unable to conceal my surprise.

My friend, while in possession of some of the keenest instincts of anyone I've ever met, made terrible choices when it came to men. She'd been married four times and already had her sights set on number five—the town's new bookstore owner. Although he seemed like a nice guy and owned a bookstore (how dreamy was that?), they had only known each other for less than a month. Even for Tori, that wasn't enough time between the first meet and the getting serious phase to start planning her next wedding.

And my goodness, Tori and I were both in our thirties. Shouldn't there be a rule that you couldn't have more marriages than the number of decades you've lived? Or a rule that you should give your best friend the chance to marry at least once before slipping a fifth golden ring onto your own finger? I had to say something.

"Rushing the romance a little recklessly, don't you think?" I asked, surprised that I sounded like a bitter old maid.

She gave me a startled look. I pointed to the title of the magazine she was still using as a shield.

"This old thing? I subscribed to it while planning my wedding to Number Three and decided it would be easier to keep the subscription going after the wedding. That way I wouldn't have to play catch-up learning all the new styles and trends the next time I walked down the aisle."

"If you were thinking like that when you were planning your wedding to Number Three, why did you go through with it?" Canceling that wedding would have saved me from having to buy that hideously expensive neon-green bridesmaid gown that did unspeakable things to my complexion. Every conversation I had at her reception started with someone concerned about my health.

"Don't get me wrong," Tori said. "Number Three was a nice guy. We're still good friends. We talk on the phone every Saturday night. And before you start to feel bad for the guy, I don't think he thought our marriage would be the forever kind either. In the two and a half years we were married, we never did open a joint banking account." She suddenly jerked the magazine up so it covered her face. "Whoops. He's looking over here. Sit down before he sees you."

I tried to figure out who I wasn't supposed to be looking at, but soon gave up and slid into the booth next to her. "What's going on?"

"It's Charlie," she whispered. "He's over there. No, don't look!"

Needless to say, I looked.

Charlie Newcastle, Cypress's newest resident, was Tori's prospective Mr. Number Five. He'd moved to Cypress from Las Vegas last month to open a used bookstore a few doors down from the public library. While I loved the idea that our town was finally getting a bookstore, I thought he looked, well, dangerous.

Tori had been enthralled by him from the first moment they met. Likely because she also thought he looked dangerous.

"Who is he talking to?" I asked.

"I don't know," Tori cried with true distress. "But look at her. She's gorgeous."

He was sitting at a table near the front of the diner across from a woman with flowing red hair. She wore a clingy green dress with a plunging neckline. It was exactly the kind of dress Tori liked to wear. Two steaming mugs of coffee sat untouched on their table. Charlie had his head tilted toward this beautiful stranger. She seemed to be doing all the talking, her hands gesturing to emphasize whatever she was telling him. She said something that made Charlie frown. He answered her, which in turn made her frown. She tossed both hands in the air.

He reached across the table. Almost immediately she dropped her hands into his grasp. The gesture looked automatic . . . and intimate.

"Look at them." Tori's voice was tight with anguish. "Sitting there together. They ordered nothing but a coffee."

"How did you know to follow him here?" I asked.

"The Sunshine Diner's coffee isn't even good," she said instead of answering. "If she was an *old friend* from his past or a *business associate*, why did he bring her here instead of Perks? My coffee is the best you can buy in the state. Why wouldn't he treat his friend to the best? Why is he hiding her from me?"

"Did he tell you he was meeting someone?" I asked, trying to figure out why Tori felt so threatened. My friend had no reason to be worried. Yes, the woman sitting with Charlie was pretty. But Tori was striking in her beauty. And from how Charlie acted around her, I suspected our new bookseller was just as crazy about Tori as he was about the valuable books he'd collected for his shop.

"He didn't tell me *anything*," she confessed.

"Then how did you know to follow him here?" I asked again.

"Cora texted me to tell me about his straying ways shortly before I texted you. That dirty, lying dog."

"I see." *Cora.* This was why I couldn't invite that woman to the secret bookroom. She couldn't keep anything to herself. "Would you like me to walk over there and see if he'll introduce me to his friend?" I started to slide out of the booth.

"No!" Her hand shot across the table to grab hold of my arm. "Don't go over there. If he saw that I was here, he'd think I didn't trust him."

"Clearly, you don't trust him," I pointed out.

"But he can't know that," she wailed a little too loudly.

Charlie froze. He slowly turned his head in our direction.

Tori jerked the magazine back up over her face.

But not soon enough.

Charlie stood. He winked as he made his way toward us.

"Good afternoon, ladies," he said once he stood right next to the booth.

"Don't know who you are," Tori said in a fake gruff voice.

"Oh, I think you do, love." Laughter sparkled in Charlie's eyes.

Tori slowly lowered the magazine. She cleared her throat several times. "Darn allergies," she said, and cleared her throat again. "Have you been scouring the local restaurants looking for me, you sweet man?"

"Alas, no, Tori. I'm here lunching with a friend. But you've known that ever since Cora over there texted you." He tapped the magazine Tori was now using as a shield. "Is there anything I should know about?"

She looked at the magazine's cover—which touted "Ten Ways to Plan a Quick Wedding"—and then back at Charlie. "It's not . . . it's not . . ." She blanched.

Charlie raised one brow. "Are you trying to give me a sign that you want to move our relationship to the next level?"

"No. Heavens, no. No. No." When Charlie's smile slipped, Tori quickly added, "Don't misunderstand. It's not that I don't want to. I mean, things are great between us. But we've just met. The magazine isn't for me. It's for . . ." She tossed her copy of *Brides Today* at me, which I instinctively caught like a bridesmaid catches a bouquet. "It's for Tru."

"Me?" I squeaked. I wanted to help my friend, but this . . . this could cause me trouble.

"I'm helping Tru," she said before I had a chance to protest. "The poor dear has no clue. She's never done this before. She doesn't know a tulle from a crepe."

"Oh! I didn't realize things had gotten so serious so quickly between you and the detective," Charlie said. "Wow. Congratulations."

"What? No," I said. "No. No. It's nothing like that."

But my protestations had come too late. Cora, who was only a few tables away, already had her phone out. She was smiling to herself as she texted furiously.

Chapter Five

———◦———

I'm sorry," Tori cried through my screen door that evening when she arrived at my doorstep with a tub of take-out spaghetti and a tray of cinnamon rolls. "A million times sorry." She held up the cinnamon rolls so I could get a whiff of the warm, sweet spices. Hmm . . . they were fresh from the oven and one of my weaknesses. "You were already having a terrible day, what with having to deal with the police and the murder. You should have told me what was going on when we met for lunch instead of letting me heap all this new trouble on your head." She heaved a deep breath. "I really am sorry."

Even though I was still angry at Tori for tossing me to the gossips of Cypress, I opened the screen door and let her in. Of course I let her in. There was no way in the world I was going to turn away fresh cinnamon rolls.

As she rushed inside, a flyer for Doris Heywood's essential oils fluttered to the floor. Doris had been leaving a flyer on all the doors in the neighborhood every couple of days. I scooped it up and pushed it into my pocket.

"You do realize Mama Eddy has already been here," I told her. "And my dad. They arrived at the same time. The two of them. In the same room."

Dewey let out a long, plaintive meow.

Tori winced.

"They both wanted me to explain why they were the last ones to know about my engagement. Being angry at me about not telling them I was engaged has been the only thing they've agreed on in over a decade." To describe my parents' post-divorce relationship as acrimonious would be an understatement. If one parent said it was day, the other would claim it was night.

"I can only imagine how difficult that must have been. And I am sorry. Truly, I am. That's why I brought the cinnamon rolls." She waved the fragrant bag under my nose. "But I don't understand why your parents came here. I thought Cora had promised to send out a text explaining it was all a mistake."

"Well, Cora did say that. But then she came over to tell me this afternoon that she'd changed her mind. Gossips, like her, keep hearing around town how I'm keeping a secret, a *big* secret. She figured we'd finally let slip what it was: that I've been secretly dating Jace, and that we were planning a quickie marriage, which (you know) means only one thing." I pointed to my belly.

"Gracious, I never imagined that neighbor of yours—who keeps thinking she needs to tell the world a thing or two about a thing or two—would think *that you'd been storked.*"

"I swore to her I wasn't. I told her that it was impossible since I hadn't even been on a first date with Jace."

"Because you're a fool," Tori grumbled. "That boy clearly wants to date you."

"But Cora refused to listen. She said she'd heard talk around town that I'd been spending mornings in the bathroom at the library, which only proves that she's right."

"What?" Tori wrinkled her nose. "Why are people saying that you've been hanging out in the bathroom?"

"Because that's the excuse Flossie has been using to explain why I've been missing when I've been downstairs cleaning up the bookroom after it's been vandalized. Ever since the first time it happened, Mrs. Farnsworth has been constantly lecturing me on how to improve my colon health. Anyone who's come into the library has probably over-heard her rather graphic advice."

Tori shook her head. "I knew this was somehow Flossie's fault. That woman—"

"No, it's not her fault. You can't blame her when you're the one who put the idea that I'm romantically involved with Jace in Cora's head. And I was the one who had to convince her that none of it is true by telling her what my secret really was."

"No!" She grabbed my arm. "What did you tell her?"

"Not the truth, obviously." Lies kept piling upon lies, which made me terribly uneasy. "I told her that what she heard was partially right. I told her that Jace and I had been on a few dates. On the sly."

Tori's eyebrows shot up into her hairline. "You lied? You? But you don't lie."

"It seemed necessary. And apparently that's what I do now—lie. All. The. Time."

"And after you told her that, did she retract her text?"

"She did. But by then it was too late. You know how this town likes to gossip. Word had already spread as far as Hell Hole Swamp by the time she sent that second text taking back the first one. A friend who works at the regional library out in the middle of Hell Hole texted to tell me that he heard a few people talking about it at the Crossroads Grocery."

"That's got to be fifty miles from here."

I nodded. "More like sixty miles and down a dirt road."

"I am sorry." Tori carried the take-out food to the kitchen. I took two bowls out of the cabinet. She retrieved a serving spoon from a drawer and started to spoon the spaghetti into the bowls I'd handed her. "I hope your parents believed you."

"I think they might have come around to seeing the truth . . . eventually, although my mom did keep patting my belly. She told me I either needed to fess up or go on a diet. Plus, she found my stash of chocolates I'd hidden under the kitchen sink and took it with her when she left."

Tori shook her head. "Mama Eddy and her ever-helpful diet advice. You don't need to lose weight. It's your mama who needs to look in a mirror. She's been looking absolutely skeletal lately. And there's nothing wrong with eating chocolate. Scientists now say it's health food."

"Thank you." My friend's rush to my defense made me smile. "Were you able to find out who Charlie was meeting?"

Since I had to run over to Cora's table at the diner, I missed the end of Tori's conversation (or should I say confrontation) with Charlie.

"He told me that *that woman* was an old friend from Vegas." Tori made an ugly face.

"What?" I asked. "What's wrong with that?"

"I don't believe him."

"Why? The guy is crazy in love with you. And you're lucky that he's so smitten. If he wasn't, that stalking stunt you pulled at the diner, hiding behind a bridal magazine and all, might have sent him running into the nearest swamp."

"What do you mean?" Tori sounded genuinely surprised. "Guys love it when we lose our minds over them."

"I don't think that's true." But then again, what did I know? I'd never dated a man long enough to get to the point where he proposed marriage. Or to the point of stalking him.

"Well, it doesn't matter." She set her bowl on the dining room table and then sank into one of the chairs. "It's over between us. Hate to see it end. At least it was fun while it lasted."

"It's over? Why?" I started to pour us glasses of red wine. I added a little extra to hers. "Don't you think you should let him explain himself?"

"I did let him explain." When I handed her the glass of wine, all she did was stare at it. "We talked things over at his bookstore before I came here. He told me that he worked with *Candy*—that's her name, *Candy Cane*—at one of the Vegas casinos." She made a gagging noise. "He said she was a colleague and friend and that she was passing through the area and had wanted to see his new shop. What a crock of lies."

"How do you know that he's lying? That all sounds reasonable to me."

She downed half her glass of wine in one gulp. "Because when they left the diner, I followed Candy. You know where she went? To the alleyway behind the library. She stood there for a long time, watching the police clean up the crime scene. If she was simply in town to see Charlie's bookstore, why would she visit a crime scene? A man died there. Who would want to see that?"

"That does sound suspicious." I took a small sip of the wine. "Why *would* she be interested in seeing where Owen had died?"

"That's the question, isn't it? The killer always returns to the scene of the crime. Isn't that how the saying goes?"

"It is, but why would she kill Owen? Did you see if she talked with any of the policemen working the scene behind the library?" I asked.

"That's the thing. She didn't talk to anyone. She watched for a while, took a few pictures. She then drove to a motel out on Interstate 95. That's where I left her."

"Did Charlie know Owen?" I didn't want to add the bookshop owner to my super-short suspect list. I liked him. Plus, he was a big supporter of our efforts to preserve the library's printed books.

Tori thought about my question for a moment before she slowly shook her head. "I don't know. Shoot. Clearly, I don't know squat about lover boy."

"But it sounds like you suspect he was involved with Owen's death. Is that right?" *Please say no.*

"I really don't know what to think," Tori said, her voice gruff. Her eyes welled up with tears. She swiped at them with the back of her hand, but they kept falling.

"I'm sure it's a misunderstanding." I put my arms around my friend like she had for me many, many times before.

"How can you know?" She sniffled.

"Because not only was Owen murdered behind the library last night, someone also broke into the bookroom."

"What?" Tori took a long sip of her wine. "You mean it happened again? And you're sure it happened last night?"

I nodded and tried not to take offense at the hopeful tone in her voice. Of course she sounded hopeful. She didn't want to think her boyfriend was lying to her or, worse, helping one of his "friends" get away with murder.

"And like before, nothing was missing?" she asked before taking another sip of her wine.

"The books were damaged. The shelving torn off the wall. But so far as I can tell, nothing was taken. And if Candy only came into town today, she couldn't be responsible for what happened in the library the other two times. I mean, if the two crimes are connected." I still hoped they weren't, but I felt like I needed to say something to help Tori feel better.

My friend blinked the tears from her eyes. "You're right." She sighed and then gave me a wobbly smile. "I'm so glad I came here. You always know the right things to say." She twirled the spaghetti onto her fork but didn't eat it. "Who do you think would do such a thing? Destroy the bookroom, I mean."

"Hubert Crawford came in shortly after I found the mess this morning. He told me he thought a poltergeist was the cause of the mayhem."

Tori snorted. "He also thinks the Nazis stationed spies in Cypress during the Second World War. His theories are crazy."

"This one does sure sound crazy. I don't believe a ghost is tossing around the books. But I am worried about why Owen was parked behind the library. Did he see something he wasn't supposed to see?"

Tori leaned forward. "Like stumble across our book-hating vandals in the act?"

"Exactly. But why would a vandal kill a person to keep from being caught? That seems extreme."

"What does Flossie think?" she asked after eating some of her spaghetti.

"She says there's no way the two incidents could be related. She suspects Owen was killed because he made the wrong person angry. Maybe he botched someone's car repair. Anne sure was angry with him this morning. She said he'd fixed her car with used parts, charged her for new, and her car broke down again right away. Flossie thinks that only proves her point that people routinely want to kill their car repairman."

"Well, that's good enough for me. Flossie is a smart cookie. But we do need to do something about our vandal." She ate some more of the spaghetti. "I know! You need to convince Mrs. Farnsworth to trust you with a key to the library so we can set up a stakeout."

That would never happen. I'd asked Mrs. Farnsworth for years to trust me with the library key, and she'd yet to agree. "We could watch the place from the outside," I suggested instead.

"Would that be safe? Owen was killed out there."

I thought about that for a minute. "If we invite the right people to help us, it might be safe."

"Yeeessss." The way Tori's eyes twinkled as she agreed with me made me nervous. A twinkling-eyed Tori had led me into trouble more than once. "You could ask your detective. You know, the one you're not marrying but—by your own admission—are dating?"

"I can't ask Jace." Was she as crazy as Hubert Crawford? "I can't tell him about the bookroom. I can't tell him about what's been hap-pening."

"Sheesh! I wasn't suggesting you tell him."

"He already knows I'm hiding something from him. You know that. This tension between us makes him unhappy and makes me act more than a little crazy."

She grabbed my hand. "Tru, listen to me. I wasn't suggesting you tell him about the secret bookroom or what you're up to. I've spent many fine hours parked behind the library in the middle of the night, especially when dating Number Two."

"Are you suggesting I ask Jace out on a date?" I yanked my hand away from hers. "And then you want me to lure him into a stakeout behind the library with me? Is that really what you're suggesting?"

Tori nodded enthusiastically. "Two-for-one deal. And on the upside, you'll be making that lie of yours true, which should be a relief for you. I know how much you hate lying."

Her suggestion shouldn't have surprised me. Her thoughts often ran in the direction of dates and dating. And this one did have its merits. However . . .

"You do realize there's a good reason that I've not gone out on a date with Jace, don't you?" I asked her. But before I had the opportunity to explain and before she had the chance to try to change my mind about it, the doorbell rang.

Tori and I stared at each other for a moment.

"I suspect that's Mama Eddy returning to lecture me some more on why I should never date a cop," I said finally. "Thank goodness for her bias against law enforcement officers. I think that was the only reason she was relieved to learn I wasn't secretly engaged to him. She offered to talk to some of her friends to see if any of their sons would make suit-able husband material."

I excused myself from the dining room table and went to let my mother in.

There, standing on the other side of the screen door, wasn't my mother. Who I saw there made me wish my mother had returned to scold me.

Detective Jace Bailey, looking as dangerous as ever in a black T-shirt and faded blue jeans, had casually propped his arm against my front door's frame. "Hey, babe, I heard we've gotten engaged."

Chapter Six

I don't know how long I stood at the door. I remember noticing how the sun was just starting to set, smearing fall colors across the darkening sky. A few crickets were chirping in the distance. And Tori, who must have slipped out through the back door, was tiptoeing toward her car.

"Tru?" Jace said, sounding less sure of himself than he had a moment before. "Are you going to let me in?"

I was tempted to say no and slam the door in his face. But running from my troubles never made them go away.

With a sigh, I unlatched the hook that held the screen door closed and pushed it open.

"You might as well get inside. Cora lives over there." I nodded toward the small Craftsman cottage across the street. "I'm sure she's already texting everyone she knows that you're standing on my porch."

He crossed the threshold and paused to look around before entering my tidy living room. Dewey greeted him with a happy meow. Jace smiled and scratched my kitty behind the ears.

"Missed you, buddy," he murmured, which made my lanky kitty purr loudly.

After their mutual lovefest, Jace went directly to the bookshelves that lined the walls on either side of the small brick fireplace. Dewey followed. "Is this where you keep all those books you've been loaning out?" he asked as he traced his finger along the spines. "Seems a little full, don't you think?"

Whenever we talked, he often asked questions like this, obviously probing for clues about that secret he knew I was keeping. The secret he'd once promised to uncover. Sure, he'd also later promised to let me keep my secret. But by how he acted—and by the questions he'd ask—I didn't think he could help himself. The detective in him was too strong.

He glanced at me and then back at the bookshelf. An unspoken question crinkled his brows and twisted on his lips.

The bookshelf in question was orderly, divided by section and then alphabetical by author. And yes, it was full. I'd have trouble squeezing any more books in. If I was pulling books to loan out from my personal library, there should be gaps on the shelves. And I had a feeling those were the thoughts that were going through his mind.

"There are bookshelves all over the house," I explained, which was the truth. He didn't have to know that those bookshelves were just as stuffed with books as these. "I have a floor-to-ceiling bookcase in my bedroom."

"Your bedroom, hmm?" He turned toward me. An easy smile spread to his lips. "Is that an invitation?"

"No!" I said a little too quickly, a little too forcefully.

"I don't see why you don't invite me into your bedroom to—*ahem*—look at your books?" His fingers made air quotes as he said *books*. "No one in town would blame us. Not when we're already engaged," he teased.

At least, I hoped he was teasing.

"There's spaghetti in the kitchen." Which is where I fled. "I'd just sat down to dinner when you knocked," I shouted from where I was standing next to the kitchen counter.

He followed me into the room. I glanced at him as I retrieved a bowl from the cabinet.

"I am sorry . . . about the mix-up." I stumbled over my words in my haste to explain myself. "I mean, about the rumors. About us. I'm not telling people we're engaged. Honest. I'd never do that. My neighbor, Cora, misheard a conversation, a conversation I was having with Tori and Charlie, an innocent conversation that, I swear, had nothing to do with you."

"I figured it must have been something like that, seeing how you keep refusing to go out with me."

Yes, I had turned him down. Several times.

Dating Jace would be dangerous. For the library. He hadn't been in my home for more than a few minutes and he was already busy teasing out holes in the stories I'd been telling people about loaning out the books. Those who hadn't been invited to the secret bookroom assumed the books I carried around in my tote bag and loaned out to fellow residents came from my personal hoard.

I doubted Jace could switch off his detective skills even if he wanted to. If we went out for dinner, he'd likely uncover enough clues to conclude that I was hiding a bookroom in the library's basement before the dessert arrived.

With that worrying thought, I spooned out heaping amounts of spaghetti from the container and handed him the bowl. "Here. Consider this a consolation prize for having to put up with the town thinking we were engaged today."

"So, are you saying we're having a date? Now?" His likable smile knocked me slightly off-balance.

"Not a date. Dinner." I hurried into the adjacent dining room, where a cold bowl of spaghetti was waiting for me. I poured him a glass of wine and set it on the table in front of him.

"Sorry, Tru. As much as I'd like to enjoy this concession you're giving me, I'm still on duty. I can't drink the wine." Being on duty didn't stop him from finishing off the bowl of spaghetti I'd fixed for him or from refilling the bowl and eating that as well. "I stopped by because I needed to ask you a few questions about Owen's murder," he said once he'd finished the meal.

I wiped my mouth with a napkin and looked down at the spaghetti I'd barely touched. "I didn't see anything more than you saw. And I already gave a statement to Detective Ellerbe."

Detective Gregory Ellerbe worked for the state law enforcement department. Cypress was too small to have a crime lab. Instead, the police chief called in assistance from the state for the more complicated crimes, such as murder.

Talking with the state detective had actually made me feel better. "Detective Ellerbe told me he suspects that Owen's murder was a random event perpetrated by an outsider who was passing through town. He thought drinking was likely involved." I took a sip of my wine. "Because of the circumstances, he seemed to think we might never learn who did it."

Jace crossed his arms over his chest and tilted his head toward me. "And you believed that?"

I nodded.

"In Cypress?"

I shrugged.

"When was the last time you encountered some random passerby in our town, which is—need I remind you—miles from the nearest interstate?"

Well, Jace did have a point there.

"We have the lake," I said, grasping on to something—anything—to make me feel like the trouble outside of the library wasn't at all related to the trouble happening inside the library. "Strangers come to fish on Lake Marion from all over."

"They rent houses. Or own summer cottages. And they are coming to do something in the town. They aren't just passing through."

He was right, but I wasn't in the mood to agree with him. Thankfully, Dewey sauntered into the room and started to meow for his dinner. I excused myself to go feed my intelligent tabby.

Jace followed me to the kitchen. While I spooned wet food into Dewey's dish, Jace started washing the spaghetti bowls.

"You don't have to do that." I reached over and turned off the water.

"Yes, I do." He turned the water back on. "You fed me. I'll clean. If my mama ever heard I'd done it differently, she'd have my hide."

I chuckled at the image of the dainty Hazel Bailey taking on her very much grown son.

"We still need to talk," he said. "When we were at the library, I had asked you if you'd noticed anything odd that had been happening around there. Before you could answer me, Flossie tried to distract me with one of her travel stories."

Oh, he'd noticed that?

"I do love her travel stories," I said as I put Dewey's food dish on the floor. My kitty made the cutest purring-meowing noise as he gobbled the cat equivalent of canned beef stew. "Did you know she's visited every continent, even Antarctica?"

"I did not know that. Though I'm sure I'll hear about it from her soon enough."

"You should ask her about her trek across Siberia. Listening to her talk about her travels makes me want to get a passport. You know I've never been anywhere."

He wiped his hands on a dish towel and slung it over his shoulder. "As interesting as Flossie's travels must be, that's not why I'm here. I need you to talk to me, Tru. I need you to be honest with me. What's been going on at the library that you don't want to tell me?"

"Oh . . ." I waved my hand in the air as if I weren't feeling guilty or nervous. "Nothing that could be related to Owen's death."

I hoped.

That darn hand I was waving around started to tremble.

Jace leaned toward me. "Humor me, Tru, and tell me what's been going on anyhow. Pretend you're recounting one of Flossie's travel tales and don't leave out any detail."

I drew a breath and closed my eyes for a moment before coming up with something safe to tell him. "Well, you know the changes that happened at the library last month?"

"Kind of hard to miss, especially considering how a man was killed in the middle of all those renovations."

"Yeah . . . um . . . those . . . well, they're causing all sorts of troubles. I'm worried that if I don't learn how to use all those machines Anne brought in, I'm going to find myself out of a job. If that happens, what am I going to do? Like I've said, I've never been anywhere. Other than those few years I spent attending the University of South Carolina, Cypress is the only home I've ever known. Am I going to be forced to leave it?"

He nodded and looked honestly concerned. "That must be hard. I do feel for you. But is that really what Flossie didn't want you to tell me? That you're worried about job security?" The skin around his eyes crinkled. I got the prickly feeling that he knew I was holding back potentially vital information. But, I told myself once again, it was kind of farfetched to imagine that someone making mischief in the secret bookroom would be driven to murder just because Owen spotted him.

"Oh, you know Flossie." I tried to nonchalantly wave my hand again, but it was still trembling. I ended up flapping my hand around as if I were an angry duck, before tucking it behind my back. A spoon went flying off the counter and clattered to the floor. I quickly picked it up. "Flossie is a big believer in the maxim that if you put voice to something, you will inadvertently make it happen." Which was true.

He frowned and we had a staring contest for several seconds before he shrugged unhappily. "Well . . . if you think of something, please let me know. I'll let you enjoy the rest of your evening in peace."

He started for the door.

I should have felt relieved he didn't push me harder to spill my secrets.

I should have let him go.

Maybe it was because I'd spent too many hours lost in the pages of novels or perhaps it was because I'd read too many mystery stories. But no matter the reason and despite how many times I told myself that the library break-ins and Owen's death had nothing to do with each other, part of me refused to believe it. I was seriously worried that Owen was dead because I'd created that basement bookroom and made it this huge secret. And I didn't know what to do about it. My conscience nagged and nagged at me to tell Jace the truth.

"Wait," I said.

I held up the box of cinnamon rolls.

"You can't go yet. I have dessert."

The lusty smile he gave me made the butterflies in my stomach dance. We didn't bother with plates. We stood side by side at the kitchen counter, eating the buns straight from the box. They were sticky and sweet and spicy and perfect.

"You're wrong about one thing, you know. There *was* someone who was just passing through town," I said between bites. "Charlie's old friend. Tori told me her name is Candy. Candy Cane. I can't believe that's her real name. Can you? She surprised Charlie as she was traveling through." At least that was the story Charlie told Tori. "Tori happened to notice that Candy had stopped to watch the police work the crime scene behind the library on her way out of town." He didn't need to know that Tori had been following the woman at the time. I took a bite out of my third cinnamon bun. "Don't you think that sounds suspicious?"

"Hmm . . ."

Did that sound mean Jace was agreeing with me, or was he simply enjoying dessert? I waited to see if he'd say something. Perhaps he'd even share some information the police had about Owen and the events that led up to his demise.

When he didn't, I added, "I also learned today that Owen was the vice president of the museum board. Don't you think that's interesting? You know, I've never seen Owen at the library. Most of the members practically live there."

"They do?" Jace asked. "Even after the change to a bookless library, those history geeks from the museum still come to the library to do research? I thought they were all antitechnology."

Whoops. I couldn't explain to him that they came to the library only to conduct their research in the basement where the papers and books and even paper card catalogs still existed. So, instead, I looked away as I muttered, "Uh-huh."

"Hmm . . ." Jace said again.

"Cora told me that the museum board's previous vice president, Fenwick Harrington, also met an untimely end."

"This is the same Cora who told the entire population of Cypress that we're engaged?"

"Unfortunately, it is."

"Hmm . . ." He wiped his mouth with a napkin. "Thank you for the dinner and the delicious dessert." The box of cinnamon buns was empty. I tried to count in my head how many I'd eaten. "I don't suppose you'd let me return the favor and take you out to dinner on Friday?" Jace asked.

Had I finished off three or four of those large gooey buns? Either way, I'd eaten too many. I had a bad habit of overeating when I felt stressed.

"What?" I asked when I realized Jace was waiting for an answer.

"You. Me. Dinner. Friday?" he asked, with a chuckle.

"Oh. I'm sorry," I said while twisting my own napkin into a wrinkled mess. "I can't."

"Can't? Really?" He sounded hurt. "You're turning me down again? The man everyone in town already thinks you're going to marry?"

"I am sorry, but it wouldn't—"

"No, Tru. I'm the one that's sorry," he said softly. He headed toward the front door. Dewey and I followed. Jace stepped out into the night and then turned back toward me. "If you see anything strange happening at the library—anything at all—give me a call. Please."

I nodded even though I knew he would be the last person I would call about strange happenings at the library.

Dewey looked up at me and meowed in that disapproving manner cats mastered so well.

Chapter Seven

———o———

"WWMMD?" Flossie asked Tori and me the next afternoon as we moved chairs into a circle for our Mystery Book Club. The book club met every fourth Wednesday. It used to meet upstairs in the library. But since the renovations, we'd moved the meetings to the secret bookroom. I'd signed out from work and had taken a late lunch break so no one in the library upstairs would come looking for me.

"Are you having a stroke or something, Flossie?" Tori grumbled. "You're speaking gibberish. No one can understand you." She still hadn't made peace with Charlie and had been as prickly as a sandbur ever since she'd arrived.

"I said"—Flossie spoke slowly, enunciating each letter—"W-W-M-M-D, or in other words, 'What Would Miss Marple Do?' Our book club members have read enough mystery novels for us to qualify as professional investigators. We need to start pooling our combined knowledge to figure out who is making a mess of this room and why. What would Miss Marple do if she found herself in this situation?"

Tori shook her head and muttered, "You're crazy."

Although Tori had been coming to my Mystery Book Club meetings ever since I'd started the group way back in high school, she never read any of the books. She rarely took the time to sit down to read for pleasure.

"No, she's not crazy," I said. "Flossie has a point. If our group members put our heads together, I don't see why we can't figure out how our library saboteur is getting into the building. We should also be able to come up with a list of people who might have wanted Owen dead. It's a great idea."

After Jace had left last night, I did some hard thinking and came to an important conclusion: the fastest way to prove to myself that the break-ins and Owen's murder weren't related was to figure out who was breaking into the library and who killed Owen. If I knew those two things, I could happily keep everything down here in my basement bookroom secret without feeling a morsel of guilt.

"Flossie's idea of asking the book club to help in the task of solving both mysteries is a fabulous idea."

"Thank you, Tru." Flossie wrinkled her nose in Tori's direction. "I knew *you'd* agree with me."

"Do we know who'll be able to make it today?" I asked before my two friends started arguing. Again. They both had personalities that were about as powerful as a hurricane, which was one reason I loved them. But those strong personalities sometimes rubbed each other the wrong way.

"I suppose Charlie will show up," Tori said with a grimace. "He said he wanted to become a regular after attending last month's meeting. But that's just me making an assumption. It's not as if I've heard from him since yesterday or anything. Because I haven't."

"Delanie told me she planned to come," Flossie offered after an awkward silence. Delanie Messervey was one of the library's biggest supporters. She was also Anne Lowery's aunt and close friends with Mrs. Farnsworth. Delanie and Mrs. Farnsworth even went on vacations together. The fact that Delanie knew about the secret bookroom made me nervous. But there was no way to turn back time and undo telling her about what we'd been doing in the basement. That Delanie knew about this place was my fault, since I was the one who had invited her to its opening. "She said she's bringing a friend."

"A friend?!" Tori shrieked. "The silly woman will probably end up bringing Mrs. Farnsworth. You know how those two women are." She held up two fingers and pressed them tightly together. "What will you do when she fires you, Tru? Where will you go?"

"Cool your jets. Delanie knows to be careful when telling others about this place," Flossie said in that soothing tone I needed to hear. "Tori, you need to stop scaring Tru. She's doing the best she knows how in balancing her duties upstairs with keeping this bookroom going, which we all know isn't easy. And she makes sure anyone who walks through those doors understands their responsibility to keeping our secret as well."

"I just don't want to lose you." Tori threw her arms around me and hugged me so tightly my ribs hurt. "If Mrs. Farnsworth fires you, you'll have to move away in order to get a job at another library. And then what will I do? You know I'd be a wreck without you, you know that. You're my rock."

I wiggled out of her embrace. "I'm not going anywhere. Cypress is my home." *This library is my home.*

Dewey nudged my leg as if agreeing with me. He then rolled onto his back and bit my ankle.

"Ow, why did you do that?" I rubbed my ankle, but he hadn't bitten it too hard. The skin wasn't even broken.

While still lying on his back, the naughty kitty stared up at me with his vivid green eyes and seemed to grin as he waved his paw at me.

"Who gave Dewey catnip this time?" I asked.

"Miss Tru," Hubert Crawford whispered.

I turned to see the president of the museum board.

"You gave him catnip?" I'd never noticed Hubert ever paying much attention to the library tabby.

"No. I . . ." He turned to the man standing next to him. I sighed. Hubert had brought a friend with him. Perhaps Tori had a point about too many people being told about the library without our knowledge. Maybe I needed to come up with some rules about bringing new people into the bookroom. A nomination process?

While I wanted this place to be open and welcoming, at the same time we needed to protect it.

"Oh, hello." I didn't recognize his friend.

This new man was much younger than Hubert. He looked to be about my age. Also, unlike Hubert, he dressed as if he lived in this century, with a polo shirt and khaki pants. His dark hair was slicked back with some kind of hair product. He flashed a toothy smile.

"Hubert has sneaked me into this room a couple of times over the past several weeks so I could help him with his research." His voice possessed a charismatic quality that made me feel like I was the most important person in the room. He took my hand in his. "You must be Trudy Becket. Our Hubert has been singing your praises as well."

"Actually, my name is Trudell, not Trudy. And you are?" I asked as I slipped my hand from his.

"Calhoun. Frank Calhoun. I beg your pardon about the name mix-up. I'm usually a crackerjack at remembering names. Comes in handy in the car sales business."

Hubert slapped him on the back. "He's our newest member on the museum board. Calhoun here had taken a keen interest in assisting with my research a few months ago. He's listened to all the stories my maw-maw used to tell about the library back in her day. And now he's going to shift his research to help me dig up something in the library's original papers that will explain our poltergeist. I hope you don't mind that I let him in on our secret." He touched a finger to the side of his nose. "There's very little in the museum's archives that even mentions our library. I'm hoping to find more information in the documents that you have over yonder." He nodded to the local documents section of the bookroom.

"Well, Frank, I hope Hubert has already gone over the rules with you. But in case he hasn't, let me briefly review them. You're welcome to come down here during library hours. The room isn't always manned. If you need to check anything out and none of the volunteers are available, there is a self-checkout process." I went on to walk him through the low-tech way we checked out books using book slips that were prestamped with due dates. "The most important thing to remember is that this room doesn't officially exist. You don't tell people about this place unless they are the kind of person you can trust with the location of your favorite fishing spot. If word gets out about our bookroom to the wrong people, it will be shut down. Do you understand that?"

Nerves had made my voice sharper than usual.

"Yes, ma'am." Frank gave me a salute. "I see you and your friends are setting up for some kind of meeting. I'll not detain you. We have work to get to as well."

"Thanks to some new information Frank has already brought to the table this morning, we're on the verge of revealing some important facts," Hubert said. "I'll bring the results to you when we're done finding some backup sources to prove or disprove what he's found."

"That would be wonderful," I said, even though I doubted anything the two of them learned about the distant past would have any relevance to the vandal attacking the bookroom today. However, gathering historical information and putting it together in a usable format for future readers was always a worthy endeavor. I looked forward to watching our local history section grow.

Before they left to bury themselves in the historical documents, I felt as if I needed to say something about Owen's death. Hubert's lack of reaction to the news about what had happened to a member of his museum board behind the library still bothered me.

"Let me offer both of you my deepest condolences over Owen's death. Losing a member of the museum board must have been a shock," I said.

The two men exchanged glances before Hubert said, "Yes, well, no one on the board really knew Owen Maynard that well."

"Is that so? But I heard he was serving as vice president." How could a stranger step into such a high position? The museum board seemed to be a close-knit organization.

"He was. He was." Hubert cleared his throat. "But it was . . . um . . . just a temporary thing. He stepped up to the position after Fenwick Harrington"—he cleared his throat again—"after old Fenny passed."

"What happened to Fenwick?" I asked. The old fellow would come to the library when it still had its full collection of books, but he'd preferred to talk with Mrs. Farnsworth. I never had a chance to get to know him well. And after we'd opened the bookroom, Hubert had warned us not to invite Fenwick since he couldn't be trusted to keep any kind of secret from Mrs. Farnsworth.

"He died . . . unexpectedly," Hubert said. He cleared his throat a third time. "Look, we have quite a bit of work to do and not much time before Frank has to return to the dealership."

I bit my lower lip as I watched the two men hurry over to start their research. Why was Hubert, who usually talked the ear off anyone he met, suddenly reticent? I worried even more about what was happening with the museum board to make him act that way.

I couldn't help but wonder if Hubert knew more than he was saying about why Owen was killed.

Chapter Eight

———•———

By the time I returned to where my friends were setting up for the book club, the seats were already in place. Flossie was pulling the plastic off the fried chicken salad platter I'd picked up from the Grind. The scent of spiced fried oil filled the air. Tori set paper plates, napkins, and little plastic forks on the table beside the platter. Cups and a jug of sweet tea had already been set up on the table.

Flossie had taken one look at the sweet tea and grumbled that there wasn't any Coke for her to drink. With a sniff she pulled out a warm bottle of water from the bag hanging from her wheelchair and took a sip.

Pleased to see everything was ready—save for having forgotten Flossie's Coke—I grabbed a copy of *Murder at the Vicarage*, the Agatha Christie classic we were all rereading. Well, not Tori, who had never read an Agatha Christie mystery in her life. But she had watched several of the movies.

After her marriage with Number Two had crumbled and she was acting as if she was planning to murder the man, I'd invited her to my house to watch every murder mystery show I had on DVD to convince her that she wouldn't get away with anything she might have been planning. Cypress was too small a town and had far too many busybody neighbors.

Tori and Flossie seemed to be getting along again, I was glad to see. Tori looked almost happy as she filled her plate. Her good mood lasted until Charlie walked through the door.

She spotted him. Her smile instantly dropped, and she got the same look on her face that she wore after Number Two had left her. It was downright scary. I jumped between the two of them before Tori had a chance to toss her plate of salad at him.

"Charlie, it's so good to see you again," I said, sounding artificially chipper. He frowned at that.

"Good afternoon, Tru. I brought this for you." He handed me a book. I looked at the spine. It was an old copy of Agatha Christie's *The Body in the Library*. "It's signed," he said as he sidestepped me to get to Tori.

I flipped the book open to the title page. *Glory be!* The queen of crime had scrawled her signature across the page. My heart beat double time as I lightly ran my finger over the slightly faded black ink.

"Is this . . . is this real?" I stammered.

"It sure is. When I saw it, I knew you'd give it the best home in town."

I started to gush my thanks when Tori pushed me aside. "Oh? You're here? You had nothing else to do, Charlie? No old 'friends' popping in for a quick visit, so you decided to grace us with your presence?" Despite Tori's sharp tone, I could hear the hurt in her voice.

I closed the book.

Dewey meowed worriedly.

"Um . . . Tori . . ." Flossie started to say. She looked as concerned as I felt. Tori's passionate nature, while usually one of her strongest qualities, could sometimes be her downfall.

"Surely, you aren't feeling jealous, love?" Charlie asked.

Dewey arched his back and hissed.

Flossie groaned.

The poor man seemed unaware of the imminent danger he was facing.

I tried again to step between Charlie and Tori with the hopes of keeping a new world war from erupting. But Tori raised a hand and blocked me.

She tossed her hair.

"Jealous?" he asked.

She laughed. "Me?" She flashed Charlie a toothy smile. "Why should I be jealous? It's not like we've been dating long enough for things to be exclusive. What you do with Candy is your business."

"I'm not doing anything with Candy. She's an—"

"An old friend," Tori finished for him. "Yes, you've already told me that. And you told me she was simply passing through town, which—*come on*—we both know was a lie."

Still, Charlie looked nonplussed. He shook his head and gave up when Tori didn't say another word. Instead of arguing, he headed to the lunch table to pour himself some sweet tea. "Your instincts about people astound me, Tori," he said. "You are right. You've caught me in a lie. Candy did come to Cypress for a specific reason." He held up his hand as if reciting an oath. "And that reason had nothing to do with me. But a man has his ego and likes to pretend that pretty girls flock to him."

"Give me a break." Tori shook her finger at him as she bit off each word. "You expect me to buy that? We might be living in a small town, but I'm not some green girl who doesn't know what's what in the world."

I was thinking the same thing. Charlie was an exceptionally handsome man. And well read. There was no reason women wouldn't flock to him.

"Mind you, it used to happen." He took a sip of his tea before placing a hand on his chest. "Women would follow me around. But I'm not in my prime anymore. And as surprising as it might sound, my interest in old books seems to discourage the ones that do take the time to flirt with me."

I scoffed. Certainly, that couldn't be true. A man who loved books was my idea of a perfect catch.

"Yes, I can see that," Tori said, her voice a touch less menacing. "Your obsession with books can be off-putting. I mean, who wants to hear 'blah, blah, blah,' about some dead writer that no one has ever heard of."

"You're crazy," I blurted, and then blushed hotly when both Charlie and Tori turned toward me. "The two of you are being silly. Books are cool. The fact that Charlie loves them means he has a brain in his head, which isn't something you can say about most of your exes, Tori. And, Charlie, you need to grovel a little because Tori has been hurt in the past, and seeing you having lunch with Candy in that dress that plunged practically to her skinny navel has left her feeling shaken."

Charlie started to say something to Tori that I was fairly confident would be charming enough to melt all our hearts, but before he could utter even the first part of a groveling apology, Delanie burst through the door in typical Delanie style. "Sorry I'm late. I was working on improving my apple pie recipe for the contest and completely lost track of time. Is the rumor true? Did your aunt Sal decide not to enter the contest this year?"

Aunt Sal wasn't planning on entering the apple pie contest? This was the first I'd heard about it. I was about to tell Delanie that, but she kept talking without pausing for a breath.

"It's about time she let someone new win. My goodness, it smells good in here. What's for lunch?"

She was dressed in a vintage powder-blue swing dress from the 1950s with a cute matching leather purse. Her bleached blond hair was done up in a refined updo that I envied.

"Dang, y'all have opened a speakeasy down here," her much less flashy companion, Doris Heywood, drawled as she took in the room. She adjusted her vintage cat-eye tortoiseshell glasses. "A speakeasy with old books. Who would have guessed we'd find something like this down here? I sure wouldn't. Not in a million billion years. No, ma'am, not I. Oh, is that a card catalog?" She pulled open one of the drawers. "Oh! And there are actually cards in it. I've never seen one that was being used for its intended purpose. These old things sell like hotcakes in the vintage market."

"I hope you don't mind that I invited my friend," Delanie said, her tone happy even though she had cringed at Doris's strong reaction to seeing the library's secret bookroom for the first time. "I was comforting her yesterday after the . . . um . . . *ordeal*." She whispered the last word. "That's when she mentioned how much she enjoyed reading old mysteries. We both love all sorts of old things. Did you know she operates several online stores that sell vintage items? Well, we were talking about those old books we both like to read and then started to reminisce about how the library used to be filled with books instead of computers, and it just hit me. I should invite Doris. That's what I told myself. And before thinking to ask you if it was okay, Tru, I blurted it out that I was coming to a book club down here and that she should come. I do hope you don't mind." Her speech came out all this in one breath. "Ah, fried chicken salad. Did this come from the Grind?"

"Of course I don't mind," I said, even though I kind of did mind. "The books in the library belong to everyone." I then repeated the same rules of the bookroom that I'd given to Frank not more than ten minutes earlier, putting extra emphasis on the need for secrecy. "And yes, the meal did come from the Grind. It's one of my favorite places."

"It is delicious, even though she forgot to buy Cokes to drink. There's some kind of overly sweet tea in the jug that everyone raves over. Shall we get started?" Flossie asked as she wheeled to her regular place in the circle.

"I do enjoy a good Agatha Christie novel," Doris said, her voice positively vibrating with excitement. "They are quite popular in my online used bookstore. People from everywhere like to buy them. Did you know that Agatha Christie was quite a mysterious figure herself? She went missing for eleven days and triggered a nationwide manhunt in England, and to this day no one knows why."

"Yes, I have read a bit about it." I fixed my plate, poured a drink, and then picked a chair in the circle. "It's an interesting puzzle."

"The leading theory is that Agatha Christie had learned her husband was cheating on her," Charlie put in. "The jerk may have even asked for a divorce, so she fled." He glanced over to Tori. "Clearly, the man was an idiot."

"Clearly," Tori agreed with a deep nod. But when she took her chair, she chose one that was as far away from Charlie as the small circle would allow. Delanie's straw purse had been on that seat. Tori moved it to the empty seat beside her. After getting settled, she smiled at Doris, who had already taken the chair to her left.

Seeing that there was no way to sit close to her, the poor man sighed and sat in the chair next to mine. Charlie himself was a mystery. The owner of the used bookstore had moved to Cypress from Las Vegas. But when anyone asked him about what work he'd done in that glittering city, he'd only answer vaguely that he'd worked in security. Tori liked that about him. I didn't.

I tried not to worry that he'd been mixed up with anything illegal, like the mob. Yet he had come to town with loads of money, enough to buy one of the downtown's historic buildings, and he wore the most fashionable suits despite how little he must be making running a used bookstore in a small rural town. I also couldn't help but wonder about Candy—his friend from Vegas—coming to town for a reason other than to visit him. She had a reason to visit our cozy little town other than to see her old friend? Another reason to visit *Cypress*? I couldn't imagine that she would travel halfway across the country for a spot of fishing or boating. What could she be up to? Was she involved with the mob too?

Did Owen overhear or see something Candy was doing behind the library that he shouldn't have?

The more I thought about it, the more the mystery behind her visit unsettled me.

"Speaking of mysteries," Delanie said as she gracefully slid into her chair, the one beside Tori, "I still cannot believe what happened to that poor Owen Maynard. I mean, he drank to excess far too often and could turn surly, but the thought that someone in town would kill him chills my blood."

I glanced over at Charlie. His expression remained inscrutable. He seemed more interested in eating his lunch than paying attention to the conversation.

Delanie lowered her voice and added, "Do you suppose his long-suffering wife finally snapped and bopped him over the head with one of his own bottles?"

"I don't see how Gracie Mae put up with his antics for this long," Tori said. "I certainly wouldn't stick around longer than a day with him acting like that." She was looking at Charlie as she said it.

But I was thinking the same thing. I wondered if Jace and Police Chief Fisher considered sweet Gracie Mae Maynard a suspect. Did the woman have an alibi? Would she even need an alibi? I mean, it really was hard to imagine Gracie Mae getting upset at anyone. Besides which, if she hadn't been driven to violence by Owen periodically drinking himself silly over the past sixteen years, what could have possibly changed to make her break now?

"What would Miss Marple think about the mystery unfolding behind our own library? Would she have any insights that none of us have yet considered?" Flossie asked with a glance in my direction. It was her turn to lead the group discussion and she certainly caught everyone's attention with that first discussion question. But before anyone could say anything, she said, "While Owen's murder is interesting to ponder, let's set it aside for now. In the meantime, I'd like us to start the meeting. I do hope y'all enjoyed visiting with Miss Marple in St. Mary Mead." Instead of launching into a short summary of the story, like she usually would do, she said, "Let's do something different today. We all know how Ms. Agatha Christie is a master at tucking in her clues within the story. And we've worked hard over the years to match her cleverness while trying to suss out those clues. I was thinking we could use the mystery we all read as a springboard for solving a little mystery ourselves."

"Oh, that sounds delightful," Delanie said. She balanced her lunch plate on her lap so she could clap. "I've always wanted to try my hand at playing amateur sleuth."

"You don't mean we're going to talk about Owen's murder, do you?" Doris's leg stopped bouncing and all the color drained from her face. "Y'all do remember that I found him?"

"No, no, no," Flossie was quick to say. She held up her hands like twin stop signs. "Nothing morbid like that. It must have been horribly upsetting for you to find him like that yesterday, Doris dear. No, I'm sorry to have made it sound that way. What I'm suggesting is that we look into something different altogether. There have been three break-ins to our bookroom over the past couple of weeks. Nothing has been taken, but whoever has been coming in here has been leaving the place in a shambles. Since the secret bookroom doesn't officially exist, we can't ask the police's help in tracking down the culprit. So, I was thinking that if we could figure out why someone would want to toss the books off the shelves, we could find a way to stop it from happening."

"Oh." Doris breathed out a relieved breath.

"I think that's a fantastic idea," Charlie said. He also sounded curiously relieved. "No need to poke our noses in police business. And the police don't need to poke their noses into library business either."

"Where do we start?" Tori asked.

Flossie set aside her plate and pulled one of her many notebooks from the tote bag hanging from her wheelchair. "How about we brainstorm possible motives?"

"Sorry to interrupt," Frank said. "I couldn't help but eavesdrop." He pulled a chair over to our circle and wedged it between mine and Doris's. He sat down and propped his elbows on his knees. "Care if I join in? I do love a good mystery."

"It appears you already have joined us," Doris said as she scooted her chair away from his.

"Of course we don't mind," I said, even though, again, I did kind of mind. It seemed to be a common refrain for the day.

There wasn't enough room for him to be sitting where he was sitting without having his leg press against mine. I scooted my chair back to make the circle bigger.

"Are we planning to catch the killer?" Frank asked. He slid his chair back and once again put his leg in close proximity with mine. "Everyone is talking about how you single-handedly captured a killer last month."

"I didn't single-handedly do anything. My friends and I"—I gestured to the rest of the group—"merely helped the police catch a murderer."

He patted my leg. "That's not how I heard it, but I understand why you'd want to downplay your involvement. I've heard from more than one person that you've proved yourself to be a brilliant sleuth. I've never believed that real-life amateur sleuths existed. And here we have had one living in our little town all this time with no one knowing."

I gritted my teeth. Sure, he was charming and perhaps I should feel flattered—more often than not people tended to ignore a plain Jane like me—but I had too much on my mind to enjoy some unexpected compliments and (maybe even) a bit of flirting.

Tori, on the other hand, was making all sorts of suggestions with her eyebrows. Suggestions like, *go for it, girl.* "That's our Tru," she said, sounding more like her happy self. Perhaps getting some lunch into her stomach had helped her get control of her emotions. She was well known for her "hangry" explosions. "Tru hides her light under a bushel, as my gramps likes to say."

"I'm not hiding anything . . . other than this bookroom. Now let's get back to the matter at hand. We're not doing anything dangerous like going after a killer," I told Frank. I then briefly explained to him that we were looking into the break-ins. "While there are signs that the lock to this room has been picked, there are no signs of forced entry at any of the library's entrances."

Frank furrowed his brows. "Sounds like a locked-room mystery."

"Exactly what I was thinking," Charlie said.

"And that's our first main clue," Flossie added as she jotted notes onto the paper. "What are some elements that most locked-room mysteries share?"

"They are all seemingly impossible crimes, but there's always a rational explanation," Charlie said. "Mystery author John Dickson Carr is a master of these. I have a first-edition copy of his 1935 classic, *The Hollow Man*, for sale in my shop."

"I've read a few locked-room mysteries. I seem to remember that someone could hide inside the room, so they are in the room even after it was locked," Delanie added.

"There could be a mechanical device, like a robot being controlled remotely, that is already in this room somewhere that is doing the damage," Frank suggested.

Tori rolled her eyes and then said, "Or someone could block a door open, so even if the room is locked, the perpetrator can still get in."

Flossie nodded while writing down all the ideas.

"Someone might have left a window unhinged," I said. There were a few operable windows in the building. I made a mental note to check that they were securely locked.

"Whoever is breaking in might have access to the main library."

Delanie lowered her voice before adding, "Like an inside job. Someone who already has a key."

Flossie wrote that into her notebook.

"Oh! I know," Doris said. "There could be a secret door in here. A secret panel of some sort."

"That is definitely one of the more fantastic plots that often show up in these kinds of stories," Charlie said, with a kind smile for the younger woman.

Tori snarled.

Doris didn't seem to notice the tension between them. She leaned forward. "You know what we all should do? We should go on a search of the library, to see if there's a secret button or lever that could open the hidden panel."

Everyone smiled awkwardly at this idea.

"Let's check out some of the other ideas first, dear," Flossie said. "We have quite a list. We could—"

"Do any of the other library employees know about this place?" Doris interrupted to ask. She seemed to really be getting into the spirit of our investigation.

"No" was my quick answer. But then I thought about how Anne liked to taunt me relentlessly about keeping Dewey down here. Had she been poking around in the basement? "Anne might know," I amended.

"Anne would never do something like this." Delanie practically leaped from her seat as the words shot out of her mouth.

Anne wasn't just Delanie's niece, she was her *favorite* niece.

"I agree with Delanie," Tori said. "If Anne knew about this place, she'd report it. She is a zealot about the library's new format and would view this room as a mark against what she's trying to achieve."

"How about Mrs. Farnsworth?" Charlie asked Delanie. "Do you think she suspects anything? From what I've seen of the head librarian, not much happens in the library that she doesn't know about."

Delanie shook her head slowly before answering. "She doesn't know."

"If she did, do you think she'd say something to you?" I asked.

"Definitely," she answered without having to stop and think about it. "We talk about what's going on at the library all the time."

"Would anyone else have a key to the library?" Flossie asked.

"I don't even have a key," I grumbled. I couldn't understand why Mrs. Farnsworth refused to trust me with opening up the library. If I had a key, I could come in extra early and get Dewey down to the basement without having to walk past the rest of the library staff.

"But certainly, someone at town hall or with the maintenance staff has a key," Flossie said.

"Not the maintenance staff. Mrs. Farnsworth wouldn't allow that. But I suppose the new town manager would," I offered. They'd recently hired the town clerk, Gretchen Clark, to take the reins at running the town. "But I can't imagine that she'd come to the library to periodically wreck the bookroom. After what happened last month with the murder and the arrests, she has her hands full down at town hall. I've only seen her at the library once since she's taken the position."

"My Anne has a key," Delanie said after she finished chewing a forkful of salad.

"She does?" That was news to me.

Delanie shot a guilty look in my direction. "With all the work she's been doing with getting the electronic equipment up and running, she needed to have access to the building after closing."

I bit my tongue to keep from saying something I'd regret. It was unfair of me to feel jealous. Anne was the only person who fully knew how to work the various equipment she'd installed upstairs. I'm sure Mrs. Farnsworth had no choice but to grant Anne access to her precious machines.

"Maybe if we asked ourselves why someone is sabotaging the library, that might lead us to who would be doing it," Tori suggested.

"From time to time I have someone leave bad reviews about one of the many products that I sell in town and online," Doris said in a rush. "Just last month, someone wrote a review saying that my essential oils were nothing more than overpriced, spiced-up olive oils, which is absurd. My products are of the highest quality. The ingredients are sourced from—"

"How does this relate to the library, dear?" Flossie gently interrupted.

"Oh, it's related. You see, the reviews . . . they are never really about my products, are they? Someone calls the antique and vintage items I sell online cheap crap. But what they're really saying is that they are jealous of my success. Couldn't that be what's happening here? Someone is jealous of what's going on in this bookroom. Someone is jealous of you, Tru."

My first reaction was to scoff at the idea. I'd spent my entire life living first in the shadow of my mother and then the shadow of the formidable Mrs. Farnsworth. Most people in Cypress had trouble remembering my name.

"Doris might be right," Flossie said. "You're being portrayed as a book-bearing Robin Hood around town. Someone could feel threatened that you are getting so much attention. Maybe that person feels as if you're pulling attention away from them?"

"But who would be jealous *of me*?" I asked, still unable to believe it.

"Mrs. Farnsworth has been walking around like she has a bee in her bonnet ever since your rise in the community," Tori said.

"But she wouldn't harm the books," I pointed out.

Everyone nodded.

"Anne is unhappy that she isn't being hailed as some kind of techno wonder woman. She might want to discourage you from providing books to the community," Flossie suggested.

Before I could point out that Anne could stop me by simply telling Mrs. Farnsworth about the bookroom, Delanie shot out of her chair again. "My niece would never do something like that! She's a gem. It's Tru that has been doing everything possible to sabotage Anne's hard work and turn the community against her. Everyone thinks Tru is this sweet, kind librarian, but you're not sweet. You're bitter."

As she spat her accusations at me, her plate of fried chicken salad sailed across the circle and landed in my lap. Whether it was an accident when she'd jumped up from the chair or whether she tossed the plate at me, I don't think we'll ever know. But one thing was clear. The chicken and lettuce swimming in spicy mayonnaise had splattered all over my face and my white sweater set.

Everyone gasped and gaped at Delanie. Everyone except Tori. She had, I noticed, turned her troubled gaze toward Charlie. Charlie, who owned a used bookstore. Charlie, who dreamed of creating a literary community in his shop. Charlie, who was always around and knew as much about the bookroom as any of us.

"*It's him,*" she mouthed.

Chapter Nine

O h my goodness." Delanie rushed at me with a handful of napkins. "Oh my goodness, that's going to stain." She dabbed at my sweater and pants with a ferocious energy. "Oh my goodness, I can't believe I did that."

"It's not him," I said as I plucked chicken from my cheek.

"What's that?" Delanie asked.

"Nothing," I said.

"It is," Tori countered.

This wasn't the first time one of us had suspected Charlie of being a villain.

"Can I have a few of those napkins?" Charlie asked. He must have been within my splash zone. Chicken salad had splattered across his expensive tailored pants.

Tori thrust a wad of napkins in his direction while giving me the side-eye.

"I'll get the mop." Flossie moved toward the door. "I suppose our meeting is adjourned for the month."

Frank chuckled as he dabbed at some chicken salad that had landed on his khakis. "If I'd known book clubs were this exciting, I would have joined one years ago."

"I found it!" Hubert crowed, seemingly oblivious to the drama that had erupted not a few feet away from him. He shot up from his chair and waved a piece of paper over his head.

No one paid him a whit of attention.

"Anne is such a sweet girl," Delanie was saying as she kept dabbing at my sweater. I tried to push her away. "If you would simply give her a chance, I know the two of you would be the best of friends." *Dab. Dab.* "She moved to town not knowing anyone, save for family. All of us are as old, older than her parents. Plus, she doesn't like baking or apple pie. She needs friends closer to her own age." *Dab. Dab.*

"Please stop." I snatched the napkins from Delanie's hands. "I hear what you're saying about your niece. And I understand that you're trying to be a good aunt and all. But friendship is a two-way street. Anne thinks I'm a dinosaur. I have serious doubts that she wants to be my friend."

"Nonsense." Delanie tried to come at me with a new stack of napkins. "You intimidate her. You're capable and well-liked."

"See, that only proves my point. Anne is jealous of you." Doris clapped her hands. "She has to be a suspect."

Delanie stiffened. "She's not!"

"Let's not start this again. I think we've had enough chicken salad tossed around for today," I said.

"Sorry." Delanie's face flooded with color. "Sorry."

"Are all y'all's ears clogged up?" Hubert complained. "I said I found it. I found the proof we've been looking for." He shook the paper he was holding. "It's right here."

"What is?" I asked as I plucked some chicken from my shoe and tucked it into a napkin.

"The focus of our research, dang it." When I didn't immediately react, he gave a long-suffering sigh. "You know, the reason there's a poltergeist haunting your bookroom? My maw-maw was right. This basement has been hiding secrets for a hundred years." He hurried over to us and stood in the center of the circle. "You see, my maw-maw worked in this library when she was a teenager. It was the 1920s. Times were good for the town. Many people relied on farming . . ." While he launched into a long-winded history of Cypress's economy, Tori pulled me aside.

"Think about it," Tori whispered. "Without this bookroom, Charlie's store would be the only place residents could go to get printed books. You're cutting into his business. What better way to discourage what we're doing here than to pretend to help while quietly sabotaging your work?"

"He could simply let word slip to Mrs. Farnsworth what we're doing," I pointed out. "That would put a quick end to things."

"No." Tori shook her head. "No. If he did that, he'd anger the book-loving public he needs for his store. No, he has to act in a clandestine manner . . . like a secret agent. And who knows? Perhaps he enlisted that gorgeous Candy to help him with his sabotage plans and something went wrong. And 'boom,' poor Owen is dead."

"I hate to interrupt," Charlie whispered from directly behind us.

Both Tori and I jumped. Had he overheard Tori's crazy musings?

His jaw looked tense. "It seems as if we're done here, and I need to get back to the shop." His gaze narrowed and his eyebrows flattened. "Tori? Perhaps we can talk tonight?"

"Perhaps." Tori crossed her arms over her chest and matched him glare for glare. "You'll have to come to Perks, though. I'm working the night shift."

He nodded and left just as Flossie returned with a mop and bucket.

"I never knew you to work on Wednesday nights," I said.

"I'm not scheduled to work, but I'm also not some horror-movie bubble brain. If he wants to talk to me, he's going to do it in front of a roomful of witnesses."

While I respected Tori for protecting herself, I still had a difficult time picturing Charlie as the villain of this mystery. For one thing, he would never do anything to harm the books. And for another, he'd just brought me a signed Agatha Christie novel. A signed copy!

Anyone who would do that had to be one of the good guys.

Didn't he?

"Thank you for a fun lunch, Tru," Frank said as he passed by us and headed toward the doors. "I do hope you'll welcome me back next week."

"Of course you can come back. But we meet the fourth Wednesday of every month, not every week. Next month, we'll be discussing . . ." I paused and thought about the book that was scheduled for October—a charming gardening mystery set at the White House. It was a novel I had been looking forward to discussing. But if we were to use Flossie's "Miss Marple" method of detection, we needed to keep reading Agatha Christie novels. I mentally scanned through the list of Agatha Christie mysteries and landed on Christie's thirteenth Miss Marple mystery. "*The Sleeping Murder*," I said, picking a book that was filled with decades-old motives and even hints of a ghost.

Frank raised his brows. "That's a good choice. I'll see you then. If you ever need to buy a car, I can get whatever you need." He slipped his card into my hand. "Or if you need anything else, I'm your man. Ladies."

Before I could even think to respond, Delanie pulled me into a big bear hug. "I do hope you can forgive me. I don't know what came over me. I've been under so much stress lately, but that's no excuse. I should have never taken out my stress on you."

What did Delanie have to be stressed about? She spent her days spearheading charity causes and spending her family's inheritance money. Of course, she had mentioned that she was working on her apple pie recipe for the upcoming festival. Many women in the community treated the competition quite seriously. But Delanie had never entered her pie in the contest before, so I couldn't imagine that she would be stressing about her first go at it. No one expected a baker to win on her first try. Only Aunt Sal had managed to do that.

Why wasn't Aunt Sal entering this year?

Just what I didn't need, another mystery.

I asked Delanie about Aunt Sal, but she hadn't heard any specific reasons for her dropping out. Delanie then let out a long, soulful sigh.

"What's been going on with you?" I asked. I was truly concerned. "You can trust us." I indicated Tori and myself. "We're good at keeping secrets."

"I know, dear." She patted my shoulder. "You two are like the daughters I never had. Well, I need to be going."

And without telling us anything of importance, she left.

Hubert, apparently unaware of his dwindling audience, continued his lecture about life in Cypress in the early 1900s. How anything he was telling us related to his supposed poltergeist was anyone's guess. "In the twenties, a connection between our town and nearby Hell Hole Swamp grew," he was saying.

Flossie deftly maneuvered her wheelchair around him so she could mop up the mess Delanie had made. The only person paying the man any attention was Doris.

She had settled back into her chair and was biting her lower lip as she listened to Hubert's history lesson. Her leg started bouncing again. "That is so interesting. Hell Hole Swamp is where all those mobsters operated their bootlegging stills during Prohibition, isn't it?"

Hubert nodded, pleased to have found someone who shared his interest in history. Her comment caused him to wander down another tangent about the history of Hell Hole Swamp and its brief brush with fame.

"I hate to leave you to clean up," I walked over and whispered to Flossie, "but I need to get back upstairs."

My friend paused in her mopping and looked me up and down before clicking her tongue. "Go. Mrs. Farnsworth will want you to change your clothes before she'll let you get back to work."

My sweater was hopelessly stained with a mixture of mayonnaise and the special spices the Grind used to make their fried chicken salad taste so addictively good. "That means I'll be late returning from lunch. She'll be putting another black mark against my name. Text if anything else happens down here." I started for the door.

"Miss Tru," Hubert called. "You can't leave yet. You haven't heard the best part."

"It'll have to wait. I have to get back to work."

"But"—he shook the paper he was holding—"the poltergeist. Surely you haven't forgotten that I found proof that it exists."

He had proof? Weirdly, part of me wanted to stay and hear the ghost story.

"Please, make it fast," I said, although I already knew that this was a hopeless request. He wasn't the sort who did anything quickly.

He took several deep breaths and cleared his throat before saying, "Here's the thing." His speech cadence thankfully did pick up speed. "A man was killed behind the library back in August of 1921. Does that sound familiar?" He thumped the newspaper article. "Like Owen, this man was drunk. Unlike the situation with Owen, drinking was illegal at the time."

I nodded.

He looked at me as if that should be enough information to convince me to believe in the poltergeist.

"Thank you," I said, and pulled the door open. "That's something I'll have to think about very carefully."

"She doesn't understand," I heard him complain as I rushed through the basement hallway. "Someone needs to make her see that this man—"

The bookroom's heavy doors slammed closed, cutting off the rest of this sentence.

Sure, I was curious about what he was saying. His cool reaction to

Owen's murder still bothered me. Was he pushing this poltergeist tale to distract us from looking at him as a suspect in Owen's murder? Oh dear, those questions were going to have to be put on hold. I didn't have time to wait around and see where his lecture was going. I needed to get changed and back to the library upstairs before Mrs. Farnsworth decided to fire me. School would be out in less than an hour. I had a reading program to lead this afternoon.

Inspiring young children's love of books—even if those books were now being read on computer tablets—was far more important than investigating Owen's murder. That was the police's responsibility.

Chapter Ten

———•———

Step back!" Anne cried shortly after the library had opened the next morning.

"No! I will not. I cannot let this happen." Hennie Goodloe blocked the entrance of the largest meeting room the next morning. She'd crossed her arms over her chest. A scowl creased the corners of her mouth. "I cannot let people come inside this . . . this . . . den of sin."

Anne was standing just inside the room. She was dressed in loose pants and a T-shirt that read "Slow Down and Tai Chi On." Her rainbow-colored hair was pulled up into a high ponytail.

"You can't block this door," Anne said from behind clenched teeth. "For one thing, blocking doors in a public building is a fire hazard. For another, this class is—"

Mrs. Farnsworth came hurrying over. "You have nothing to be upset about. Anne is teaching an exercise class."

"It's an exercise in sacrilege," Hennie shot back. "That's what it is."

Mrs. Farnsworth opened her mouth and shut it again. Very few in the community had ever talked back to Mrs. Farnsworth. The head librarian pressed her lips tightly together.

I took a step backward.

Mrs. Farnsworth looked around. "This is *my* library, not your husband's church. Within these walls, I am in charge, and I get to make the decisions about what classes we hold."

"That may be so." Hennie's voice had grown louder. "However, *we* will not allow the community to be infiltrated by the occult."

Mrs. Farnsworth shushed her. But it was too late. Several of the patrons began moving toward us to watch. Hubert Crawford and Frank Calhoun were two of the first to make their way over to us.

"There is nothing occult about the practice of—" Anne had started to say.

But Hennie was on a roll. Her voice grew even louder. "The good people of this community will not stand by silently and let Satan take over our governmental institutions!"

Mrs. Farnsworth drew a long, slow breath.

I took another step away from Mrs. Farnsworth and from Hennie.

"She's going to regret she said that," Frank murmured.

"Missy—" Mrs. Farnsworth's whispery voice had become nearly inaudible. "I've known you ever since you first came in here and that distracted mama of yours let you chew on the corners of all our picture books. Don't you dare question my faith."

"We. Will. Boycott," Hennie warned.

"You do what you need to do, but if you say one more word right now that disrupts my library, I will ban you from this building." Mrs. Farnsworth's voice was still the softest of whispers. And yet there was no doubt that everyone listening had heard her. Personally, I was shivering deep in my bones from the chill in her words. "I'll ban you for right now . . . and forever."

Hennie clutched her golden cross necklace and paled several shades.

"I'm . . . I'm leaving. But I'm not giving up," she muttered with none of her previous bravado.

Banishment from the library was Mrs. Farnsworth's harshest punishment. And Hennie had five young children who all attended library events. Even if Hennie didn't believe in reading novels, she depended on the library for free entertainment for her children. As she rushed off, she passed by me. "Heard about the engagement, Tru. If you need a place to hold the ceremony—"

"Rumors are wrong," I was quick to correct. "I'm not even dating anyone."

"Oh?" She stumbled to a stop and turned to look me up and down. "I'm surprised. I wouldn't have ever thought that you . . ." She shook her head. "I know several young couples who are looking to adopt."

"I'm not—"

"I can be discreet," she said as she hurried away. "Call me."

"Delightful woman," Frank murmured.

"Should we be worried about her?" Anne asked Mrs. Farnsworth.

"That church her husband founded is as much a cult as what she thinks she's protesting," the head librarian said with a sneer.

That might be true, but everyone knew the Goodloes had some powerful friends in town hall. I had a feeling this wasn't the last we'd be hearing from them.

"Well?" Flossie grumbled as she wheeled up to the meeting room. She was dressed in tight exercise leggings and a rainbow-colored tank top that matched Anne's hair. She had a towel draped over her shoulders. "Are we planning to stand around and stare at each other or are we going to go in and move our chi around?"

In an effort to show Anne that we were all on the same side, I had planned to attend her classes. All. Of. Them. Including this one, even though I wasn't a fan of organized exercise.

"Let's go," I said with a long sigh.

"Where are we going?" Frank asked as he followed us into the meeting room.

"This is a tai chi class," Anne answered before I could. "Beginners and experts welcome."

"Men and women?" he asked. He was the only man in the room.

"Everyone is welcome," Anne said. "It might be slow movements, but I assure you, every part of your body will get a workout. Even your mind."

Only a handful of people attended the inaugural tai chi class. But everyone left—myself included—feeling slightly sore, energized, and excited about next week's class. Who knew tai chi could be so fun?

"I'm going to tell everyone about this class," Delanie promised Anne on her way out. She hadn't said two words to me and blushed deeply whenever our gazes met. As we left, she stayed glued to Anne's side. "Imagine, my dear, getting a workout like this at the library. And for free. You are a wonder."

"I hate to admit it," Flossie said to me as we left the room, "but not all the changes Anne has made to our library are bad. Some things had been getting stagnant around here. No offense to you," she was quick to add. "But you have to admit that we've been seeing a few new faces coming to Anne's classes, or to use a sewing machine, or one of the computers."

"No offense taken," I said, although it was a prickly subject. All over the country, libraries were expanding their roles and reaching out to their communities in new ways. And that was a good thing. But at the same time, only one of those libraries had chucked all their books in favor of an online reading system like ours had.

"Can you believe how wild Hennie Goodloe acted? She should be ashamed of herself. That woman certainly had a bee in her bonnet," Frank said as he fell in step with me. "You do know that Hennie and that idiot husband of hers only took up the cause against the library because of Owen."

"What do you mean?" I asked.

"Hadn't you heard? Owen had been on a crusade against the library's changes. He said it was unnatural. He said the library should have kept the books."

"I'd heard him grouse about that a time or two myself," Flossie said. "He sounded a lot like you, Tru."

"While I'm mourning the loss of books, I do support the programs. If I didn't, I certainly wouldn't have signed up to learn how to knit. Mrs. Farnsworth is teaching that one."

I was not like Owen.

"While we're on the subject of Owen," Frank said. "Have you made any progress with the investigation?"

"I, um . . ." Truth be told, I hadn't made much progress. But since I didn't know Frank very well, I wasn't comfortable including him in our discussions, not even to tell him that we hadn't discovered anything.

"We were just heading down to the basement to share notes now, weren't we, Tru?" Flossie said, obviously not sharing my inclination to keep the investigation just between friends.

"Splendid!" Frank's face lit up. "I was supposed to spend the afternoon helping Hubert with his research. But an exercise class filled with beautiful ladies seemed so much more enticing." His eyes twinkled as he said it. "And I'd much rather talk about Owen's murder with you than dig through old papers searching for proof that a poltergeist is terrorizing the place. I mean"—he laughed—"poltergeists? That's got to be the craziest theory Hubert has ever come up with. Not that I've known him that long. But *really*. Am I right?"

He was right. But it felt mean to agree with him. Besides, for all I knew, he might go back to Hubert and tell him how I thought his theories were insane.

So instead of saying a word, I shrugged.

Flossie did the same.

If Frank was disappointed in our reaction, he didn't let it show. As we made our way down the back stairs, he chatted happily about his used car business, about fishing in the lake, and about how several of his business's cars were locked up in Owen's shop waiting to be fixed. "It is really a bother. A few of those cars had buyers waiting for them. And now, well, I suppose it can't be helped. Owen was causing trouble when he was alive, why shouldn't he continue that after his death?"

"What do you mean?" Flossie asked.

"As you know, Owen had taken over as vice president on Cypress's museum board after Fenwick Harrington croaked. Taking over meant that he had access to Fenwick's research papers—a fat lot of primary source documents. Fenny had been compiling a history of the neighboring Hell Hole Swamp. Had been working on it for years. Supposedly, he wanted to put on an exhibit at the museum about the swamp and the community living there. When Hubert asked for it, Owen acted as if he had no idea what he was talking about."

"Wait." I stopped in the middle of the basement corridor. "You're saying Owen stole Fenwick's work?"

"That's what I think. He stole it. How else could you explain where Fenny's work went? I mean, how could every last scrap of paper disappear like that? It's all irreplaceable too."

"What did Hubert do?" I asked.

"He exploded, of course." Frank shook his head. "Threatened to kick Owen off the board. Threatened to sue him even. Still, Owen stood by his story that he had never seen the papers and didn't know what Hubert was talking about."

"Why did you think Owen was lying?" Flossie asked.

Frank shook his head again and then flashed us one of his blazing smiles. "Why should I have believed the guy? He was awfully quick to volunteer for the position of VP. And it's a thankless position at that. The vice president is called on to do all the tasks Hubert doesn't enjoy doing. Fenny once told me Hubert would routinely call him at three in the morning to brainstorm ideas for research projects. Hubert is a great guy and all, but he doesn't understand personal boundaries."

"Then why in blazes did *you* accept the VP position?" Flossie demanded. "Do you have rocks for brains?"

Frank's smile widened. "I've been trying to get on the museum board for years now. When a position opened up, I jumped at the chance before anyone else could, even if it was the worst position on the board. I figure in a year or so, I can move into a better position, like fundraising. That's where the real networking happens. It's good for business to have a place on as many boards around town as possible."

I was still having a hard time trying to understand why Owen would want to steal research about a nearby swamp community. Nothing ever seemed to happen in Hell Hole Swamp. Heck, only a handful of people even lived in the area.

"Why would Hubert—or Owen, for that matter—care so much about a research project that doesn't even involve our town?" I asked.

"Dunno." Frank shrugged. "But everyone got real crabby about the subject real quick."

"Crabby enough to kill?" Flossie asked.

"Dunno. You'll have to ask Hubert."

Chapter Eleven

———— o ————

Unfortunately, I didn't get a chance to talk to Hubert about whether or not he'd been angry enough to kill Owen. As soon as I'd entered the bookroom that afternoon, Tori pounced on me like a cat on a mouse. Dewey, who was watching from his perch in the travel section, meowed as if impressed.

"It's him. I know it is." Tori dug her fingers into my arm. "I have proof that he's a filthy murderer."

"You do?" She had proof? That surprised me.

Her accused *him* clearly wasn't Hubert Crawford, whom the rest of us were all wondering about at that moment. Tears sparkled in Tori's eyes. My friend's heart was breaking, which could mean only one thing. She was talking about Charlie.

"Are you sure?" I asked.

"Yes, I'm sure." She thrust a piece of paper at me. "Charlie and that 'Candy' woman have been br-breaking into the library and th-they killed Owen when he saw them sn-sneaking out of the library that night," she sobbed.

"I don't believe it." The words shot out of my mouth before I had a chance to consider how my quick dismissal might hurt Tori. But honestly, my friend had to be wrong about him. A book lover would never throw books around and damage them like that. No book lover could do it.

With another distressed sob, she tapped the paper I was now holding with her purple-polished nail.

"What is this?" I asked.

"Isn't it obvious?" She sniffled.

"If it was obvious, dear, Tru wouldn't be asking you," Flossie pointed out gently.

"It's a transfer-of-title form," Frank said as he peered over my shoulder. "Deal with them all the time at the car lot. Never heard one used as evidence of a murder, though."

"Look at the *names*." Tori tapped her nail against the paper again.

"Charlie Newcastle," I read aloud. "And it looks like he's transferring title of an old truck from the 1990s to a Candice Newcastle. I didn't know he owned a truck. Did you?"

She shook her head. "Apparently I didn't know anything about him, the filthy liar."

"Where did you get this?" I asked.

"I'd stopped by the bookstore to bring him some coffee. You know, to show that I still cared about him and that I was willing to listen to him. And then I saw this"—she attacked the paper with another vicious series of fingernail taps—"sitting on his desk. I swiped it because it's evidence."

"Evidence that he's sold an old car to some woman," Frank said flatly.

"Doesn't anyone else see it?" Tori cried as tears spilled down her cheek.

"I'm afraid I think I do," Flossie said as she took the paper from me.

"But, Tori dear, there might be a simple explanation. Don't you think you should give him the chance to tell you his side of the story?"

"Give a murderer a heads-up that we're onto him?" Tori snapped. "No, thank you. I don't have a death wish."

"I don't understand," Frank said while looking from Flossie to Tori and finally to me.

I wasn't quite sure I understood either. But the longer I stared at the transfer-of-title form, the more pieces started to fall into place. "Are you suggesting that the Candice Newcastle named on the form is Candy Cane's real name?"

"I told you that Candy Cane had to be a stage name," Tori said, her voice growing even more brittle. "Fake. Just like Charlie. Everything he told me about her is clearly a lie. Remember he told me they were old friends? Old friend. Ha! I've been such a fool. Would you do that to someone, Frank? Would you lie? Tell me, and please be as candid as possible. Is this something all men do?"

"I'll . . . um . . . Hubert must be wondering where I've been," Frank said softly before rushing away.

"You need to talk with Charlie about this," Flossie said.

"I'm sure there must be a reasonable explanation," I said.

Tori started to tremble. "We all know what that reasonable explanation will be, don't we? Candice Newcastle and Charlie Newcastle. Same last name. Not a coincidence. Happens all the time in Vegas." Her voice turned high-pitched and strangled. "The jerk is married."

"They could be separated. Or even divorced. Perhaps she's having some financial troubles and came to him for help," I said, talking slowly as if I needed to talk Tori out of jumping off a high ledge. "Nothing on this paper tells us that they're still together or that they're collaborating on some devious plan to destroy our bookroom. Nothing on this paper tells us that he or *Candy* killed anyone. All it tells me is that he's selling or giving away a truck."

"A truck no one has ever seen," Tori pointed out angrily. "Charlie doesn't drive a pickup truck. And his—his"—she choked back another sob—"wife was driving an ugly rental sedan. He must have used the truck when carrying out the murder and now he needs to get rid of it. Fast."

Flossie handed the title transfer form back to Tori. "It's something we can look into. Don't you agree, Tru?"

"Yes, of course we'll support you and help you investigate what's going on with him." Not that I thought that title transfer form was evidence that Charlie had committed a crime.

Besides, Charlie was a smart guy. Even if he was breaking into the bookroom—which obviously he wasn't—I doubted he would have been so startled by seeing Owen passed out behind the library that he committed murder. But Tori was upset, and she needed us to stop her from doing what she had done in the past when she was *this* upset with a man. "Do you think you'll be able to get this form back onto Charlie's desk without him seeing you?"

"I suppose I could. But I'm not sure I'll want to go back to that scheming snake's store. Maybe we should let him know that we have this and let him sweat over it. That would serve him right."

"But, as you've already said, we wouldn't want to tip our hand," I said gently. "We wouldn't want to give him a reason to come after you, or any of us." That is, if he was guilty, which I was *fairly* sure he was not.

Tori chewed her bottom lip. "I suppose not. He might take his frustration at my thievery out on you, Tru, and if that happened, I'd never forgive myself."

"Good. Now, I need you to be careful. Don't let him see you return it." I wouldn't want her to do anything rash that she might regret later, especially if Charlie had a completely innocent explanation for the title transfer form.

"You could bring him another coffee tomorrow morning and push the paper under the desk when he's not looking," Flossie suggested.

"That way, when he finds it, he'll think it slipped off and fell to the floor."

Tori nodded as she slumped into the nearest chair. "I suppose I can do that."

"In the meantime, we do have another line of inquiry I'd like to follow," I said as my gaze traveled over to where Hubert and Frank were bent over a stack of papers. Whispering, I briefly outlined for Tori what Frank had told us about the tension between Owen and Hubert and Fenwick's missing research materials.

"But Hubert looks so frail," Tori said. "I can't imagine that he'd be able to hit anyone with a bottle with enough force to leave a bump, much less to kill a man."

"Looks can be deceiving," Flossie, who hated it when people underestimated her just because she was in a wheelchair, pointed out.

"Fine. But the Hell Hole Swamp isn't even remotely related to our library or Cypress. I don't see how some missing research could be related to the troubles we're having down here in the bookroom," I said.

"I don't think Owen's death is related to the secret bookroom," Flossie reminded us. "The swamp research might be a motive for his murder. That makes more sense than thinking that some stranger from another town has been breaking into our library and then one night killed someone who saw her committing the crime."

Tori harrumphed.

"We can still keep an open mind about everything," I said quickly, "but I don't think it will hurt to keep an eye on both Hubert and Frank."

Thankfully, both Tori and Flossie agreed.

I checked the time and saw that I needed to get back upstairs. "Text if you need me for anything," I told them. "And, please, be careful. Y'all are my best-besties."

"You know me. Careful is my middle name," Tori said, unable to keep a straight face, because we all knew that even if she could pick out her own middle name, it would never be *Careful*. And for the record, her middle name was Kaitlyn. A name that Mama Eddy only used when she felt like Tori was leading me astray. "Victoria Kaitlyn Green," she'd say. When we heard that, we knew a scolding would follow.

"Just be careful," I told my friend. "And don't do anything rash when it comes to Charlie. Please."

"I'll make sure she keeps her head on straight," Flossie promised.

Dewey echoed her sentiments with a loud meow and a narrowed gaze that he'd directed toward Tori. Silly, I know. But I found his green-eyed kitty glare more comforting.

With Dewey taking charge, Tori would be safe from herself. And also from the killer. But, mainly, from herself.

Chapter Twelve

That evening, after the library had closed for the day, I carried Dewey in his tote bag down Main Street toward Charlie's bookstore, the Deckle Edge. Tori had texted constantly all day, each text more frantic than the previous one. First, she couldn't bear to face Charlie. Then, if she did confront him, she would kill him. She'd put a knife straight through that lying heart of his.

That was the gist of the texts, that is, before they'd turned downright scary.

I'd texted and called and even showed up at her café to hug her neck. Knowing as I did how fragile and hurt she was feeling, there was no way in the world I was going to let her go to the bookstore and confront Charlie alone. She needed someone at her side as she faced him. And even though she had originally planned to meet him in the morning, I convinced her to meet me outside Charlie's bookstore as soon as I'd gotten off work. I didn't want her stewing and growing even more upset overnight.

I had managed to get away from the library early. But as I approached, I spotted Tori pacing in front of the bookstore. She'd styled her hair in a romantic updo, and she'd donned a slinky red dress with matching red heels that made her look like a fashion model. Her outfit was quite a contrast to my light blue sweater set, loose-fitting khaki pants, and pair of thick-soled orthopedic shoes that one of the older library patrons had recently given me.

As soon as my friend saw me, she grabbed my arm and pulled me close. "I'm nervous," she whispered. "He keeps texting. You don't think he knows I suspect him?"

"We'll cross that bridge when we come to it," I said. "Hopefully, we won't have to come to it."

Dewey stuck his furry head out of the top of the tote bag and greeted Tori with a sound that was part meow and part purr. Tori blinked at him. He reached out a paw and placed it on her hand as if trying to calm her.

"Hiya, kitty." She smiled as she scratched his head. He pressed his head into her hand as his purrs grew louder.

"Where's the coffee you were going to bring for Charlie?" I asked. We had planned over the phone about an hour ago that she'd give him a coffee and chat with him while I slipped into his office and returned the title transfer form. But Tori wasn't carrying anything other than an oversized purse.

The last time she carried that purse, she'd packed it with cans of spray paint that she'd used to paint rude words all over Number Two's brand-new BMW. This had happened after she had discovered he was cheating on her and she'd decided that everyone else in town needed to know about it.

She'd worn the same red dress and heels on that occasion as well.

"He doesn't deserve my coffee," she said bitterly.

"Tori? What's in the purse?" I asked, speaking slowly. "What are you planning?"

Dewey punctuated my question with a series of insistent meows.

She hugged the purse to her chest. "Nothing."

"Come on. What's in there?"

Instead of answering, she chewed on her lower lip.

"I want him to feel how much he's hurt me," she finally said.

I pulled my friend into another hug. "Of course you do, Tori. But we need to focus on the investigation. A man is dead. If Charlie or Candy is responsible, we need to stay focused on finding the kind of proof we can take to the police, don't you agree?"

She nodded. Slowly.

Good.

I shuddered as I imagined her turning her spray paint on all those innocent books in Charlie's store. "Perhaps I should hold on to your purse?"

"But I might—" she started to protest.

I held out my hand and gave her my best impersonation of Mrs. Farnsworth at her sternest.

Tori sighed and handed it over.

"Shall we go in?" I asked, sounding more confident than I felt. This meeting promised to be a disaster. The last thing I wanted to do was go in there. "Actually, I could do this myself. I don't really need you to cause a distraction," I said.

"Tru!" a woman shouted.

Both Tori and I turned to watch as Hennie Goodloe hurried toward us. A crowd of little kids followed behind her like a line of baby ducks.

"What could she possibly want?" Tori whispered.

"Tru!" Hennie panted a bit as she jogged up to us. "I wanted to make sure you understood I was sincere earlier."

"There's no need," I said. "It's all a misunderstanding."

She glanced over at Tori and then at her wide-eyed children, who were gathering around us. "Of course it is," she said dryly. Her gaze shifted to Charlie's shop window, which displayed novels, cookbooks, and histories with fall themes. "You aren't going in there, are you?"

"Books are my avocation," I pointed out.

"Oh, it's not the books I'm against. Well, novels can lead one astray. But I've already talked with you about that. It's the owner." She lowered her voice. "He's from Vegas, you know?"

"What does that have to do with anything?" Tori was quick to demand.

"Oh, you know. That place attracts all kinds of bad apples. And I've heard Charlie was just as bad as the rest of the criminals in *that* town. I wouldn't step foot in *his* store. Oh no, I wouldn't. One has to guard one's own soul. It's turning into a full-time job around here with all these 'people from off' moving here."

"That's the truth," Tori said. "They should build a gate at the town entrance and keep out everyone but the natives. My family, for example, has lived in Cypress for the past one hundred and fifty years." She tilted her head to one side. "How long has your family been part of our town?"

Hennie's parents had grown up in the upstate of South Carolina. They'd moved to Cypress after their car repair shop in Greenville had failed. Hennie's father had gone to work on one of the farms just outside town. Hennie's mother had taken a job as a maid. One of the houses she'd cleaned was Tori's parents' home. In terms of family histories, Hennie and her family were as much outsiders as Charlie.

"It's not the same thing," Hennie said, bristling. "At least my family roots are Southern."

"I don't know anything about Charlie's roots. They might be Southern," I said. I reached for the door handle. "How about we go in and ask him?"

"No! Landry would never forgive me if I led his children into that place." She hugged a newborn baby protectively to her breast. "Besides, it's getting late. I need to get dinner on the table. I just wanted to make doubly sure that you knew you could call me, Tru. It's bad enough that you have to work at the library. I fear for everyone who has anything to do with *those* classes. But, Tru, you can count on me to help you. When the time comes, I have resources."

"Resources?" Tori asked as Hennie and her brood hurried away. "What is she talking about?"

"Hennie thinks the library is going to hell in a handbasket," Doris answered before I could say anything. She had run up from behind us. It appeared that she had been chasing after a few of Hennie's straggling kids. Her cat-eye tortoiseshell glasses sat at a crooked angle on her face. "Go find Mommy," she said to one of the little boys before adding, "Hennie also has a bee in her bonnet when it comes to Charlie. If you ask me, it's because he's holding his book club meetings on the same day as her Bible study group. She's lost a few of her members—all younger women. It's stung her pride something awful."

"Are you working for Hennie?" I asked. Doris seemed to have an endless list of jobs. She cleaned houses, delivered mail part-time for the post office, had an online business, and now this? I wondered how she found time to do it all.

"I've been her part-time nanny for several months now. I help out around the house three times a week. If she had more money, she'd hire me full-time. Those offspring of hers are more than one woman can handle. *Noah! Don't stick your finger there!*" She pulled a tissue from her pocket and managed to wipe the boy's grimy hands before he ran off again. "Hennie says I'm a godsend. *Noah! I said don't—!* I'm going to have to run. But I did want to tell you that after I left the book club meeting the other day, I thought about the break-ins. *Noah! I'm warning you!* That boy." She shook her head. "I think there must be something hidden in the basement." She ran after Noah. "Look for a secret room!" she called out as she darted down the street.

"She's nuts," Tori said, with a laugh.

"Not too nuts. After all, *we* have a secret bookroom in the basement. Could there be something else? Maybe. Some*one* is definitely looking for some*thing*." I stepped on a crumpled old newspaper article on the sidewalk. Had it fallen out of Doris's pocket? I picked it up. The headline read, "Local Kershaw Man Hits the Jackpot with Hell Hole Swamp Bootlegger Bottles."

Huh.

"Now, you've really got to tell me what Hennie was talking about," Tori went on, not noticing that I would rather crawl in with a rhumba of rattlesnakes than tell her. "What resources does she think you need? Certainly not an exorcist."

"A what?" I jammed the crumbled newspaper into my purse. "Hennie wants to help find an adoptive family for that baby I'm having with Jace."

Tori's mouth dropped open. Her eyes bulged. That was an odd over-reaction. It wasn't as if she didn't know the rumors about me and Jace were still flying wild around the town.

But then I noticed that her gaze wasn't directed toward me but at something (or someone) beyond my shoulder.

"He's standing behind me, isn't he?" I said.

"I am," Jace replied.

Chapter Thirteen

You're pregnant. Well, that explains all these texts I've been getting from my mom today," Jace said. "The tone of them vacillated between giddy and dismayed."

"No! I'm not pregnant! Please, assure your mother that it's all a misunderstanding," I said. My face, my neck, the top of my head, and even the tips of my ears burned from embarrassment.

Tori poked me in the side. "Obviously, the entire town has no trouble thinking y'all are a couple."

"Our town is gullible. Last year everyone was all up in arms because they believed that there was a creature from outer space living in the bottom of Lake Marion," I reminded her.

"What kind of creature?" Jace asked. This had happened before he'd moved back home.

"A slimy one," I said, and wiggled my fingers. "With tentacles."

"Cool. I'm sorry I missed that."

"A classic case of mass hysteria," I said.

"Mass hysteria?" Tori cried. She'd loved the outer-space creature. It had brought both monster and UFO hunters to Cypress and into her café. She'd reaped record profits. "The creature ate a cow! You can't tell me that mass hysteria goes around eating cows."

"An alligator ate a cow," I told Jace. "The Department of Natural Resources was called out to remove it. After they'd handled it, the 'monster' never showed up again."

"An alligator." Tori made air quotes. "That's what the government wants us to think."

"Don't listen to her. She's just teasing."

"No, I'm not. I'm always serious when it comes to conspiracy theories," Tori said, but laughed as she said it. She believed in conspiracy theories just like she believed she'd find a pair of comfortable high-heeled shoes. They simply didn't exist, but that didn't stop her from having fun with them.

Jace looked at me and then at Tori as if he didn't know what to think. I started to laugh as well. He shook his head.

"Well, since that's all cleared up," I said, still chuckling. "Please, do apologize to your mother for me. Tell her that there's no truth to the rumors. But I don't need to tell you that. We're not even dating."

"Ouch." He rubbed the back of his neck. He then moved toward me in a way that made my heart do a little flip. "You do know, however, that my offer to take you to dinner still stands. Come on, Tru. Say yes. Come out with me."

"Now isn't a good time for us to be seen together. It would only fan the rumor flames." The last thing I needed was for more people in town to start noticing me and what I was doing. "Now, if you'll excuse us. We've got to go." I reached for the door handle to Charlie's shop.

"Actually . . ." Jace beat me to the handle and pulled it open. In a move that would have made his very proper Southern mama proud, he stepped aside and gestured for us to enter ahead of him. "That's where I'm heading as well. Police business."

"You mean the investigation-into-Owen's-murder kind of police business?" I asked. Had he reached the same conclusion that Tori had? That Charlie and his . . . his *wife* . . . were somehow involved?

"I can't discuss it," he said. "But, at the same time, I can't stop you from listening in."

Charlie's bookstore was in an iconic, historic, two-story redbrick building that could be found in almost any downtown. Charlie had bought the building and had worked hard to transform the first floor into a charming bookstore. Bookshelves that reached all the way up to the tall tin tray ceiling ran the length of the two sidewalls. There were several aisles of bookshelves. In the center of the store were sofas and armchairs and little wooden side tables. And throughout the shop were groups of comfortable armchairs inviting the shopper to linger and enjoy the rich scent of leather binding. The warm lighting hanging from the ceiling served as the cherry on the top of the cozy space.

There was also a back room that Charlie used as his office, which was where I needed to go to return the transfer-of-title form that Tori had taken. The upstairs had been converted into Charlie's personal residence. While I'd never seen the upstairs, Tori had reported to me that it was quite luxurious.

"Tori!" Charlie had been standing on a ladder as he slipped books onto the shelves in the mystery section. When he saw us, he jumped off the top step and landed as gracefully as a cat. "I'm so glad you're here. And, Tru, it's always good to see you. Is that Dewey in your tote? You can let him out. I'm sure he'll enjoy looking at the books."

"If you don't mind," Jace said as he stepped forward. He paused for just a moment to scratch Dewey behind the ears. My kitty had fallen in love with Jace and had jumped out of his tote bag to make a beeline to the detective so he could butt his head against Jace's leg.

Tori and I moved over to the nonfiction section, where we could watch Jace work without being overly intrusive. Jace gave Dewey a bit more attention before straightening. My kitty, seeing that the rubs were over, ran with his tail high in the air over to sniff a book about ghosts of the Lowcountry.

"Charlie, I need to ask you some questions about Owen Maynard's murder," Jace said.

Charlie glanced over at us and gave a troubled look as if he thought we were the reason a police detective was in his shop. I didn't blame him for that look. He had, after all, overheard Tori accusing him of committing Owen's murder. "I would be happy to assist the investigation in any way I can," he said.

"Thank you." Jace sounded all business. "We're, of course, following several lines of inquiry. But we found this on the victim's body, and we're trying to trace where it came from." He withdrew a hardcover book from a paper bag.

Charlie took the book and turned it over in his hand.

As soon as I got a glimpse of it, I inhaled sharply.

Jace looked over at me. "What?"

"Nothing," I lied.

It wasn't nothing. That book. It was a library book.

"I remember you took several boxes of the old library books to sell in this shop." Jace turned back to Charlie and asked, "Is this one of the books?"

Charlie retrieved a pair of reading glasses from his trousers' pocket and slipped them on. He looked at the spine. "Agatha Christie's *Death on the Nile*," he said, reading the title. His finger traced over the library call number taped to the spine. He generally removed the call numbers from the spines of the old library books before he'd sell them, but not always. "Classic mystery novels are my best sellers." He opened the book and looked at the front matter. He took the book slip from the front pocket with the due date stamped on it. He glanced at me and turned over the slip before returning it to the book's pocket.

"Did you sell this book?" Jace asked. Thankfully the detective hadn't spent enough of his youth in a library to realize that Charlie was hiding a recent (or even future) due date when he'd turned over the book slip. "And do you know who you sold it to?"

"Hmm." Charlie glanced over at me again. "I don't know. I'll have to check my records."

"I can wait."

"It'll take a while, perhaps several hours, to dig through files in the back office. And as you can see, I'm busy with shelving inventory right now. I can call you as soon as I have a name."

"I see." Jace started to say something else, but abruptly changed course and asked, "Did Owen Maynard ever buy books from your shop?"

"He stopped in once," Charlie said.

"Do you remember if he bought anything? This book perhaps?"

Charlie shook his head slowly. I had a feeling he could remember every book he sold in his store and whom he sold it to. He treated the old books on these shelves as if they were strays in search of a good home.

After a moment of contemplation, Charlie said, "Owen wasn't interested in novels. He was looking for books on local history. He was especially interested in anything I had about the Hell Hole Swamp area."

"Really? Why?" Jace asked.

"I think he mentioned that his family was from there?"

"Did he buy any books on that subject?" Jace asked.

"No. I didn't have any. But he did buy a book on Southern antiques. He pointed out a few pieces of furniture in the book that he said looked like the furniture he'd inherited from his grandmother."

Jace frowned and then looked over at us. "Do either of you two know why Owen might have wanted to buy a book on the history of the Hell Hole Swamp?"

Tori and I looked at each other before shrugging almost in unison.

"Well, I might have heard that he may have been doing some research on the swamp. It's possible that he'd picked up where Fenwick Harrington had left off when he died. When Owen took over as vice president for the museum, he should have had access to all Fenwick's old research," I admitted. "But I was told that Fenwick's research has disappeared."

Jace eyed me carefully as if trying to decide if I was telling him everything I knew.

I shrugged again, because I *was* telling him everything. This time. But his watching me like that made me jumpy. "You should talk with Hubert Crawford. He's the president and the lifeblood of the museum, you know."

Jace nodded. "I'll do that."

He rapped his knuckle on the checkout counter before heading toward the door. "And, Charlie, please let me know after you have a chance to go through your sales records. I really need to know who that book belonged to."

"I will." Charlie frowned as he said it.

"Hey, Jace. Wait. How did Fenwick die?" I called to him before he could get out the door. "I've heard it was an unexpected death. Was he murdered?"

Jace appeared to be taken aback by the question. "Not that I'd heard."

"You might want to look into his death," I said. "I mean, he died and now his research on the swamp has disappeared. And Owen jumped at the chance to become vice president on the museum board, but I heard that it's a thankless board position. Did he take the position because he wanted to get his hands on Fenwick's swamp research? It sounds extra suspicious now that we know he came to Charlie's bookstore looking for books on Hell Hole Swamp. I think you should add Fenwick's death to your investigation."

"I don't know." Jace glanced over at Charlie, who was still holding the library book. "It sounds like it is a long shot."

"But you'll look into it?" I pressed.

He nodded, but he still looked unconvinced.

As soon as the bell over the door chimed when Jace left, it seemed as if the three of us let out a collective sigh of relief.

"Why did you go on and on about Fenwick Harrington?" Tori demanded.

"Because Jace needed to know about him. His death might be related to Owen's. Why shouldn't I have mentioned it?"

Instead of answering, she scowled at Charlie. "The police have enough evidence. They don't need our help."

Charlie did a good job of pretending not to notice Tori's killing glare. He picked up the book Jace had left and crossed the room to hand it to me. "I figured you didn't want the police to know that the book came from the basement bookroom at your library."

"You're right. I wouldn't want that," I said. If Charlie wanted to destroy the secret bookroom, Jace had handed him a golden opportunity. Cooperating with the police on a murder investigation—no one would blame him for telling the truth, even if it did expose what we'd been doing in the library's basement. "Thank you."

"I'll keep telling the police that I haven't found the buyer's name until you have a chance to go through the library records. You can tell me who checked out the book, and I'll relay that information to Detective Bailey. No need to involve you or your books."

I opened the book's cover and pulled the book slip out of its pocket. The latest due date stamped on the slip was for a week from today. I chewed my bottom lip. One of my trusted patrons had checked out this book.

How could a patron be so careless with their checked-out material? Leaving a library book with a dead body. That wasn't how one should take care of a library book. Oh sure, I did also realize that the police finding this book must mean that the patron who checked it out was also a murderer. And that was worse. Yes, much worse.

Just thinking about it made my chest ache.

Charlie, who'd avoided looking at Tori, finally turned her way and gave her a crooked smile. "Please, join me?" he said as he headed for the seating area in the center of the store. He stopped next to one of the armchairs. "When you came in with Jace, I'd—" He pinched the bridge of his nose and then cleared his throat. "I'd assumed that you'd brought him here to question me, or that you'd followed him here to watch Tru's clever detective arrest me."

"He's not my detective," I corrected.

"What were you expecting to happen, Tori?" Charlie asked. "Were you hoping he'd drag me away in irons?" He pressed his wrists together.

Tori didn't answer. She remained rooted to her spot in the store near the nonfiction section and I kept my place beside her.

His shoulders dropped a bit. "When am I going to stop being the main suspect for every crime that happens in Cypress?"

"You're not from here. You're not one of us," Tori said as if that should explain everything. She crossed her arms over her chest. "We can't trust you."

"I'm working hard to help the town," he countered without missing a beat. "When will that count for something? When will the towns-people stop looking at me like I'm about to steal their firstborn?" He slashed his hand in the air. "It's not just you. It's half the residents in this place. They come in here to glare."

"To ogle, more like," Tori grumbled under her breath.

"What's that?" Charlie asked.

"I said, you won't stop being an outsider until someone new and more 'outside' moves to Cypress. Until that happens, you're the one everyone will want to blame. You are the enemy at the gates."

"What an apt image, and very literary of you," I said, impressed by my friend's reference to a nonfiction book about the battle of Stalingrad.

"Book? No, it's not a book. *Enemy at the Gates* is the title of one of my father's favorite movies," Tori said with an embarrassed shrug.

"Even so, it is an apt description," I said. "I am sorry, Charlie. But I agree with Tori. I don't think you'll win over most of the residents until they start to feel like they know you, really know you."

"What she's saying is that you have to stop lying to us," Tori cut in to say.

"I don't lie," he countered.

"You don't disclose the truth," she was quick to reply.

Charlie's jaw tightened. "I know you took the title transfer form, love," he said, and held out his hand. "May I have it back?"

"I don't know what—"

Charlie didn't let Tori finish her lie. "While I didn't see you tuck it away, it was on my desk before you arrived and gone after you left."

I looked at Tori, expecting her to snap at him or even burst out in a rage of passion. Charlie was also watching her with what looked like a healthy dose of trepidation.

Tori kept her arms crossed over her chest and her lips tightly sealed. She reminded me of my grandmother's ancient teakettles. It simmered silently before exploding with a startlingly loud whistle.

Charlie's attention never wavered from Tori as he spoke as if watching her would keep her from boiling. "I am sorry that my unfinished business with Candy has created this rift between us." He seemed to be picking his words with great care. "I assure you that what you saw on that paper has nothing to do with us."

"Nothing to do with us?" Her voice rose. The teakettle was boiling now. "That paper says you are married to that . . . that *woman!*" Tori shouted. "But you're saying that your decision to keep that information from me doesn't affect our relationship? I see. I see."

"Well, um, when you put it that way." He gestured toward the seating area again, as if imploring us to join him there. But he didn't say anything other than "I'm an idiot."

"Now you decide to start telling the truth?" Tori bit off. "Now?"

Charlie chuckled.

And strangely, so did Tori.

I suddenly felt like a cart's third wheel. "I'll leave and let the two of you discuss things," I murmured.

But as I edged toward the door while calling for Dewey, Tori grabbed my hand. "No. Please stay. I need you. I can't face him alone."

"Very well, but the moment you two start making googly eyes at each other, I'm out of here." I copied the stance Tori had taken and crossed my arms over my chest and pressed my lips together.

The two of us glared at Charlie and waited.

He finally eschewed good manners and sank down into the arm-chair he had invited Tori to take. Dewey appeared from wherever he'd been exploring to leap onto his lap. Charlie gently stroked Dewey's back as he spoke. "It was fifteen years ago. Candy got herself into a tough situation. I won't go into details because it's really her story to tell. But suffice it to say, we were both working in Vegas at the time. There are people in that town who will kill someone for sticking a toe out of line. Most of those same people, however, live by a code of honor so rigid that if you know the code you can use it to your advantage. You can use it to save a life." He drew a long breath. "And that's what I did. Once I slipped that ring onto her finger, the people who wanted to hurt her had to weigh their choices. Did they let Candy slip through their fingers? Or did they cross me and the men I worked for? Luckily, for everyone involved, they made the right decision."

"Such a dramatic story," Tori said with an impressive eyeroll.

"It's the truth, though. As you might have already noticed, I don't enjoy talking about my past."

"Yeah, we hadn't noticed that about you," Tori said dryly. "And the tale you've so briefly recounted leaves out all the details. I still feel as if I don't know you."

"This is my life." He gestured to his shop. "This is what I've been dreaming about and working toward my entire life. This is all I want to be."

"But you're married. That's not a detail that you can simply leave in your past," I pointed out when Tori refused to say anything.

"Candy and I only stayed together for a few years. We've been divorced and living separate lives for ten years."

"Then what is she doing here? In Cypress. It's a long way from Vegas, you know," I asked.

"It is," he agreed. "But Cypress isn't that far from Washington, DC. She made the move to DC shortly after we split up. It was a good move for her."

"And so, let me try and understand what you're trying to sell me," Tori said, her voice as sharp as a knife. "Candy just happened to stop by. And you just happened to have a truck that no one has ever seen you with that you needed taken off your hands. And you signed ownership over to her because—I don't know—it was give-your-ex-a-vehicle day?"

He rose from the armchair and slowly started walking toward us.

Charlie was a tall man with a dangerous presence. His shoulders were broad. His hands opened and closed into fists with each step.

Having him stalk toward us made me want to back up.

Tori, on the other hand, loved his air of danger. Her arms loosened. Her tongue ran along the seam of her lips. And a corner of her mouth kicked up.

Perhaps Charlie, who was a master at reading people, knew that his bad-boy behavior would win points with my friend. For both our sakes, that's what I was hoping.

"Tori, Tori, Tori," he said. "When Candy left me in Vegas all those years ago, she took my truck. Stole it, actually. Man, I loved that truck. But instead of chasing after her and having an ugly scene about trying to get Gertrude back, I went out and bought a new car."

"Wait. Gertrude?" Tori snorted. "That's a silly name for anything. And what's the name of that Maserati you're driving now? Jolene?"

"As a matter of fact, it is. How did you guess?"

"I'm psychic."

She wasn't.

But like Charlie, she could read people. And, like most of the population in Cypress, she listened to classic country music.

"Was Candy in town because she wanted you to sign over the title to her truck?" I asked.

"It was my idea. She still has the truck because without the title, she couldn't sell it or even give it away."

"If she didn't come to town to get the truck's title, what was she doing here?" Tori demanded. "Was she trying to hook up with you again? Because that's sure what it looked like in the diner. She wanted you. And I felt like a world-class fool."

"No, that's not what she wanted. She had come here to . . ." He shook his head. "I'm sorry. I told her I wouldn't say."

"It's not gossip if you tell me," Tori pointed out. "I'm not just anyone, am I?"

"I'm sorry," he repeated.

"You're sorry?" Tori drew back as if he'd hit her. "You might enjoy living in that man-of-intrigue, need-to-know world of yours. But honestly, I'm sick of it. You either tell me what's going on or I walk out that door, and I'll never come back."

No, Tori.

That was an ultimatum I was sure my best friend would come to regret.

"This can't leave this room," he said after a long, tense span of silence.

"You already know we can keep secrets," I whispered.

He drew an unsteady breath. "Candy is an agent with the FBI now. Thanks to her—er—experiences in Vegas and her knowledge of the inner workings of some of the organizations she'd worked with, the folks at the Bureau recruited her. What was supposed to be a short undercover assignment led her to a career she loves. And that's why she was in town. She's investigating a suspected crime ring. Please, don't ask me what crime is being committed in our town. Candy wouldn't tell me. All I know is that it is connected to a case her team is investigating in Florida."

Tori barked a laugh. "You can't be serious. A crime ring? In Cypress?"

Charlie, however, looked dead serious.

And I couldn't help but wonder—despite how crazy it sounded—was *this* the reason why Owen was dead?

Chapter Fourteen

The next morning, I hurried toward the library with Dewey in one tote bag and Agatha Christie's *Death on the Nile* in the other. *The book* seemed to make the tote bag sag. This, of course, was nonsense. It wasn't any heavier than any of the other books in my bag. But, nonsense or not, toting *the book* felt as if I were carrying a flashing sign that signaled to anyone who saw me, "Look! Damaging Evidence Here."

Besides which, the wiggling tote bag on my other arm would attract much more notice than a bag weighed down with books.

"What are you doing in there?" I whispered to Dewey. He didn't usually make such a fuss. He loved coming to the library and would jump into the tote as soon as I picked it up in the morning. But this morning, he twisted and turned, making it look as if I were carrying live fish. "Are you okay?"

Dewey stuck his head out of the bag. He looked at me with his big green eyes and meowed.

"I wish I spoke cat," I said. He was obviously trying to tell me something.

"I can't imagine what a cat would say, beyond 'look, there's a rat,' or 'ooh, tassels.' Not really illuminating conversation that," Frank said as he walked up to me. He was dressed as if he was planning to take in nine holes at the local golf course.

"Good morning, Frank," I said. I was still a few storefronts away from the library, but close enough to see Anne on the front steps waiting for Mrs. Farnsworth to arrive, which was interesting. If Anne had a key, why didn't she simply let herself in?

"It's a beautiful morning," he said, his eyes still on my kitty. "Hello, puss-puss. I assumed you lived at the library full-time."

He reached out to scratch Dewey behind the ears.

Dewey hissed and dropped back into the bag.

"He lives with me. I just bring him to work," I said, wondering at Dewey's odd behavior. The last person he'd hissed at turned out to be a killer. "I hate to leave him home alone all day. And I would hate to leave him alone in the bookroom all night. So, I take him with me pretty much everywhere I go."

"Ah, good morning, Doris," Frank said as she dashed past us. "Where are you off to in such a hurry? I hope that Mazda of yours is still working out for you." He then whispered to me, "She's missed three payments on that old sedan. If she misses another, she'll lose the car."

Doris was dressed in sweatpants, pink high heels, and a fitted gray T-shirt with the slogan "Essential Oils Are Essential for Happiness." Underneath the curlicue lettering on the shirt was the logo for the essential oils she had recently started selling. It almost looked as if she'd dressed herself in the dark. One ponytail was much higher than the other.

"Doris?" Frank called after she'd passed us. "Are you okay?"

"Oh!" She whirled around and seemed startled to see us. She paused only long enough to adjust her eyeglasses before continuing to trot away from us. "Can't stop to chat. I have a few deliveries to make this morning. Was babysitting over at the Goodloes' last night. They were out until dawn. Without a full night's sleep, I'm useless. Perks sells an extra-dark brew on Fridays. I'm hoping it'll wake me up."

"I'm sure it will," I called after her. "Tori swears by that stuff."

"Come by if you need anything for the car," Frank shouted. He then said to me, "I hate to see any of my customers lose their wheels. I pride myself on matching the right car to the right person. You know, I've never sold you a car." He tilted his head to one side as he studied me. "Why is that?"

Embarrassed, I looked away. "Mama Eddy always gives me her castoffs."

"Ah, the last time she came in, she fell in love with a bright blue SUV that she needs steps to get into. I tried to tell her that it was all wrong for her, but your mama is one strong-willed lady."

"You don't have to tell me. Mama Eddy could scare the quills off a porcupine."

He chuckled at that. I looked up to find him smiling at me. "If she gives you her old cars, you'll be driving that blue SUV before the end of the year." He then studied me some more. "But her SUV isn't the right car for you either. When she gives it to you, bring it to the showroom. I'll give you a good deal on the trade-in and get you into something that fits your personality."

"Like what?" I asked, curious what a professional car salesman thought I should drive. *Please, don't be a boring white sedan.*

He surprised me when he said without hesitation, "A red sports car. Something small, but at the same time sleek and fast." His eyes darkened. "And sexy."

"Oh, you're good. No wonder nearly everyone in town is driving around in a car from your lot."

He widened his too-handsome smile. "Helps that I own the only car lot in town."

"People can drive to Columbia or Charlotte. And yet most don't."

A Perfect Bind

"Busy sidewalk this morning," Frank said before hollering, "Good morning, Mrs. Goodloe" as Hennie passed us. "How's that minivan working out for you?"

Hennie was dressed in a dark blue smock dress with a high-collared white blouse underneath. The blouse looked hot and uncomfortable. Her sensible shoes clacked on the pavement as she hurried in the same direction as Doris had gone. She acted as if she hadn't heard Frank. And perhaps she hadn't. She, quite literally, had her arms full. She was carrying a crying baby while pushing a tattered old baby carriage.

"I told her to go for a full-sized van, but she didn't want to pay for it. She'll be sorry in about nine months. Those minivans can fit only so many car seats."

"She's expecting?"

"Don't know for sure, mind you. I'm not her doctor. But when I spoke with Doris yesterday about her late payments, she told me that she was considering going to work for the Goodloes as their full-time nanny. Apparently, they're planning to offer her the position since they're expecting their family to grow. And since Hennie recently gave birth to that infant she's carrying, I figured that the blessed event wouldn't happen for at least another nine months. Of course, it might not even be true. You know how rumors are. I, for one, take them only with a grain of salt. Don't you agree?"

"Certainly. Cypress loves passing around rumors," I said.

"It does seem like a community-wide obsession."

"More like an affliction."

He seemed to consider something serious before saying, "Speaking of rumors, I heard a surprising one about you."

"It's not true," I was quick to say.

"It's odd, really. Until very recently, I'd never heard your name come up in conversation. And now you're the new 'it' girl. You should be flattered."

"It's still not true," I felt it necessary to repeat.

"Aren't you even curious what people are saying?"

"I've heard several rumors, and they are all lies. So, no. I'd rather not hear it repeated to me now."

He seemed undeterred as he ticked the rumors off on his fingers. "You mean to say that you're not pregnant with Jace's baby, you're not running off to marry Jace, and you're not hot on the trail of Owen's murderer?"

"Well, I *am* investigating. A bit. You already know that from the discussion we had at the book club. As for the others? No. I'm not dating anyone."

"Oh!" Frank's smile returned. "I'm glad to hear it. Then, can I take you to dinner? Tonight? We could discuss Owen's death while enjoying each other's company. I've been thinking about some of the details of his murder and might have a few ideas to share. What do you say? Eight o'clock?"

"Um . . ." What should I say? He was handsome. (Perhaps too handsome.) He had confidence. (Perhaps too much confidence.) And he might have information that could help lead us to Owen's killer.

And why shouldn't I go out with him? Being seen with another man would quiet those silly rumors that Jace and I were carrying on in secret. What was wrong with me? Why didn't I say yes? I should have SHOUTED IT.

What I did do was stammer unintelligibly. It was embarrassing.

Thankfully, Mrs. Farnsworth walked by with her usual grace and dignity. She glanced at me before heading up the library's grand front steps, the key to the building jingling in her hand. I glanced at the clock. It was eight thirty on the dot. Mrs. Farnsworth was as punctual as ever.

"I've got to go." I trotted up the steps with much less grace than the head librarian. Dewey complained with a soft mew.

"What about tonight?" Frank called after me.

"Let me think about it."

Inside my tote bag was a book. A heavy book. I needed to find out who had checked it out before I could think clearly about anything else . . . even the prospect of dating a handsome man who thought I should drive a sports car. A sexy sports car at that.

Chapter Fifteen

———•———

When the library opened at ten that morning, I still hadn't had an opportunity to look through the files to see who had checked out *the book.*

Aunt Sal had called my cell phone immediately after Mrs. Farnsworth had unlocked the front doors to the public. My sweet aunt (who'd once mistaken salt for sugar when baking chocolate chip cookies for the fire department) wailed into the phone for several minutes before I could get her to talk to me. Had she blown up her kitchen again? No, that wasn't it. She finally (tearfully) explained how her favorite bakery in New York City had unexpectedly closed, and she didn't know what she was going to do. I wasn't sure why she was so broken up about it. Sure, Aunt Sal loved to travel to New York City, but she rarely made the trip more than once a year. I'd pointed this out to her, which had only made her cry harder. She was sobbing so hard that I didn't have the heart to ask her why she wasn't planning on entering this year's apple-pie-baking contest, which had been the reason I'd called her yesterday. Instead, I promised I'd stop by tonight and bring her something from the Grind to help cheer her up. Maybe I would be able to figure out what was going on with her and the apple pie contest then.

"What's wrong?" Tori asked. She was one of the first to come into the library this morning.

"Aunt Sal's favorite New York bakery closed," I explained as I sat down at the front desk.

"I don't understand why you and your aunt are so upset about a bakery. Doesn't New York like have one on every corner? What's so special about this one? Do they have like the best cheesecake in the world?" my best friend asked. "This doesn't seem worth an SOS text."

"Oh, the text!" No wonder Tori was confused.

This morning I'd texted her an SOS. I'd sent Flossie the same text. Flossie had texted back with a profusion of apologies that she had an important phone call with an editor and she couldn't come in until after lunch.

"Yes, the text," Tori said. "What's wrong?"

"Ahhh . . . It's . . . nothing," I said with a false smile. There were too many people around for me to tell her the real reason I'd texted her. For a small library, the building got a surprising amount of foot traffic. I had thought that removing the books from the building would have turned the place into a ghost town. But really, the opposite had happened. In the last couple of weeks, the library had become more of a community center. We'd doubled the number of classes offered. The café and sound studios attracted a younger crowd who hadn't come to the library since grade school. And community members of all ages came to use the sewing machines and 3D printers.

"Personal nothing? Or other business nothing?" Tori asked. She was dressed in tight jeans and a Perks T-shirt, which meant she had left her coffee shop to come help me. Part of me regretted texting her. I hated to waste her time.

I glanced around and noticed that a few people had moved closer to the front desk—most likely so they could hear us better.

"Nothing." I shook my head. "How did things go with you and Charlie after I left?"

Tori blushed. "He's good at groveling."

I enjoyed seeing her smiling again.

I was about to tell her that when Anne rushed by. I waved my arms to catch her attention. She pointedly looked the other way.

"Drat. She was supposed to work the front desk this morning," I grumbled.

"I'll take care of it," Tori said, and sprinted after Anne.

Although Tori had never been interested in any kind of sports, save for high school cheerleading, she was surprisingly fast in her chunky heels. Less than a minute later, she returned with Anne at her side.

"Your friend says you need to take a break?" Anne said.

"If you don't mind." I was trying to be nice.

"I suppose if you need to sneak off to play with your cat, I could cover for you for a few minutes. But just a few minutes."

I bit my tongue. If I got her riled, she might go to Mrs. Farnsworth and tell her about Dewey living in the basement. "Thank you," I mumbled.

"Do hurry back. Some of us have real work to do in this library," Anne said, sounding important. Yet her voice was a touch too loud.

Mrs. Farnsworth came out of her office and made a beeline for the front desk. She slipped on the reading glasses that hung from a golden chain around her neck, picked up the jobs sheet, and silently read through it. "What are you doing working the desk?" She whispered the question.

"Tru said she has to take a break," Anne answered, although I was fairly certain Mrs. Farnsworth had asked me the question.

"While I understand that you find working with your electronics immensely challenging and rewarding, Anne, there is more to running a library than playing with things that squeak and beep. According to the schedule, it is your turn to work here. It's important that we present ourselves as pleasant and professional and available to be of service to all our patrons. Tru, I know you're busy with your projects. You don't have time to visit with the public when it's Anne's turn."

I didn't know if I should have felt insulted that Mrs. Farnsworth was scolding me for shirking my duties or pleased that she told Anne that she needed to attend to the desk and leave me alone. After a moment of reflection, I decided to go with the latter. There was too much to get done in the basement for me to worry about my pride.

"Yes, Mrs. Farnsworth," I said, and jumped up from my chair. Without even a backward glance, I hurried toward the back stairs.

"Now can you tell me what's wrong?" Tori asked as she followed me.

"Too many ears," I whispered.

"Did you find out who checked out—?"

"No, I didn't," I snapped, feeling more frustrated than angry.

Tori didn't say another word. And I didn't offer any until we reached the secret bookroom.

"It happened again last night," I said as I opened the doors. "And this is why I sent the text."

Tori cursed when she spotted the damage.

Dewey stood in the middle of a jumble of loose papers. It looked as if he had been trying to sort out the mess. He meowed at us as we entered. It sounded as if he was scolding us for letting this happen again.

"It was the local documents section this time," I said, pointing to the far wall, where Hubert and Frank had been spending most of their time. File cabinets had been pushed over and their contents had been spilled out. The shelves where we kept one-of-a-kind documents and maps had been knocked over. Many of the irreplaceable documents were crumpled and bent. A few had been ripped.

"Didn't Anne scan this section into her computer for safekeeping?" Tori asked.

"She only scanned the documents she and the town manager thought were important. And after she was done, she shipped those documents to the town hall archives. These documents were deemed unnecessary. But"—I reached down and picked up a handbound leather book that was now missing several pages—"this was a diary from the late 1800s. It recorded common day-to-day life in Cypress. The author described in meticulous detail special events, purchases, prices, holidays, and mundane chores around the house. This is something stats and figures can't give us."

"I'm sure we'll be able to sort out the papers and put it all back together," Tori said.

"It's going to take time," I warned. "And what happens when our vandal returns? Do we start all over again?"

"We'll have to come up with a better plan. For one thing, we need to get a camera set up to record what's happening at night. Charlie might be able to help with that." Tori started tapping out a text on her phone. "Plus, we'll need to get Hubert down here. He knows this section better than anyone else."

She was right. We needed to be more proactive. And we needed to include more people in helping with the cleanup. I didn't have the hours it would take to piece this area back together.

Dewey batted at a stapled copy of a research document detailing Hell Hole Swamp's history. I scratched him behind his ears before taking his toy away from him and putting it on a nearby table to look over later.

"Frank Calhoun asked me out," I blurted.

Tori nearly dropped her phone. "He didn't!"

"He met me outside the library before Mrs. Farnsworth arrived."

"A little stalkerish, but sweet. He's a good-looking guy. And he can get you a deal on a used car. A win-win situation."

"He said I should be driving a sexy red sports car." Saying it aloud made me feel all bubbly inside.

Tori set her hands on her hips. "Tell me you agreed to go out with him."

"I didn't say no." I scooped up some more papers. "Mrs. Farnsworth arrived before I really could say anything. I told him that I'd call him."

"I should have guessed it. You always do this. You put him off."

"I haven't been asked out by enough guys for my behavior to be a pattern," I said.

"Oh yes you have. Do you want me to list them?"

I didn't.

"I think maybe I should go," I said. "On the date. He told me that he had some ideas about Owen's death that he wanted to talk with me about."

"Wise man. He knows the right lure to put on his fishing hook for you."

"I put his card somewhere around here." I searched the desk for it. "I'll give him a call and accept."

Tori nodded. "Maybe going out with Frank will cure you of your obsession with Jace."

"I'm not obsessed with Jace," I said a little too quickly. "He's nothing to me."

"Uh-huh." Knowing Tori, she would have teased me relentlessly if my kitty hadn't caught her attention. "What's Dewey doing?" she asked.

The lanky tabby was standing on his hind legs. He'd stretched his front paws above his head and was batting at something along the wall where the local documents section used to be.

"It looks like he's found something." I joined him at the wall. The wall here was made from several sheets of metal welded together to form a sturdy bomb shelter. The metal had been covered with layer after layer of white paint. There were scratch marks in the paint.

"Was the poltergeist trying to write us a message?" Tori joked.

I ran my finger along the scratches. It didn't look like letters. There were several sets of them. "Why would someone take a knife and try to slash at a wall?" I wondered.

"To spook us," Tori said as she hugged herself. "And it worked.

Those marks are creepy. Like a mad serial killer from a horror movie slashing his knifelike hands across the wall."

"I don't know . . ." Whoever was breaking into the bookroom was going to an awful lot of trouble just to make a mess. I couldn't imagine that their sole purpose was to scare us.

"I'll get the camera in here," Tori said. "Even if I have to buy one myself, I'll get one set up. You call Frank. Find out what he knows. We need to put a stop to this before someone gets hurt."

"Someone *else*," I corrected, thinking of Owen.

"Right." Tori had lifted her phone and was snapping pictures of the slash marks. "I hate that we can't call the police. This does seem like something they should know about. Whoever is doing this is one troubled individual."

I hurried back over to the old, battered circulation desk. I remembered that I'd slipped Frank's card into the top drawer. "I suppose I'll need to tell Jace about everything that's been going on down here if we can't figure out who's doing this in the next few days. In the meantime"—I held up Frank's business card—"I have a dinner date to set up."

Tori stood over me, making sure I dialed the number correctly. The call went to voice mail. I left a message asking Frank to call me so we could set up a time and place to meet. Tonight no longer worked, since I was taking dinner over to my distraught aunt's. But I told him I was free this weekend. Maybe Sunday? After hanging up and laughing a little manically at the thought of going on a date on Sunday, I went back to work cleaning up the mess the vandal had made.

"I wonder if the break-ins are somehow related to the crime ring that Charlie's ex is investigating," Tori said about a half hour later. We'd been sorting through the loose papers and putting them into piles that would make it easier to file them in the cabinets. "I wish we knew what that crime ring might be."

"Could be anything," I said as I tried to figure out if an article about the end of Prohibition in Cypress should be filed under *regional history* or *political science*. I finally put it in a small stack to be filed under *law*. I looked up at Tori. "I did hear an odd thing about the Goodloes this morning."

"What's that?"

"Well, two odd things. Doris walked by when I was talking with Frank. She had bags under her eyes and was yawning. She told us that she had very little sleep last night because she'd been babysitting for the Goodloes. According to her, they had stayed out all night."

"That couple doesn't drink. They won't even touch coffee. They don't dance. What were they doing?" Tori asked.

"They could be holding an all-night prayer vigil. Or they could have been"—I looked over at the scratches on the wall—"doing something else."

"You don't think that they . . . ?" Tori's gaze followed mine.

Dewey was still investigating the scratches.

"I don't know what to think."

"You said there were two things," Tori said. "What's the second one?"

"This one is mostly wild speculation on my part, mind you."

"That's the best kind. Go on," Tori urged.

"Doris has been offered a full-time nanny position with the Goodloes because, supposedly, they're expecting another child."

"Gracious. Don't those two have any self-control? They already have a newborn."

"Now stick with me. Hearing that got me to thinking about babies."

"No," Tori gasped. "Please tell me you're not actually wishing that you were . . ." She cleared her throat meaningfully.

"No. No. Nothing like that. Maybe one day. With the right man. But not on my own. Mama Eddy would kill me. However, Hennie has been very interested in the rumors that I'm expecting a child out of wedlock. And she's told me that she'd like to place the child—that I'm not having—with a family of her choosing. This is where the wild speculation comes in. What if the Goodloes are selling babies? And maybe they've decided to keep one instead of selling it?"

Tori stared at me.

"Crazy, I know. But it is a crime. And it would be something the FBI would be interested in investigating. At least that's what I've read."

"I don't know," Tori said slowly. "It's mighty farfetched, but that doesn't mean it's not worth looking into. If it is true, I wonder how Owen is involved? And why is he dead?"

"Perhaps he found out that his close friends were profiting from an illegal adoption agency and threatened to turn them in? Or maybe he tried to blackmail them in exchange for his silence, and they decided to assure his silence in a more permanent way? I don't know. Do you think if we told Charlie our theory, he would run it by his ex to find out if we're on the right track?"

"I could ask. But don't hold your breath. You know how hard it is to get any information out of him. Now, don't you have a children's program starting soon? I can work here until Flossie arrives. Where is she? I thought she lived down here now."

"She's supposed to come in after lunch. Are you sure you don't mind staying? It's slow this morning. We could leave a note asking patrons to work around the mess."

"Where is Hubert? He's another one who practically lives down here."

"I don't know. He sometimes gives presentations to civic groups and will come in pretty late."

"When he does arrive, I'll hand him a tissue to mop up his tears and put him to work. Now get out of here before someone comes looking for you."

I reluctantly set the papers I was sorting on a table. "Wait! I still haven't looked up who checked out the Agatha Christie mystery. This won't take a moment."

I slipped into the chair at the circulation desk and flipped through the cards until I found one for *Death on the Nile.* "Here it is."

My heart dropped into the pit of my stomach.

"No," I whispered. "No. No. No."

"Who?" Tori demanded. "Who checked it out?"

"It's—it can't be right." But no matter how long I stared at the name on the card, it refused to change.

"Don't leave me in suspense like this. Who is it?" She was inches from snatching the card from my hand.

"It's Frank," I said.

Please tell me I hadn't just agreed to go to dinner with a killer.

Chapter Sixteen

What a fool I was. I should have known better. I should have seen the signs. But I hadn't.

Reading Frank's name on that card felt like a semitruck had slammed into the side of my body. Of course Frank Calhoun was the patron who had checked out the book the police had found with Owen's body. Of course he had.

Why should I have expected it to be anyone else?

Gad, he was handsome. His pretty words and intense gazes had flattered me. Heck, he'd told me I should be driving a sexy sports car.

Me?

Jace would have laughed his head off if he'd heard that.

Well, reading his name on that card certainly put me in my place.

After leaving the basement bookroom, I hid in the staff bathroom and dabbed angrily at my tears with a tissue.

How gullible could I be?

Clearly, Frank had feigned interest in me so he could wangle his way into our group. If I hadn't been blinded by his attention, I would have suspected what he was doing from the beginning. He'd only started to flirt with me after he'd overheard the book club talking about investigating Owen's murder.

There was no getting around it. He'd asked me out as a ruse to gather information.

I drew a deep breath, determined to pull myself together. Frank wasn't tear-worthy. He wasn't even sniffle-worthy. The jerk. A *murderous* jerk who couldn't be trusted with a library book.

As soon as I'd shown the card to Tori, she'd texted Charlie, who'd promised to pass Frank's name to Jace. It would all be handled. I wouldn't even have to text Frank to tell him that I'd changed my mind about dinner. Because he would be in jail.

Good gracious, I felt another round of tears coming on. I didn't have time for this. There were a dozen kids in the children's area waiting to hear a story about a clever beaver who'd constructed a neighborhood for his woodland friends. After the story, I was going to help the kids build their own log houses out of Popsicle sticks.

I huffed several deep breaths, wished all sorts of painful ailments on the male of the species, and then marched out of the bathroom with a giant, fake smile plastered on my freshly painted lips. (Thank you, Mama Eddy, for teaching me ways to hide my emotions beneath thick layers of cosmetics.) I might rarely wear makeup, but I was awfully glad to have a repair kit in my purse for this purpose.

A few minutes later, the kids were laughing loudly at the beaver's silly antics in the book I was reading to them. Afterward, they then excitedly smeared white glue everywhere as they constructed an elaborate (if messy) neighborhood for their imaginary animal friends. The two hours that it took to complete the program flew by.

Mrs. Farnsworth stepped into the children's area just as the kids were filing out. She smiled at the creative mess.

"I'm impressed with the quality of the programs you've been developing for the children," she said, which coming from her was high praise indeed.

"Thank you. The little ones are a joy to work with," I said. "They are always eager to try whatever craft I bring. And they are always so creative. The ideas they come up with astound me."

Mrs. Farnsworth smiled and nodded. "Children can be that way." She started to leave, but then stopped and turned back around. "I wonder," she said, tilting her head to the side, "you're so good with kids. Have you ever considered having one of your own?"

"Why?" I took several breaths before stammering, "I—I—"

I still felt a sharp sting in my chest from Frank's betrayal. I was feeling unloved and unlovable. And didn't she know that it took two people to make a child? I'd been single the entire time I'd worked for her at the library. Sure, I'd gone on the odd date now and then. But I'd never found anyone I could see myself getting serious with. *Was there something wrong with me?*

"Men are . . . trouble," I finally managed to get out past the despair squeezing my heart.

Mrs. Farnsworth nodded knowingly. "That they are," she agreed as she left the children's area. "That they are."

Somehow, her words made me feel both worse and better. In all the years that I worked for her, I'd never heard her mention her husband or what her married life was like. Her husband was a loan manager at the local bank and just as stern and precise as Mrs. Farnsworth. He seemed like a perfect match for her. But perhaps he left his dishes in the sink or dirty clothes on the floor or slurped his soup loudly. One never knew what happened behind the closed doors of a marriage, which made me only all the more wary about letting a man get too close. Especially now.

Still, the part of me that loved reading romances longed to be swept off my feet. Why couldn't I have a man tell me how he thought I should be driving a sexy red sports car and mean it? Why couldn't I take a chance on someone without having my heart stomped all over?

"Doesn't Hennie usually bring her brood to your programs?" Flossie rolled into the children's area as I scrubbed a thick blob of paint off one of the tables and asked. "I stuck my head in when you were reading that charming book and noticed she wasn't in the audience. Tori told me how you heard Hennie and Landry had stayed out all night. And now Hennie is changing her pattern of bringing her children to the library to take part in the crafts. That's interesting, don't you think?"

"I'd been so wrapped up with . . . other thoughts, I hadn't really noticed." I didn't want to admit to Flossie just how badly Frank's deception had upset me. "But you're right. Hennie didn't bring her boys today. And that is unlike her. The last time she missed a program was when she was giving birth to Josiah. I hope she's okay."

"Maybe you should call on her and make sure," Flossie said as she raised one brow. "You could also ask her about"—she cleared her throat meaningfully—"you know, other things at the same time."

"Maybe I'll do that." Hennie's absence today would be a good excuse to pay a visit to the Goodloes' house. While I was expressing my concern, I'd let slip a few questions about her relationship with Owen and even see if she had a good explanation for why she and her husband had stayed out so late last night.

I could also drop a few hints about baby adoptions and see if she thought those good families who are waiting to adopt children were required to pay a high price in order to get a baby.

"Would you go with me?" I asked Flossie. "We could leave shortly after the library closes."

She readily agreed and offered to drive us in her wheelchair-equipped sexy red sports car. Now, she was a woman born to drive that car.

• • •

After Flossie left to help out in the secret bookroom, Tori emerged from the basement. My mind kept circling around to Frank's deception and why it had stung so badly. Sometimes it was hard being friends with someone as beautiful as Tori. She looked amazing, even when she was wearing jeans and a Perks T-shirt. Her clothes hugged her gentle curves. I glanced down at the tan slacks and peach sweater set that I'd thought looked adorable this morning. Now it felt as if I was wearing a couple of oversized, lumpy sacks.

Tori had offered more than once to give me a makeover. I waved her over to me.

"Hubert came in. After he recovered from the vapors, he set to work organizing and filing. More than half of the documents are back where they belong. Before closing time, you won't even be able to tell that anything happened down there," Tori said.

"That's good news," I said without any emotion.

"If that's so, why don't you sound happy about it?" Tori asked.

I shrugged. "I'm going to pay a visit to the Goodloes after work. Hennie missed today's children's program. Flossie has agreed to come along. Could you give me a makeover?"

"What? Could you repeat that last part? Because I couldn't have heard you correctly. You want a makeover? Why? To impress Hennie?"

My cheeks burned red. "No. Not for her. For me. I'm tired of . . ." I couldn't bring myself to admit how tired I was of being seen as *less than.*

Less pretty.

Less interesting.

Less adventurous.

"Sure." Her brows creased. "I'd love to take you shopping and do something with your hair."

"I'm ready to do it now. Not tonight, of course. After Hennie, I'm taking dinner over to my aunt Sal's. But tomorrow? Saturday night?"

"I don't know." The crease in her brows deepened.

"Oh, you have a hot date with Charlie on Saturday. Of course you do. I understand."

"No, it's not that," Tori said. "BFFs always come first. You know that. It's just that I'm concerned that you want me to act as your fashion adviser for the wrong reasons."

"I need help. I'm ready to admit it," it hurt me to say.

Tori snarled. "Frank Calhoun is a jerk. And he's always been a shameless flirt. It's part of his business model. Don't let what he did shake your confidence. There is nothing wrong with you. He's the one that has something wrong with him. Forget him."

"So, you won't go with me to Columbia to shop on Saturday?"

Tori looped her arm in mine. "Oh, we'll go shopping. I never turn down a chance to hang out with my bestie and spend her money. And we'll bust our guts at the food court while we're at it."

Thank goodness for best friends who used to be cheerleaders. Tori just being Tori lifted my mood like no one else could.

I was feeling so good about everything that afternoon, I almost started to whistle. A sharp click of Mrs. Farnsworth's disapproving tongue put a quick end to that frivolous idea. But not even her clucking tongue could quell my happiness.

After all, today hadn't been a complete disaster. Mrs. Farnsworth had complimented me on my children's programs. I knew Frank had killed Owen. I suspected that Hennie and Landry were vandalizing the library for some twisted reason only they understood. And Tori was going to give my wardrobe a badly needed update. (Wouldn't Mama Eddy be ecstatic?)

It was a win-win-win-win-win.

Oops. I almost started whistling again.

"Are you dancing?" Jace asked as he came into the children's area, where I was still scrubbing off the paste that had somehow gotten everywhere.

"Might be," I said with a little twirl.

"And you're smiling. I like it when you smile like that."

"Thank you," I said, and gave a curtsy. "Glad to entertain you."

"Go to dinner with me tonight," he said with a smile. "I'll take you dancing afterward."

"I can't." My feet no longer wanted to dance. My smile faded. I remembered how Frank had fooled me.

"Can't?" Jace's smile faded too. "Because you have a date with someone else?"

"No. Flossie and I are going to check on Hennie Goodloe. She didn't bring her children to the reading program today. And she never misses. I want to make sure she's okay. And then afterward I'm taking dinner to Aunt Sal."

"Did your aunt blow up her kitchen again?" he asked.

"No. But she's having a bad day and needs some cheering up."

Jace nodded, but he still looked troubled. "I heard a new rumor about you."

"Why can't the people in this town mind their own flipping business?" I was getting sick of people telling me what others were saying about me.

"The residents here care about you. Plus, ever since you practically captured a murderer single-handed, you've become a local celebrity. People love talking about what you're doing and wondering what you'll do next."

"Most people couldn't even be bothered to learn my name before that happened."

"That's how celebrity and notoriety work. Keep your head down and mind your own business, and eventually their attention will move on to someone else. How about joining me for dinner Saturday night and starting some real rumors?"

"Sorry." I shook my head. "I have a hot date with Tori. We're going to Columbia to shop."

He looked relieved. "So, it's not true that you're getting involved with that slick used car salesman?"

"Is that the rumor that has you so worried? Afraid your low-hanging fruit is going to be picked by someone else?"

"Low-hanging fruit? I don't know what you mean by that."

"I think you do." I didn't look at all glamorous like Tori or like the beauty queens he'd dated all through high school.

Jace shrugged. "People have been saying that you were seen getting all cozy with that used car salesman in front of the library this morning."

"I wouldn't say we were cozy. Frank just happened to be walking by this morning, and we chatted." I wasn't going to tell him that I now knew Frank had been flirting as a means to get close to the book club's investigation. Maybe Frank had even planned to feed us information to misdirect us.

"If it becomes more than that, I want you to avoid him."

"Are you jealous? He is awfully good-looking."

"He looks like he's been dipped in plastic," Jace shot back. "Anyhow, he isn't as nice as he wants us to believe. So, if he comes sniffing around again, you need to send him away."

I crossed my arms over my chest. "Now, why would I do that?"

"Because an officer of the law is warning you," he said stiffly. "I cannot say more."

"Does this have something to do with the investigation into Owen's murder?" I moved closer, enjoying playing with Jace a bit. "Did Frank off the poor guy? Was Owen overcharging him to fix up his used cars? Is that what put him over the edge?"

"Now, Tru, you know I can't discuss it." He backed away from me.

I followed. "Was Frank flirting with Owen's wife?" I tapped my chin. "No. No. That couldn't be it. Owen would have killed Frank. Not the other way around."

"This isn't one of your mystery novels," Jace said. "This isn't a game. A man was killed. You need to take care, Tru. I'm serious."

"I know you are," I said. "But that doesn't mean you get to come in here and start dictating to me who I can and cannot flirt with."

Jace sighed. "Charlie called me and told me who had purchased that Agatha Christie novel from his shop."

"And?" I picked up a tablet a child had left on the floor and made him follow me as I returned it to the charging cart. "I assume you'll be arresting the man."

"Man? Did Charlie already talk to you?" Did he sound relieved?

"Haven't spoken with Charlie since last night," I said. "But am I wrong? Was Owen killed by a man? By Frank Calhoun? Will you be making an arrest soon?"

"We're still gathering evidence. I can't arrest someone based solely on a book he purchased and lost."

"But you can warn me away from flirting with him," I said.

"You don't sound surprised that Frank is our main suspect right now," Jace said. "Why is that? Who told you?"

"No one. Don't forget that my friends and I have been conducting our own investigation. And we've come to the same conclusion you have about Frank."

"Ah, that's why you were flirting with him, wasn't it? You were trying to get information from him?"

"I might have been," I said, still too embarrassed to admit that Frank had duped me.

"And?" he said. "Don't hold back on me. Do you have anything you need to share with the police?"

"Not yet," I said. "Only suspicions so far."

Jace blocked me. "No. Tru, you need to promise me that you'll end it here. Now that you know there's a cloud of suspicion hanging over Frank's head, don't go and put yourself in a situation where he might hurt you. Please, Tru. I don't want to see anything happen to you."

"I'll be careful."

"By staying away from Frank?"

I nodded.

"Then come have Sunday supper with me at my mother's. She'd be thrilled."

"Have you lost your mind? If I did that, she'd have the wedding planned before dessert was served. She already thinks I'm carrying her grandchild."

"I straightened her out about that."

"But now the image is in her head. And I know she's been complaining around town that she's the only one of her friends without a grandbaby to coo over." I gave him a little shove toward the door. "Now go. Leave me alone." I had trouble thinking straight when he was around.

He gave a laugh as he headed toward the door. "That would explain why she suggested I invite you. And here I thought it was because everyone enjoys your overly friendly personality."

Gracious, Jace was good. He sent me a look as he left that made my heart do a flip, proving he was a bigger flirt than Frank. He liked to joke around with me, but I knew he couldn't really be serious about wanting to date me, not when he could date just about any other single woman in town. And this is a town that has produced more beauty queens per capita than any other town in South Carolina. "Whatever you decide to do, Tru, please be careful."

"You too," I said, far too softly for him to hear. "You too."

Chapter Seventeen

That evening I drove up to a modest farmhouse on the edge of town where the Goodloes lived. Bikes and toy guns littered the front yard. Yet the grass was neatly trimmed, and the flower beds looked full and healthy.

"Why couldn't Flossie come with you? What's she doing now?" Tori asked from the passenger seat as I pulled the car to a stop at the curb. "It's not like her to back out at the last minute."

"She said she had an idea for the book she was working on and had to go rush off to write it down. According to her, the best ideas are fleeting. If she doesn't get them down on paper, they'll vanish on her."

"That's nuts, you know."

"It's how she writes." I turned off the car. "Thank you for canceling your date with Charlie to come with me. I do appreciate it."

"That's what friends are for. Besides, forcing Charlie to wait will make him all the more appreciative of the time he gets to spend with me."

We both emerged from the car. I retrieved a box of cinnamon rolls that we'd purchased from the Grind while picking up Aunt Sal's dinner.

The sweet scent of the hot-from-the-oven buns made me feel dizzy with hunger. My stomach grumbled.

"Ready?" I asked as Tori fixed her makeup.

She checked herself in her compact's mirror one more time before snapping it closed. "Now I am." We started up the walkway.

"Good evening!" Mrs. Edith Frampton called as she walked by.

"Good evening. How are the pies coming along?" I called.

"Each one is getting better than the last. My Lazlo complains that he's gaining too much weight. But I know he loves it." She speed-walked toward the downtown, her brand-new athletic shoes squeaking against the road's asphalt.

"I like her," Tori said.

"I do too. She's always so nice to everyone."

We continued up the walkway to the Goodloes' home. It was cluttered with children's toys.

"How many kids do the Goodloes have now?" Tori whispered as she stepped over a second bike.

"I think five," I whispered back. "All boys."

Tori shuddered. "Hennie is a few years younger than we are. Can you imagine chasing after five boys?"

"Not really." I rang the front bell. "But I think she enjoys it. Her boys all seem to adore her. And the older ones mostly behave when she brings them to library events."

Inside, a dog started barking, followed by the thunder of what sounded like an entire army running. The door opened a crack. A pink-cheeked boy poked his head out. The door slammed shut again. "Mama! There's some ladies at the door!"

"You don't have to shout like that. I heard the bell," we heard Hennie say from somewhere deep inside the house.

The front porch shook as the army inside went on the run again. Several moments later the door opened a crack. A spicy aroma of fried fish rolled out to greet us.

"Yes?" Hennie asked. "What are you doing here?"

"You didn't bring your boys to today's reading program. I was concerned that something was wrong. You never miss. I thought we should check on you." I held out the box of cinnamon rolls. "We brought dessert."

"Oh. Thank you. That was thoughtful." The tension from her face eased as she accepted the box. "Boys!"

One of her sons ran to the door. "What is it, Mom?"

"Please take this into the kitchen."

"What is it? It smells delicious."

"Never you mind. Just take it into the kitchen."

"Yes, ma'am." He ran off down the hallway behind Hennie. The thunder of feet followed him.

Hennie smiled and shook her head. "Those rolls will be gone before I finish this sentence. My boys are more voracious than a pack of wolves."

"And you're okay?" I asked.

"Can we come in?" Tori asked at the same time.

"I am sorry if I gave you cause to worry. An old friend of mine needed counseling. Thank you, again, for the dessert. That really was . . . kind . . . of you. Now, if you'd excuse me . . ." Hennie started to close the door.

"Can't you spare a few more minutes?" Tori turned toward me and raised her brows. "For Tru?"

It took a moment for Hennie to catch what Tori was saying but not saying. And I didn't thank her for her subtle hint that I was there to talk to Hennie about the silly rumor that I was carrying Jace's love child. But I suppose for the sake of this investigation, we needed to pretend I was in trouble and desperately in need of Hennie's help if that was what it took to get inside the house.

"Of course," Hennie said. She opened the door wider so we could enter. "You can sit in the front room. I'll be right back. Let me tell the boys to leave us alone."

The front parlor looked as if my grandmother Mimsy had decorated it. Mimsy was a traditionalist when it came to parlors and draped everything (from the sagging ancient sofa to the highly polished end tables) in lacy doilies. There was even a milk-glass dish with hard candies that was a twin to Mimsy's on the coffee table.

"I'd bet a year's salary her boys aren't allowed in this room," Tori whispered as she eyed several delicate shepherdess figurines sitting on a chest of drawers.

"There's no way I would take that bet," I said.

"Hennie would tan their hides something good if she caught any of her boys in here," a woman with dark brown hair said from an armchair that was turned toward the unlit fireplace. She peered around the arm. "She says she needs this room and the treasures it contains for her sanity."

"Oh! We didn't know anyone else was in here," I cried, cringing at the thought that she'd overheard our silly conversation. I didn't recognize the woman at first, although I knew I'd seen her around town. "Are you Gracie Mae? Gracie Mae Maynard?" Was this Owen's widow?

She gave a quick nod. "My name's the talk of the town, I suppose."

"I'm so sorry," I said with a rush. "Owen's passing must have been quite a shock."

"Yes, a shock," she agreed sadly. "But not a surprise. He drank hard and was always trying to get the upper hand over anyone he knew. I suppose it was only a matter of time before he angered the wrong person."

"What do you mean?" I asked.

"Oh." She waved her hand in a dismissive gesture as she rose from the chair. "You know . . ."

I didn't know, but I didn't want to push her. She had, after all, just lost her husband.

"We are sorry," Tori said. "I can't imagine what you're going through."

"Thank you," Gracie Mae replied.

"If there's anything we can do, please let us know," Tori continued. "Food. Coffee. Whatever."

"You could share your aunt's secret apple pie recipe," Gracie Mae said to me with a vague smile.

"Anything but that," I said. "Aunt Sal would flail me alive if I did something that foolish. Besides, I don't know it."

"That's what I thought. But I had to try." She headed for the door. "Hennie is taking good care of me. Please tell her I went up to the guest room to take a nap."

"We will," I said as she headed out of the room.

"Sorry about that," Hennie said a few minutes later when she returned. "With all these boys around, there's always a disaster somewhere in the house. Please take a seat."

"Gracie Mae was here," I said, before taking a seat on the sofa. "She wanted us to tell you that she went to the guest room to rest."

"Good. That poor dear. She's been a good friend since high school." She clicked her tongue. "She's always been too good for Owen. But she was determined to make their relationship work."

Tori sat next to me. "She told us she wasn't surprised Owen was killed. Did he have enemies?"

"*Enemies* is a strong word, isn't it? Especially for Cypress. Let's just say the poor man had a personality that rubbed people the wrong way." Hennie picked a chair across from us to sit in. She took a candy from the dish and slowly unwrapped it. "But enough about that. Tru, how can I help you? I can drive you to a doctor in another town."

"That won't be necessary. I don't need a doctor," I said. When Hennie frowned deeply, I added, "It's all too early for all that. Just speculation and all . . ."

"Gracie Mae and Owen never had children. Did they ever ask you for help finding a baby for them?" Tori asked.

"Oh no. Not them. Owen was much too brash. And I'm very picky about the kinds of homes that I'll place a child in." She said this last bit to me.

"Do you run an adoption agency, then?" I asked.

"Nothing formal," Hennie said. "I simply enjoy helping women in need. It's my calling."

"Ah," I said.

"I suppose some of those childless families you work with are willing to pay quite a lot of money for a child," Tori said.

"You're expecting to be paid?" Hennie asked me, frowning. "It should never be about money, but there are compensations that can be given."

There was a loud crash somewhere in the house, followed by a couple of hoots.

"Excuse me." Hennie jumped off the sofa. "I'll be right back."

After she left, I whispered furiously to Tori, "Why are you telling her I want a wad of cash in exchange for a baby? I don't want her to think I'm a monster. And we don't know how much of a gossip she is. Anything we say here could become common knowledge tomorrow."

"Relax," Tori said, sounding like she was enjoying this. Well, why wouldn't she? It wasn't *her* reputation that she was being so free with. "I think you were so busy worrying about what people will think of you that you didn't listen to what Hennie said. She can't come out and tell us that she gets a small fortune from selling babies. I think you were onto something with that wild idea of yours. I think we've found the crime ring that Charlie's ex is investigating."

"But how is Frank involved? He's a used car salesman." None of this felt right. I was beginning to regret coming here.

"Perhaps he helps with the paperwork? I don't know. When she comes back, let's try to figure out if there's a connection between the two."

When Hennie returned, she smiled at us. Her smile looked tighter than it had before she'd left. "I'm sorry about that. Where were we?"

I stood. "We've taken too much of your time."

"We were just talking about Frank Calhoun," Tori said as she stubbornly remained seated.

"That's the guy who sells cars?" Hennie shook her head.

"Do you know him?" Tori asked.

"Not really. Bought a minivan from him. Landry handled most of the transaction. That salesman kept trying to upsell us."

The front door opened. "Hello!" Doris's chipper voice called out.

"Oh no," Hennie muttered. "I forgot to cancel her babysitting services for tonight." She rushed to the door.

Since I was anxious to leave, I followed her.

"I'm sorry, Doris." Hennie blocked the door. "I meant to call you. You can't come in. We won't need you for a while. I'll call you next week."

The young woman looked crushed. "I don't understand. Did I do something wrong?" She glanced over at me standing next to Hennie and her voice turned tight. "Did someone say something about me?"

She had been talking to me about Hennie quite a bit lately. And with me standing there now, it must have looked like I'd come to spread rumors.

"No," Hennie was quick to say. "No. It's nothing about you. I . . ." She glanced up the stairs behind us. "It's just that we have someone staying here. Someone who might be upset if—"

"Gracie Mae's here?" Doris said, her brows lifting.

Hennie looked away.

"You know I didn't—that I wouldn't do anything with Owen. He's as old as my father. Or rather he was." She made a gagging noise.

By this time Tori had given up and joined us.

"You had a thing with Owen?" Tori cried. "Really?"

"No, not really," Doris nearly shouted.

Hennie shushed her and pushed us all out the door. "Gracie Mae is upset. Understandably so. She came to me for solace. I'm sorry, Doris. You can't be here. Goodbye." She slammed the door closed in our faces.

"This is so unfair," Doris said as the three of us stood on the front porch and stared at the closed door. She looked close to tears. "Because they have so many kids, they pay much more than most."

"I don't understand. Why would Gracie Mae think you were interested in Owen?" I asked. "That seems so . . . so wrong."

"I was never interested in Owen. He was interested in me," Doris said with a shiver.

"Ew, why?" Tori asked.

"What?" Doris cried in protest. "Are you implying that a man wouldn't think I'm attractive?"

"No, I didn't mean it like that," Tori backpedaled. "I mean, why would he think *you* would be interested in someone like *him*. You date some of the hottest guys in town—firefighters, that young doctor who lived here for a year, and that one guy who recently moved to New York to model. Anyone with a smidgen of a brain could see that Owen isn't in your league."

"Thank you," Doris said. She adjusted her glasses.

"If there was nothing between you and Owen, then why would seeing you upset Gracie Mae?" I asked.

She gave me a nasty look before shouting, "Because that woman is nuts! Whenever Gracie Mae saw Owen talking with a woman, she'd go ballistic. She came to my house, beating on the door, screaming that I needed to keep my mitts off her man. But here's the thing. I never sought him out. He came to me because my family has roots that reach all the way back to the day Cypress was founded. He'd ask all sorts of questions about my family and about family tales that I might have heard growing up. I'd tell him what I knew, but he kept coming back for more, pressing me to search my family's papers, asking me about this or that. It was really annoying. And if that's all you want to know, I need to go make some phone calls. I might still be able to find someone who needs a babysitter tonight."

She hurried off before either Tori or I could say anything. Her hair bounced with each quick step.

"I've never known anyone so hardworking," I said.

"She works hard, but not smart," Tori pointed out. "Have you noticed how none of her jobs or businesses pay very well?"

"Her heart seems to be in the right place, though." I thought a bit about what she'd said about Gracie Mae. "Do you suppose Gracie Mae followed Owen and saw him with an accomplice—or even the head of the criminal ring—and snapped? Maybe she killed Owen in a fit of rage, not understanding what she was witnessing."

"We'd never get her to admit to that," Tori said.

"No," I agreed. "But if she saw Owen doing something with Hennie—the head of our adoption crime ring—and killed him because of it, I doubt she'd be staying with Hennie now. You saw how the thought that Gracie Mae might see Doris worried Hennie. Maybe that means Hennie isn't the master criminal we're looking for. Maybe we need to look in another direction." And I was relieved for it too. "Frank sells used cars. Maybe he's selling stolen cars in addition to the ones he offers on his lot. That seems like a more logical explanation. Perhaps Owen had been helping strip the cars of their VIN numbers and the two had an argument."

"That might be our answer. Since Jace is looking now into Frank's background, I say we sit back and let the police handle things from here on out," Tori said. We'd reached the car. "What's that?" She pointed to a piece of paper tucked under the windshield wiper. "Is one of Hennie's boys starting a lawn service business?"

"They're all too young," I said. "Maybe it's Doris who's branching out into yard work. Or, more likely, it's another flyer for her essential oils."

I plucked the paper from the car and unfolded it.

"What does it say?" Tori asked.

"It's not an offer to mow my grass or to sell me a cure for my aches and pains," I said.

I read over the words a few times before handing the note to her.

Someone had scribbled on the paper: *If you don't want to get hurt, you'd better watch who you talk to.*

"Watch who we're talking to? What does that mean?"

"It means we've made someone nervous," I said. My heart started to beat faster.

"Nervous, or maybe angry," Tori corrected. She frowned at the paper. "This note sounds like a threat. Is whoever wrote it trying to tell us that we shouldn't have talked with Hennie?"

"Who else could it be referring to? Well, I suppose if someone wants us to stay away from Hennie, then Hennie is who we need to keep talking to if we want to solve Owen's murder."

Chapter Eighteen

After getting that troubling note, Tori insisted on coming with me to Aunt Sal's house. Aunt Sal lived in a small brick one-story home that looked quite ordinary on the outside. On the inside, the place looked as if a circus had set up shop in her living room. The walls were painted bright red with white stripes. Her collection of iridescent carnival glassware lined shelves in front of the windows. Antique stuffed animals hung from strings on the ceiling. And the strangest artwork I'd ever seen hung on the walls. I found that it was best not to let any of the creepy, large-eyed people in any of the paintings make eye contact.

"I'll just take this into the kitchen," I said as I hurried through the room with my gaze locked on the brightly colored Persian rug.

"That girl is always in a hurry," I heard Aunt Sal saying to Tori behind me. I was glad to see that my aunt had stopped crying.

"Um . . . what?" Tori said. "Um . . . What—what is that person doing in that painting over there? It looks like he's—"

"He is," Aunt Sal said proudly. "The paintings are all one-of-a-kind, you know."

Thank goodness. I'd hate to think there were more of those images out in the world.

"I dated the artist for a while," I could hear Aunt Sal explain from the living room. "A deeply troubled man, but oh, so passionate. That one is a portrait he painted of me."

Don't look. Don't look.

"Oh!" I heard Tori gasp. She must have looked. "I should go see if Tru needs help."

Aunt Sal's kitchen appeared normal, save for the singed bits around the oven and the stove. Over the years, Aunt Sal had learned to cook less and less. She mainly used her kitchen for storing plates and glasses, the refrigerator for storing leftovers and drinks, and the large freezer for storing frozen meals. (Although, truth be told, she could mess up a frozen dinner just as dramatically as she could a meal she attempted to make from scratch.)

I loaded up three plates with crispy melt-in-your-mouth fried chicken and the Grind's secret-recipe coleslaw that tasted like a party on my tongue, poured three glasses of iced tea, and set it all on a large decorative tray that Aunt Sal kept on the rarely used stovetop.

"Please tell me that there's some hard liquor in that cabinet over there," Tori said with a wavery voice. "I don't think I can see any more of your aunt's artwork while still sober."

"I'm sure Aunt Sal would enjoy something too. Pour three glasses of brandy. That's what she likes to drink. And she always buys top-shelf quality."

The dining room, while sporting a quirky decor of paper-mache flowers glued to the walls, felt almost welcoming. Tori, who was huddled at my back, breathed out a deep sigh of relief at the sight of it. Aunt Sal had laid out silverware and cloth napkins.

"I heard you got yourself in the family way," Aunt Sal said halfway through the meal. Honestly, I was surprised it took her that long to ask me about that particular rumor.

"It's not true," I said after I wiped my mouth with my napkin. "I heard you aren't planning on entering the apple pie contest. That can't be right."

"Oh, it *is* true . . ." Aunt Sal broke out into sobs. She grabbed her snifter of brandy and drained it before glancing in Tori's direction. "I already told you why on the phone."

No, she didn't. All she had done was cry about her favorite bakery in New York City closing down. "I don't—"

"It breaks my heart to dis-disappoint everyone," she cried.

"I don't understand. Why can't you enter?" Tori seemed to have finally recovered from the shock of seeing all that one-of-a-kind artwork.

"Well, dear, you have to understand that there are certain things I cannot purchase because a certain place where I buy them has closed." Aunt Sal gave me a meaningful look as she said the last part.

"Oh. Oh! Really?" I said as the pieces started to fall into place. Was she suggesting what I thought she was suggesting? "Aunt Sal, are you telling us that you won the baking competition every year, not because you are an apple-pie-baking savant as everyone believed, but because you had a pie express-shipped down from the best bakery in New York State?"

"It cost a small fortune to do it," she said, seemingly not at all remorseful about cheating for all these years.

"Aunt Sal!" I cried. "You didn't!"

"I think it's hilarious," Tori said. "While all the other women in town tried to figure out how Sal could outbake them, Sal kept bringing the best pie to the competition, year after year."

"It was a hoot and a half," Sal said with a sniffle. "But that wasn't why I did it."

"So, it's true. Anyone could win the contest this year," I said. "Which explains why everyone is talking about it again."

"The first year I won was the year the brawl broke out in the library.

Terrible, terrible times that was. Prissy had just died, and nearly every baker in town expected to be crowned Prissy's successor."

That was the year Mrs. Farnsworth had banned the librarians from helping anyone in their search for the perfect apple pie recipe.

"Bringing a winning apple pie to the festival was my way of helping the community. Everyone knew Prissy's daughter, Cora, was hopeless in the kitchen," Aunt Sal said.

"You're hopeless in the kitchen," Tori blurted, and suddenly realized how rude that sounded. "No offense." She flashed me a look of distress.

"None taken, dear. I have the fire department on speed dial for a reason."

"Cheating was a community service?" I asked, still unable to believe what Sal had done. I mean, I believed it. She really was a terrible cook, but she was also a kind, thoughtful person.

"I took Prissy's place in order to keep the ladies in town from murdering each other," she said.

Although her sobs had abated, Aunt Sal kept waving her napkin while looking as if she might burst into tears again. Desperate to avoid that, I tried to change the topic.

"Do you know much about Gracie Mae Maynard?" I asked her. "Her husband was the man who was killed behind the library. Did you work with her when you were waiting tables at the diner?"

"Gracie Mae Maynard?" Aunt Sal sniffled. "Never worked with her. But I do know that she could never win the apple pie contest."

"That's not what I meant," I said, trying to move her away from all thoughts of her pie.

But Aunt Sal didn't seem to hear me. She shook her head. "That woman would starve if she had to depend on her own cooking. You did notice how she'd moved into the Goodloes' home the moment her husband was dead. That's because he was the cook in the family. I've tasted one of his pies before. If he had ever entered the contest, I don't know if my pie would still have won. I suppose it'll never win again." She drew a long, shaky breath and (thankfully) didn't start crying again. "The two of you need to watch your backs. I fear for Cypress society. Until another superior apple pie arrives on that competition table, life will get as dodgy as it was after Prissy's demise. Maybe even worse."

Tori looked at me and I looked at her. It felt as if we were asking ourselves the same question.

Was Owen murdered because he could bake a pie?

No, that couldn't be right. Frank wasn't a baker—that anyone knew of. And it was his library book that was found on Owen's body. And then there was the threatening note: *If you don't want to get hurt, you'd better watch who you talk to.*

I'd scared someone in Cypress, and I didn't know the first thing about baking an award-winning apple pie. Apparently, no one in my family did.

Chapter Nineteen

W ho would write such an ugly note?" Flossie shook the letter that had been left on my car windshield as if she wanted to do it harm. We were sitting out on her wide porch, a porch that overlooked the vast and placid Lake Marion. The sun was setting on Saturday evening. This had been the first chance I'd gotten to talk with my friend about what had happened at Hennie's. "Threatening you with anonymous letters, indeed! If I find out who wrote this awful thing, I'll wring their skinny chicken neck."

Strangely, her ire made me feel better.

It'd been nearly twenty-four hours since Tori and I had found the letter, and I still wasn't sure what I should do about it. All Saturday morning I'd stewed over it as Tori took me to her favorite hair salon and then to her favorite nail salon. All Saturday afternoon I'd stewed over it as she took me to shoe stores and clothing stores where I spent far too much money on outfits I couldn't really see myself wearing.

"It's not a makeover if you buy things that feel safe and comfortable," Tori had cried when I'd balked at buying the black stiletto heels that were currently pinching my toes.

My dishwater-brown hair now had blond streaks. My short nails wore a fresh coat of pale pink polish and sported perfectly rounded tips. I wore a tight red halter top that hugged everything, a skirt that I kept tugging on because it felt as if it'd been made for someone several inches shorter than me, and the black stilettos Tori had talked me into buying. The high heels made my legs wobble. I fully expected I'd topple over before the night was over.

After finishing our shopping extravaganza, Tori dropped me off at Flossie's. She had to rush off to get ready for a hot date with Charlie. I'd made it as far as Flossie's porch before dropping into a rocking chair. I bent down and rubbed my sore feet.

Flossie had stared hard at my new look but hadn't said a word about it. However, when I told her what had happened at Hennie's house and showed her the note Tori and I had found, she'd screeched loud enough that a few of her neighbors came out onto their porches to gawk at us.

"Me and my silly books. I should have come with you last night. I'll never, never forgive myself if anything happens to you and I wasn't there to help you because I was tucked behind a computer writing."

"Tori and I were fine," I soothed. "Besides, the note is no more than words on a piece of paper, not an act of violence."

"No one knows the power of words better than me." She shot me a look. "Save for you, of course. So, I don't have to tell you that you need to treat this threat seriously. Have you shown the letter to Jace?" she asked, her voice calmer now that she'd gotten that initial burst of emotions out of her system.

"Other than you and Tori? I haven't shown it to anyone. I don't know what I'm going to do about it. If I go to the police, how much should I tell them? Do I also mention the library break-ins?"

Flossie muttered under her breath as she poured us both tall glasses of sweet tea. "I don't know, honey. I don't know."

We sat in silence for a while. I rocked in the wooden chair slowly. The neighbors who'd come out to check on us retreated back into their houses.

"You need to give the letter to Jace," Flossie said finally. "He needs to know that someone is watching you and threatening to harm you. Even if you don't tell him anything else, you need to tell him that."

"I suppose," I said as I dug around in my purse for my phone. I wondered if I should tell Flossie about Aunt Sal. Could her dropping out of the apple pie contest have something to do with everything that's been going on? Aunt Sal seemed to think it did. I opened my mouth to say something along those lines, but what came out was, "I'll send Jace a text." While I was at it, I also texted Tori and let her know that I'd invited Jace over to Flossie's house so I could give him the note.

Not ten minutes after sending that text, Tori showed up with Charlie on her arm.

"Where is he?" she demanded as she marched up the front steps.

"Jace texted back that he was having dinner with his mom," I said. "He promised to stop by when he finished."

"That's rude." Tori stamped her booted foot. She wore a slinky navy-blue maxi dress with matching leather ankle boots. Charlie, in his khaki pants and light blue linen button-up shirt, made a perfect match for her, especially given how his eyes glittered every time he looked at her.

"His mama's fried catfish is some of the best in the state," Flossie pointed out.

Charlie tsked. "I'm surprised he'd do that to you, Tru. Your life is threatened, and he's insisting on finishing his mother's fried catfish?"

"In his defense," I said, "I only asked him to stop by. I didn't tell him why."

"Have a seat, you two. I'll get more tumblers." Flossie rolled inside her sprawling, two-story lake house. It had been her husband's family home. Truman had inherited the place upon his father's demise. And when he died, Flossie inherited it, much to the chagrin of Truman's siblings.

"Why are we sitting out here in this humid air swatting mosquitoes when there's an air-conditioned house just beyond that front door?" Tori complained after she and Charlie found a spot together on a rustic bench made from logs.

"You know Flossie," I said. "She doesn't let anyone inside her house when she's working on a book. Says it's bad mojo."

"What a charming quirk," Charlie said. He leaned forward. "I do love hearing about writers and their creative processes. Did you know that in order to get her inspiration Agatha Christie would soak in the bathtub and eat apples while looking at crime-scene photos?"

"I've never heard that," I said. "It sounds rather odd. Are you sure it's true?"

"It's what I've read," Charlie said with a shrug. "I suppose all writers have their peculiar rituals."

"I bet Agatha would let her friends come inside her home to save their hair from frizzing," Tori said as she fluffed her hair that wasn't frizzing at all.

"What's that?" Flossie asked as she returned with two tall iced tea tumblers.

"It's hot out here. You should let us inside," Tori said.

"And miss this sunset?" Flossie pointed with a glass to the lake beyond the porch. "That's crazy."

Charlie poured the tea, refreshing Flossie's and my glasses as well as pouring drinks for Tori and himself.

We sat in silence some more. Frogs chirped like baby birds while a group of cicadas buzzed in the distance.

"How long does it take for Jace to eat a few pieces of fish, for goodness' sake?" Tori asked. Her leg had started bouncing, a testament to her impatience.

"You don't have to be here when he comes. I can handle it," I assured her. "Go on to dinner."

"I wouldn't leave you to handle this by yourself." Tori glared pointedly at Flossie.

"She won't be alone," Flossie shot back. "This is my house. It's not like I'm going anywhere."

"Please." Those two always bickered when they got nervous, but I knew deep down how much they cared about each other. "I know you both have my back. You don't have to prove it."

"Send Jace another text." Tori crossed her arms over her stubborn chest. "Hurry him up. 'Cause I'm not leaving."

Sending Jace an impatient text wasn't something I was going to do, and, luckily, I didn't need to tell Tori that. Jace drove up in his Jeep as she continued to complain about him and his slow eating habits. With the sun lowering behind the trees, his tall body was in silhouette as he came up to the porch.

"Stand up, so he can see your makeover," Tori hissed.

Ah. That was why she had rushed over. She wanted to see for herself his reaction to "the look" she'd created for me.

She poked me in the side until I stood up and was wobbling on those ridiculously narrow high heels.

Jace took the steps two at a time.

My mouth turned dry. I clutched the threatening letter so tightly, it crumpled in my fist. Was I about to spill the beans about everything to him? Was this the end of the secret bookroom? It'd been open for less than a month. Had all our work been for nothing?

"You wanted to see me?" he said as he came up onto the porch.

"Yes . . . um . . . you see . . . there was this . . ." I stumbled over my words.

"My goodness, Tru." He interrupted my stammering. "What in the world do you have on?" He slapped his leg and hooted with laughter. "Isn't it a little early for costume parties? It's not even October yet."

I looked down at the fitted halter top and short skirt. While these weren't the kinds of clothes I would have chosen to wear, I had felt . . . *different* . . . in them. Not comfortable, but pretty.

As he laughed, my self-confidence cracked. Sank. Buried itself down into the mud in the deepest part of Lake Marion. My cheeks burned so hot that it felt as if they'd been charred by fire.

"I . . . um . . ." I didn't know what to say. The threatening note slipped from my fingers, forgotten.

"Did you get those shoes from Doris's thrift store?" He laughed as he pointed at the torture devices strapped to my feet. "They look like something my mom would have purchased back before she got married. You should see the pictures. They're crazy."

"Dude." Charlie jumped up and caught Jace's arm. "You need to stop talking."

As I stood there feeling as if I'd been thrust back into the bad old days of high school, Charlie pulled Jace down the stairs and into the front yard.

"Your new look came as a shock to him," Flossie said quietly. "He's used to seeing you looking more natural."

"He's an idiot," Tori said as she jumped up from her bench. "All men are idiots. I don't know why we bother trying to look nice for them. Or even why we put up with them at all."

"I can't do this." I shook my head, and despite Flossie's insistence that we stay out of her house when she was working on a new book, I ran inside and locked myself in her hall bathroom. I leaned over the sink, grabbed a bar of soap, and scrubbed until every bit of makeup was gone and my skin was as red and shiny as a ripe apple. Then I plopped down on the toilet seat, rested my chin in my hands, and stared at the black-and-white tile floor.

Tomorrow, I would return every piece of clothing and pair of shoes I'd purchased. None of it was me. It was so much *not me* that people (Jace) thought I looked like some kind of badly dressed Halloween reject.

I sighed. Those same clothes would make Tori (or Jace's ex-girlfriend Sissy) look like she was heading out to have a little fun. On a Tuesday. On an ordinary Tuesday at that.

A half hour later Flossie knocked on the door. "Everyone is gone."

"Good."

When I didn't open the door, she said, "Jace told Charlie that Frank has an alibi for the night Owen was killed. He had gone out of town to a car auction. There are witnesses."

"What about Frank's library book? How did it get on Owen's body, then?" I asked through the door.

"Frank didn't know. He thought it was still at his house. But, of course, when he looked for it, it was gone."

I opened the door. "Did he tell Jace where the book came from?"

"Don't you fret," Flossie said. "Frank kept his mouth shut about that. He knows how many people he'd anger if he didn't. Our secret is still safe."

"But we're no closer to finding Owen's killer or the bookroom vandal."

"No, we're not," she agreed. "And no one told Jace about that threatening letter you got."

"Good. I don't want him to know." I sounded as grumpy as a cornered possum.

"But, Tru, your life might be in danger."

"No, it's not." I opened the bathroom door. "Someone wanted to scare me, which means someone is worried that I'm getting too close to uncovering the motive behind Owen's death. And that's probably the biggest clue we've gotten so far."

Chapter Twenty

The library was closed on Sundays. Several weeks ago, Anne had complained that our "forward-thinking technological-barrier-breaking library followed such an outdated custom." Mrs. Farnsworth, a stickler for tradition, had snarled quite forcefully that as long as she "had breath in her lungs, Cypress's library would not open up on God's day."

The usually argumentative Anne had snapped her mouth shut. And that had been the end of that discussion. The "library of the future" kept its doors locked up tight on Sundays.

But that didn't mean I didn't carry my tote bag full of books available for lending as I attended church with Mama Eddy. This week I was especially looking forward to the service. After all, one can learn a lot about people at church. Case in point, although our church was on the other side of town from Pastor Goodloe's Church of the Guiding Light and about a hundred years older, that didn't stop the congregation from gossiping about the poor deceased Owen and his connection with the Goodloe family.

"His mother will never forgive him for this," I overheard one of the parishioners whispering during a moment of prayerful silence.

"Always knew he'd come to a bad end," another twittered under her breath not that long afterward. "People hated him. Sold people used parts and charged new-parts prices."

It was the usual gossip I'd been hearing all over town—that Owen had been cheating everyone in town when he fixed their cars, not just Anne. But then I heard someone whisper while we all had our heads bowed in prayer, "It had to be the money. I heard he'd promised to return what he'd taken. He'd promised that he'd make it all right once that windfall came to him."

My ears perked up. A windfall?

My head snapped to attention. I nearly turned completely around in my seat as I tried to figure out who had whispered that new piece of information.

Mama Eddy elbowed me in the side while tapping her finger on the prayer book.

I worried my lower lip and turned my attention back to the service. Like a book out of place on a shelf, what I'd just overheard nagged at me. Owen had taken money? From whom? And he was expecting a windfall? From whom?

After the service, I wanted to actively search for the whispering gossip. But Mama Eddy insisted I stay by her side as we headed to the parish hall for coffee. It was a ritual we'd practiced for years.

"I love the new look with your hair," Cora exclaimed as she sidled up to me. "It's so modern." She slipped the apple recipe book into my tote bag. "Thanks to you, I think I figured out why your aunt wins the competition every year." Her loud voice carried in the small parish hall. Several people leaned toward us to listen in. "She's combining two recipes from this book, isn't she? I wrote them down. I have a feeling that this will finally be my year!"

Of course, since Aunt Sal didn't actually bake the pie she entered, she didn't use any of the recipes in the book I'd lent Cora. But my aunt had once enjoyed looking at the pictures. I smiled and nodded and told Cora that I was sure her apple pie would taste better than any other apple pie in the contest. I then asked her what she knew about Owen's finances. If others were talking about it, certainly Cora had heard the details. "He wasn't expecting a windfall, was he? And did he owe any-one a large amount of money?"

Her brows crinkled. "I'd never known Owen to have more than a few pennies to rub together. His people came from the swamp, you know." She'd said that as if coming from the nearby Hell Hole Swamp determined your descendants' futures. "And he wasted what money that he did have at the bars. Poor Gracie Mae had to squirrel away the money she made waiting tables at the Sunshine Diner in order to keep food on the table and the rent paid. If I were in her shoes, I wouldn't be missing him. Not. One. Bit."

The old, whitewashed parish hall didn't have air conditioning. The building's tall windows had been propped open with scrap lumber to let in the breeze. Cora's gingham dress danced.

"I saw her at Hennie's," I confided. She had looked genuinely dis-traught to me. "It seemed like she was in shock."

Cora thought about that for a moment before saying, "That's inter-esting. Not that Gracie Mae acted like she was in shock, mind you. I don't find that interesting in the least. Gracie Mae has always been a stellar actor. But it's interesting that she'd be at Hennie's. I could have sworn that I'd heard talk about the two of them having had a falling-out."

"Over what?"

"I believe it was because of some kind of disagreement over that church of Landry's. I heard Landry and Owen had had a righteous argument first. Don't ask me over what, because no one seems to know. If I had to guess, the argument was over Owen's drinking. But I'd also heard that Landry didn't like how Owen felt as if he was some kind of enforcer in Landry's church, scaring the other parishioners if they acted in a way Owen thought was unholy. Isn't that ironic? Owen, a drunkard and cheat, holding others to a higher standard of conduct."

"If that's true, I wonder if his behavior scared away some of Landry's flock."

"Might have happened. That church's congregation is small enough to fit into a living room. And the rent on strip mall space doesn't come cheap. Landry couldn't afford to lose any of his paying members."

"Do you think Owen might have stolen money from Landry or his church?" I asked thinking about the comment I'd heard about him owing someone money.

"I haven't heard anything about that," Cora seemed to hate to admit. "If you do find out something, I want to be the first one you tell."

I smiled but refused to make any promises like that. Instead, I looked around, trying to figure out who in the parish hall could possibly know more about Owen than nosy Cora.

Before I could make much progress in finding that elusive person, Krystal Capps (the town coroner and one of my inside contacts at the police department) cornered me.

"I heard you gave Cora a recipe book that gives away all of your aunt's secrets," she said, her tight pinkish-white corkscrew curls bouncing. "How could you do that to me? I thought we were friends."

"I'm not trying to play favorites. And I didn't realize you were such an ambitious baker." I slipped my hand into my bag and pulled out the cookbook with the large juicy apple on the cover. I could see why Mrs. Farnsworth had made it a point to keep the library out of the apple-pie-baking contest. Emotions were definitely running high. "It doesn't have all of Aunt Sal's secrets." *Or any of them, for that matter.* "But I think someone as talented in the kitchen as you are can figure out what's not being said. I'm sure of it."

Krystal hugged the book to her chest. "Thank you. I'm sure I can crack your aunt's secret recipe."

"Who knows, you might even bake something better," I said. "Now that I've given you the edge for the bake-off, perhaps you can help me? Have you heard anything out of the ordinary about the state of Owen's finances? I mean, I'm sure you've heard the police officers talking about things in the hallway."

Krystal, who had just gushed her appreciation for the baking help, glared at me.

"Owen drank his paycheck," she said at last. "Everyone knows that."

"Yes, but surely you've heard more than that. With a case like this one, I'm sure the detectives are digging into every aspect of Owen's life. And talking about it."

She glanced around, as if searching to see who might be listening in on our conversation. "None of the officers or that detective from the state are saying anything," she whispered, and then started to hurry away. "It's maddening."

I tried to follow her. I wanted to know why those who were working the case were keeping so quiet. Had they learned anything? But Mama Eddy grabbed my arm.

"Don't look now," she hissed in my ear after batting my hand away from a mini cinnamon bun that had been calling out to me on the refreshment table.

Naturally, I looked. But the room was crowded. There was no telling who she didn't want me to look at.

"Too late," she whispered. "He's coming our way."

He?

Mama Eddy made it a rule to never spurn male attention. After all, men could be so useful in attending to "small" household matters like killing bugs, painting bedrooms, and weeding gardens. My mother had a reputation for being a tough taskmaster. Still, men found her as irresistible as a moth found a lightbulb.

There was only one reason why she'd not bask in a man's attention.

"Did you break up with someone?" I didn't even realize she was dating again.

Then I saw him. The crowd parted like the Red Sea and there was my father, wearing his stained and battered old fishing hat with lures dangling from the rim, swaggering toward us. Unlike all the other men in the room, he was not wearing a suit or a tie. His jeans had such a large hole in one leg that his knobby knee was sticking out.

"Hey, Pops." I kissed him on the cheek.

Mama Eddy whispered in a growly voice, "What in blue blazes are you doing here? And why in all that's holy do you look as if you dressed yourself from inside a garbage dump?"

Daddy hadn't stepped foot in a church to worship since the divorce. He claimed Mama Eddy had won their religion in the divorce, but I suspect he'd always preferred fishing to Sunday services.

He was, however, a man who liked to eat good food and had attended events in the church's parish hall over the years as long as a meal was involved. He winked at me, then snatched a handful of the mini cinnamon buns from a plate on the nearby table. He tossed me one.

"Well?" Mama Eddy tapped the toe of her shoe on the linoleum floor.

He nibbled on a bun and licked his fingers. "Good morning, Edwina. Have you not been sleeping well? You look"—he paused while giving her a meaningful glance before saying—"tired."

Mama Eddy's neck turned pink. "My daughter's been running around not caring that her actions are spreading rumors that she's getting married or pregnant or worse." I wondered what she thought could be worse. "How do you think I've been sleeping?" she answered in a whispery rage. "What are you doing here?"

While my father was chatting happily with Mama Eddy and Mama Eddy was answering in ever-softer, angrier whispers, members of the parish kept coming up to shake my father's hand. He was wildly popular in town. For a short while, his friends had urged him to run for mayor. Daddy had resisted. Again, I suspected he turned down the opportunity since such a position would cut into his fishing time.

"Why are you here?" Mama Eddy demanded for the fourth time.

Instead of answering, Daddy asked, "Who is that woman over there? She's staring daggers at us." He pointed to a silver-haired woman.

"That's Mrs. Frampton," I said. And she did look about as happy as if someone had kicked her dog. "She's a nice lady."

"If that's what nice looks like"—Daddy shuddered—"I don't want to see what she looks like when she's riled up."

"Are you going to tell us what you're doing here, or will I need to shake you silly?" Mama Eddy demanded.

"No shaking necessary, Edwina," he said, with a cat-who-ate-the-canary grin. He popped another mini cinnamon bun in his mouth and answered while still chewing, "Someone left this tacked to my front door sometime during the night." He pulled a piece of crumpled paper from his pants pocket. "And I thought our daughter should see it."

He handed the paper to me.

Mama Eddy peered over my shoulder while I carefully unfolded and smoothed out the wrinkles.

Someone had hastily scrawled in pencil, *Tell your daughter to be more careful about who she talks to. She's making enemies.*

My stomach tightened with worry. The mini cinnamon bun I'd just finished eating felt like a five-pound stone in my gut. "Who left this?" I asked.

Daddy shook his head. "Found it when I headed out to the johnboat."

"Child, what are you doing that someone would write such a note?" Mama Eddy demanded.

"Just asking a few questions here and there about Owen's death." That person in the congregation this morning had been talking about his money troubles. I supposed I needed to start asking about Owen's financial situation and soon, before the unhappy note sender decided to do more than write threats.

"Your friends are so inconsiderate, Ash." Mama Eddy snatched the note from my hands and wadded it up. "Unsigned. No phone number. No direction about who these enemies are. You should have thrown that into the trash where it belongs instead of wasting our time with it."

"You know I'm prone to disagree with those assessments of yours," he said with a smile. He turned to me. His smile warmed. "And you, Tru, I know you'll take this warning seriously."

Mama Eddy shook her head. "Don't encourage her. This is why she's not married. This is why I don't have grandchildren, not that I'm old enough to have grandchildren, mind you. But you, Ashley Grainger Becket, have no clue how to raise a child."

"I'm not a child," I gently pointed out.

But this wasn't about me. This was about the past hurts between them that they still hadn't figured out how to lay to rest.

I stepped back while Mama Eddy continued to whisper furiously at my father. She would have been mortified if she had realized what a scene she was making.

I wondered some more about the note someone had tacked to Daddy's door. Did that mean I was closing in on the killer? It sure didn't feel like I was close to uncovering any answers from my end of things.

I scanned the room, searching for someone who might know Owen well enough to have a good idea of what was going on with his finances. Our friends and neighbors were keeping their distance while watching as my mother lit into my father. Since this is what happened every time the two of them got together, no one appeared overly surprised. I plastered on an awkward smile and started to move even farther away from my parents.

But then I heard my mom whisper, "It's common knowledge that the only person who really knows what happened to that Owen fellow has got to be his wife. But I'm not going to tell Tru that, and don't you dare either. I don't want her talking to a killer."

Well, well, well. Thank you, Mama Eddy. I hurried out of the parish hall and headed straight toward Perks, where I knew Tori was working. We needed to get back over to Hennie's house.

Chapter Twenty-One

Nothing about this murder investigation made a lick of sense . . . unless Owen's death was connected to something bigger, something dangerous. Like a crime ring that would attract the attention of the FBI? If that was the case, was Gracie Mae also involved with whatever Owen had gotten himself mixed up with?

Anxious to talk this through with Tori, I hurried down the steps of the parish hall. I thought I heard someone call my name, but when I turned around to look, I didn't see anyone.

"That must be Hubert's poltergeist following me around," I joked to myself.

I speed-walked, my arms pumping, cutting across a heavily treed town park as I made my way toward the small downtown.

I'd barely made it past a cluster of azalea bushes when something hit me in the back of my head.

Whatever it was, it hit me hard. Hard enough that I didn't even remember falling.

All I remember is a voice, whispery and raspy, saying, "*I could kill you.*"

And then . . . darkness.

"That's right. Sit up slowly," someone was saying gently.

A pair of strong hands helped me lift my face off the grass. I must have landed partially in one of the old azalea bushes. My arm felt as if it'd been scratched by raven claws. Why raven claws? I asked myself. That was a random thought. But then again, none of my thoughts were particularly clear at the moment.

"What?" It took far too much effort to form that one-syllable word. I swallowed. "What happened?"

Yes. That was better. Two words. One of them with more than one syllable. And they'd formed a coherent question. Progress.

"I don't know," the kindly voice answered as the hands helped me push up into a sitting position. "Don't you?"

I dragged in one long breath and then opened my eyes, eyes I hadn't realized I'd been holding tightly closed. The person who I saw crouched down beside me with an openly concerned expression surprised me.

"Candy?" What was she doing here? In the middle of the park? I suddenly imagined crime bosses lumbering into the park to sit together on one of the benches to discuss . . . What crime could those imaginary men be discussing here, in Cypress?

"I go by Candice now." Her brows furrowed. She looked troubled. "What were you doing out here?"

"I was . . ." What had I been doing? It took a moment for my scrambled mind to put the pieces back together. "I was crossing the park to get to Perks, the coffee shop," I said slowly.

"And where were you coming from?"

I pressed a hand to the back of my head. Was I bleeding? Ow. That hurt. The edges of my vision turned all gray and fuzzy. I swayed enough that Candice tightened her grip on my arms. "I was . . ." Again, I hesitated. Mama Eddy. My father. The church. One of my best dresses. "I came from church. Someone must have hit me from behind. My head hurts."

Candice nodded as she pulled a cell phone from her pocket. "You'll need to get that head injury looked at."

Today she was wearing jeans, a low-cut blouse, and black leather boots. Like the other day, she was dressed in an outfit that was very similar to the kinds of clothes Tori liked to wear. Her long red hair had been tamed into a quick bun on the top of her head.

"Charlie says you work for the FBI," I said as I cradled my head in my hands and wondered what I'd been hit with. A baseball bat?

"Charlie talks too much." She pushed some buttons on her phone. "He used to be a black hole when it came to information. He'd let nothing escape. It was the worst. This is an inconvenient time for him to experience personal growth. I suppose he also told you that we were once married."

"He didn't, but my friend Tori and I figured it out. In case he didn't tell you, Tori has been dating Charlie."

Candice nodded. "Tell your friend that I wish her luck with him. If she's serious about staying with him, she'll certainly need all the luck she can get." She then spoke into her phone, "Yes, this is Special Agent Newcastle. There's been an attack in Cypress Garden Park. We'll need EMS and some local police support. Yes. That's right. Thank you." She seemed to be finished, but then she added, "Oh, and I think you'd better tell Detective Bailey that his girlfriend is the one that was hurt."

"We're not dating," I said as soon as she'd ended the call.

Candice shrugged. "He'll still want to know."

I tilted my head to one side as I regarded her. That was a mistake. The pain in the back of my head seemed to shoot through my entire body. "Have you been investigating me?" I asked once the pain had subsided.

"I've been conducting an investigation, which no one in this town is making easy," she said as if Cypress was a thorn in her side. "Charlie . . . he knows what you are up to. But he won't tell me anything, and isn't that suspicious?"

"He once told me that he hates secrets but has found himself secret keeper for everyone in town. He then complained that this small town has far too many secrets for its size."

Candice smiled at that. "Charlie has always gotten himself in the middle of secrets and trouble. And he has always hated it. That's how we met all those years ago. Over some trouble that I'd fallen into. Ah, here comes help."

Sirens wailed as an EMS truck and a police car pulled to a stop on the nearest road. Not far down the road, I spotted Jace's Jeep speeding toward us.

"Here comes the cavalry," Candice said dryly. "Are you sure you don't remember anything? Perhaps you saw someone? Heard someone?"

I tried to remember something . . . anything. But it was all a blank. I shook my head, which was a mistake. It hurt!

"I'm sorry," I whispered. "I think the questions I've been asking about Owen's death might have upset someone."

She raised a perfectly plucked eyebrow. "Questions? Why are you asking questions about a murdered man?"

"Because it happened at my library," I said without hesitation. "I want to know why."

"I heard you were zealous about your books." She sounded almost relieved. Maybe even a little impressed.

"I am," I admitted. "And in the last few days I've received a few threatening notes warning me to stop talking to people."

"But a few harmless written words couldn't scare away someone like you?" she said with a sarcastic edge. "You're too smart to worry about upsetting someone who . . . I don't know, has already killed a man?"

"No, it's not like that."

"You do realize that those notes trying to scare you into stopping what you're doing may have been written by a murderer? I bet this investigation of yours is the secret Charlie won't tell me about, the secret everyone knows you're keeping."

"What's this about Tru's secret?" Jace asked as he sprinted up, beating the EMS crew and the pair of uniformed police officers to my personal crime scene.

Candice looked up at him. "Nothing you don't already know, I'm sure," she said, her voice sharp. "I heard the two of you are engaged."

"That's a misunderstanding. We're not even dating," I protested. My voice was too loud. It hurt my head.

Jace dropped to his knees next to me. "What happened, Tru?"

"I'm not sure." I cradled my head in my hands. "I was crossing the park to get to Perks, and next thing I knew, I was waking up with my face buried in the grass."

"And you're the one who called it in?" Jace asked Candice.

The paramedics arrived.

Jace and Candice both stepped away from me to give the men room to work. "Dispatch said you identified yourself as being with the FBI?" he asked her.

"I am. I'm here on special assignment. I'd been hoping to keep a low profile, but . . ." She looked at me and spread her hands.

"Are you suggesting that Tru somehow stumbled into a . . . ?"

I wasn't able to hear the end of Jace's question or Candice's answer. Both paramedics were talking to me, and—irritatingly—expecting me to be paying attention and responding to them. While I didn't want to do it, I told the men the day of the week, how many fingers the man on the left was holding up, and my middle name. It was all very annoying. And I would have made a point of insisting that I had more important matters to attend to if not for the hammering pain radiating from the back of my head.

So, I let the nice men poke at my head and shine a wickedly bright light in my eyes and take my blood pressure and listen to my heart. The two uniformed police officers peppered me with questions while this was happening. Useless questions, since I really had not seen my attacker.

Jace and Candice returned and saved me from having to explain—once again—that I couldn't identify the assailant since obviously I'd been hit from behind. The bump was on the back of my head, not the front.

"How is she?" Jace asked the paramedic as he watched me with a look of concern.

"The contusion appears to be minor." He went on to explain that he didn't see signs that I'd been hit hard enough to have sustained a concussion, but he recommended I take a ride to the closest hospital to have an MRI scan just in case there was some internal bleeding.

I blanched at the thought that I might be bleeding inside my head.

Jace, however, had latched on to a different piece of information. "How long do you think she was unconscious?"

"With head wounds like that, people are rarely out for more than a second or two," the paramedic answered.

Jace gave a brisk nod and turned back to Candice. "You said she was coming around when you found her, which means you must have found her moments after the attack. Did you see anyone in the park?"

Candice thought about it for a moment before answering, "Just a few elderly people who looked as if they were either leaving or heading to church services. I certainly didn't see anyone that looked capable of having done this."

"That doesn't make sense." Jace scanned the park.

"Did she tell you about the threatening notes she's been receiving warning her that something bad was going to happen to her?" Candice asked, sounding a little too smug for my liking.

"Notes?" Jace turned sharply to me. "No. Even though I saw her last night, Tru didn't say anything about—" He abruptly stopped. His face flooded with color. "Tru?" he said softly. "Is that why you texted and asked me to come over to Flossie's last night? You wanted to tell me about threats you've been receiving?"

I nodded.

"And . . ." He pulled a hand through his slightly shaggy blond hair. "I put my foot in my mouth and . . ."

I nodded again. I needed to stop doing that. It hurt to move my neck like that!

He swore softly.

"To be fair," I said, "I didn't learn about the second note until my dad brought it to me at the parish hall this morning, not more than a half hour ago."

He held out his hand. "I need to see that letter."

"I don't have it."

"You don't?" Candice asked. "Didn't you say you just got it?"

"Mama Eddy snatched it away from me."

"Mama who? Why would you let someone—?"

"If you met her mama, you'd understand," Jace said. He then turned to me. "We'll need to get it from her."

"That may involve digging through the parish trash. I'm sure she threw it away." That was Mama Eddy's style. Toss away anything that made her uncomfortable.

"Ma'am, we need to get you on the stretcher if we're to get you to the hospital for that scan." The paramedic put his face inches from mine, I suppose to remind us that he and his colleague were still there and waiting to do their jobs.

While a ride to the hospital wasn't the way I wanted to spend my Sunday afternoon, I figured it would be foolish to refuse sound medical advice. "Let me get my tote bag and purse."

That's when I spotted the books. Not only had I been knocked over the head by some unseen assailant, that same villain had dumped all my library books from the tote bag and tossed them around in a way that reminded me of the "poltergeist" that had been ransacking the library.

Ignoring the paramedic's advice to sit still, I jumped up and started to scoop up the books from the dew-dampened grass.

"Let me do that." Jace lifted the books I'd gathered from my arms. He must have noticed the library markings on the bindings, but he didn't give away anything as he and the uniformed officers helped gather up my scattered books to return them to the tote bag.

By the time they'd finished, I could tell that none of the library books were missing from the bag (thank goodness). But if my attacker was upset over my asking questions about Owen's murder, why go after the library books? It didn't make any sense.

Right now, nothing did.

Chapter Twenty-Two

Although I hadn't known it at the time, Jace had followed the ambulance in his Jeep to the nearby hospital, which wasn't really that close by, and had waited while doctors, nurses, and technicians poked and prodded my head injury. After the MRI results came back, the doctors all declared me healthy enough to head home. I had no clue that Jace had been pacing in the waiting area until the nurse, wearing a huge grin, rolled me in a wheelchair toward him. She gushed about how my sexy detective boyfriend had been driving the front staff mad with questions, questions they had no authorization to answer, which had only made him more worried and agitated.

"You've certainly got a keeper there with that one," the nurse said. "If only I could find a man who looked at me the way he's looking at you."

I looked up and saw what she saw. Jace stood just a few feet outside the ER door. He was twisting an old New York Mets ball cap in his hands. His blue eyes locked on to mine with a look of wonder and relief.

"Tru! Thank goodness. You *are* okay, aren't you?" He quickly sidestepped around Detective Gregory Ellerbe, the officer from the state law enforcement department who'd been called in to help with Owen's murder investigation. What was he doing here in the hospital? "Do you have any prescriptions that need to be filled?" Jace took my arm and helped me out of the wheelchair as if I needed assistance. I didn't, but I appreciated the gesture. I especially appreciated his gentle touch. Spending the afternoon at the hospital had left me feeling stiff and sore. Well, that and the fact that someone had slammed what felt like a brick into the back of my head.

"I'm fine. I'm fine. I just have a tiny, lingering headache," I said, and tried my best to look as if I meant it. Truth be told, my head still ached something fierce.

"Excuse me, Ms. Becket." Detective Ellerbe pushed his way between Jace and me. Ellerbe was about the same age as my father, perhaps a bit older. His bristled mustache shivered as he looked me up and down. "I heard you've somehow put yourself into a murderer's crosshairs."

"Not on purpose," I cried.

Ellerbe didn't say anything. He let his raised eyebrows do the talking for him. While he projected a nice-guy façade, he was actually a cunning detective and perhaps an even bigger danger to my secrets than Jace.

"I *have* been asking questions," I admitted.

His salt-and-pepper eyebrows refused to back down.

"I wanted to know why someone would commit a murder so close to Cypress's library. That place has always been my favorite place in the world. I have to make sure it remains safe for everyone." Every word I spoke was the absolute truth.

Ellerbe must have believed me. His accusing eyebrows finally settled back to where they belonged. He rubbed his nearly shaven scalp. "I'll need to see those threatening letters you received. And you'll also need to tell me everything you've done, every person you've talked with, and every fool question you've asked."

"No disrespect, Greg, but can't it wait?" Jace put a protective arm around my shoulder. "She's been through a lot already today. I'm taking her home. Surely, it wouldn't do anyone any harm if you waited until morning to question her."

"Do you hear yourself, Detective? We're talking about an active murder investigation. We're talking about someone who is attacking members of your community in broad daylight, on a Sunday. And you're asking me to wait?"

Jace sighed. "Can you at least wait until we get her home? Surely, we don't have to do this in the middle of a cold hospital waiting room."

"The first threatening letter is at my house," I offered. "I am anxious to show it to the two of you. I was going to report it last night, but—" I raised my hands and shrugged. "Well, things happened, and I didn't get a chance to turn it over."

"I never meant to embarrass you, Tru," Jace whispered. "I was just . . . just . . . surprised by your new look."

"You changed your hair," Ellerbe said.

I touched one of the highlighted strands. "My best friend was helping me try out a new look. It didn't go over the way I'd hoped."

"Looks nice to me. But what do I know? My wife says I have the fashion sense of a mule," Ellerbe grumbled. "And this conversation is doing nothing to help my investigation. I'll follow y'all back to your house, where I expect your full cooperation."

"You'll have it," I promised. "I have nothing to hide."

The incredulous looks both detectives gave me made me want to squirm. What I did next broke Mama Eddy's number one rule about never inviting a police officer into my home. I agreed to have Ellerbe take my statement from my living room. Nothing bad could come from such an invitation, right?

"Good gracious, Tru!" Flossie shouted as she rolled like a race-car driver into the waiting room. "I came as soon as I got your text. I didn't even finish the sentence I was writing." Which was proof enough about how worried she was . . . and how much she wanted to prove that she could be trusted to be there for me. I could tell that she was still feeling bad that she was working on her book instead of going with me to Hennie's house when I received that first threatening note.

"Tru, why did you text Flossie?" Jace asked, before I could even open my mouth to greet my friend. "I've been here all along. I'm planning on taking you home."

"And she still needs to give a statement to the police," Detective Ellerbe put in. He crossed his arms over his chest and looked rather imposing.

"All y'all need to shut y'all's mouths and git out of my way. I need to check Tru over for myself." Flossie, not at all cowed by either man, gave Ellerbe a shove and rolled right past him. "Honey, look at you." She put her hand on my cheek. "How did this happen?"

"I was walking to Perks when—" I started to say.

"I don't mean to be rude," Jace cut in to say.

"Then don't be rude, my boy," she shot right back.

He held up his hands as if in surrender. "Please, let's not discuss what happened to Tru in the middle of the hospital. Let me drive her home. I'm sure she won't be interested in cooking supper. Maybe you could pick up some food for her, Flossie?"

"Hello?" I waved a hand. "I'm right here. I might have gotten hit on the head, but my mind is still in perfect working order. You don't need to talk as if I'm unable to make my own decisions. Okay?"

Detective Ellerbe walked away. Jace looked chastened. Flossie just sat back and smiled.

"Don't keep us in suspense. What do you want to do?" she asked.

"I—" I wasn't sure what I wanted. My head ached, but not as badly as it had even a few minutes earlier. (The pain pills must have started working.) I knew I needed to cooperate with the police, especially since I didn't want to get attacked again. And Jace was right too. I didn't want to go home and cook supper. But I did want to eat. After missing out on Mama Eddy's Sunday dinner, my stomach felt hollow.

I was about to relent and agree to ride home with Jace and send Flossie out for takeout when I saw *her*.

Hennie Goodloe.

What was she doing here?

Sure, it was the closest hospital to her home. But all the same, it was still a solid hour away. And she wasn't sick. At least I didn't think so.

Suddenly the only thing I wanted to do was chase after her.

"Excuse me." I started to sprint toward her.

"Tru?" I heard Flossie call after me.

Jace caught my arm. "You're not trying to run away, are you?" He didn't stop me from chasing after Hennie, and I could tell he was joking. But he kept his hand wrapped around my arm as if ready to catch me if I was about to topple over. (I wasn't.) "You do know that everyone knows where you live. And besides which, you're not a suspect this time. Not even remotely."

"I'm not running away from you, silly. I just saw someone I need to talk to."

"I'm sure you won't mind if I listen in," Jace said.

"What if I did?"

"Then I'll have to beg for your forgiveness, because your getting hurt scared the devil out of me. I'm going to have a hard time letting you out of my sight until this is all over."

I didn't have much time to digest what he'd just said or whether I should be pleased or insulted. Hennie was moving toward the exit.

It wasn't as if I needed to keep my investigation a secret from Jace—just the bookroom—so I ended up giving in with a shrug. He might even help provide some invaluable insight. He was, after all, a trained investigator.

"Hennie!" I called out. "Wait up."

Everyone in the waiting room turned toward me to stare. Everyone, except Hennie. She kept her head down as she made a mad dash into the parking lot.

Flossie zoomed past me. "Go on home, Tru," she called over her shoulder. "Don't you worry your achy head about talking with Hennie. I'll catch her."

Jace shook his head as we watched Flossie blast into the parking lot without looking left or right. "I don't know what's going on, and I have a feeling I don't want to."

"Probably not," I agreed, suddenly remembering how Hennie still believed I was carrying Jace's baby. Having that conversation with Jace listening in would be . . . *well* . . . awkward would be an understatement.

Awkward was apparently the word for the day.

It was close to five o'clock by the time Jace's Jeep pulled up in front of my house on that hot Sunday afternoon. What I saw when we got there made me want to dive under the passenger seat.

Local reporter Betty Crawley was standing at my front door. She and my nosy neighbor Cora Parker seemed to be having an animated conversation. The last thing I wanted was to talk to the press or have my misfortune splashed across the front page of the local newspaper.

After my involvement in the last murder investigation made headlines for several days, Mama Eddy had lectured me at length that the only kind of press she wanted to see in the paper about me was a marriage announcement. Anything else would be quite improper for the daughter of Cypress's most respected cotillion instructor. She didn't want the parents in the community to think she'd failed to raise a true Southern lady.

Betty and my nosy neighbor weren't the only people populating my yard. Detective Ellerbe had his arms crossed over his chest as he stood next to his black town car. He was glaring at Betty. He too had once been a victim of Betty's melodramatic reporting tactics.

Hubert Crawford—someone I was surprised to see—was talking with the state detective. Hubert looked as if he was in full lecture mode.

I shuddered to think what tales he might be spinning for the detective. He had a manila folder tucked under his arm that was stuffed so full of papers that it looked ready to explode. On the tab was clearly written in large block letters "Cypress Library Poltergeist."

Jace parked in my driveway and turned off the engine. When I didn't move to unbuckle my seat belt or open the door, he turned toward me.

"Waiting will only make all that worse, Tru." He reached over and gently squeezed my hand. "I won't leave your side. And that's saying something. Ever since cotillion classes during middle school, the sight of your mama strikes terror in my heart."

"Mama Eddy?" Why was he mentioning her?

And there it was—the rotten cherry on the melty sundae.

Mama Eddy had opened my front door. She was standing on the threshold with her hands on her hips, looking horribly cross. Beside her stood Doris Heywood. And she was holding . . . a pie?

Chapter Twenty-Three

I t's apple." Doris thrust the pie into my hands while Betty shouted questions that I had no intention of answering.

"I knew this would happen," Mama Eddy complained. She snatched my arm out of Jace's grasp and dragged me into the house, slamming the door in Jace's and Detective Ellerbe's faces.

She'd neglected to lock the door, though. (Not that anyone ever locks their doors here in Cypress.) So while Mama Eddy lectured me about what she viewed as my endless stream of mistakes, Jace opened the door and let himself and Detective Ellerbe into the living room. He quickly pushed the door closed, leaving Doris, who looked surprised to find herself on the wrong side of my door, and Betty and Hubert, who both looked like they were prepared to storm through a castle's battlements, stuck outside.

"Thanks for the pie!" I called to Doris just as Jace engaged the bolt in the front door's rarely used lock. It was really sweet of her to think of me. The pie was still warm from the oven. The blend of sweet and cin-namon spices made my empty stomach rumble.

Mama Eddy frowned when she noticed how I'd nearly pressed my nose into the pie's flaky pastry top.

"You can't eat that." She ripped the pie from my hands and marched into the kitchen.

"Mama, no!" I cried. But there was no stopping Mama Eddy once she got an idea in her head. I winced when I heard the garbage can lid squeak. I bit back an anguished cry at the crunch of the pie's aluminum tin as she shoved the pie into the trash.

"Girl, you eat too much sugar as it is. You need to tell those friends of yours to stop bringing that kind of junk into your house," Mama Eddy declared as she returned to the living room. "You know our family's health history. You need to follow my lead and limit yourself to a strict low-carb, low-fat, and low-sugar diet."

"We could have offered it to our guests," I said, my voice quiet even though I really wanted to scream that I was an adult and that my head hurt and that I was tired and embarrassed of the way she always treated me like I was thirteen instead of thirty-seven.

"What are they—?" she bit off before she remembered that she was supposed to be the town's shining example of good manners. She plastered a grin on her face that looked shockingly real. "Officers. As you can see, my daughter is in no—"

"We're detectives, ma'am," Ellerbe corrected.

"We didn't invite you to come into this home," she continued, still grinning as if she were presiding over a dinner party. "You can't come in here if we don't invite you. At least that's my understanding of how the law works. Not without a warrant. My daughter has been through an ordeal. She needs her rest. If you'll excuse us, I'm sure she'll be happy to meet y'all at the police station tomorrow with our family lawyer present. You can call his office in the morning to set up an appointment." She started to dig around in her purse. "I'm sure I have a card for him somewhere in here."

"Mama Eddy," Jace said. He shrank back a bit when she snapped her head up and in his direction. "We—um—Tru did invite us to come over."

Mama Eddy whirled toward me. Her eyes narrowed. Her smile grew brittle and more than a little frightening. "Have you forgotten everything I've ever said to you?" she asked through clenched teeth.

My head suddenly started to pound again. How did I explain to her that it was either invite the police to my home or spend the rest of the afternoon at the police station? Why should I even have to explain it? My decisions were my business. But since my bruised head was in no condition to handle that level of confrontation, I simply closed my eyes and pictured the spines of some of my favorite novels.

Comforting old friends waiting for me to return to their pages.

I smiled.

"Since these nice men are already here," I said, after regaining my composure, "I suppose I should offer them my hospitality. Please, Detectives, have a seat while I show Mama Eddy to the door."

I kissed my mother on the cheek, whispered my thanks for her love and concern while I hugged her tight, and then nudged my momentarily stunned parent out the front door.

"Whew-wee, Tru, that has to be one of the bravest acts I'd ever witnessed," Jace said after I closed and locked the door behind me.

After spending nearly an hour with Detective Ellerbe and Jace, I started wishing my mother would come back. I had dutifully described to them what had happened in the park and whom I'd been talking with in the church parish hall. But that wasn't enough. They continued grilling me.

"Please stop," I whimpered when my stomach and my head demanded that I'd had enough.

Jace knelt down beside the armchair where I'd been sitting. He put his hands on the arms.

"Tru," he said softly. "We need you to be honest with us."

"I am. Everything I told you is one hundred percent true."

He nodded. "I believe that."

I let my head fall back onto the chair's cushion and sighed. He wasn't going to push me to say anything that would lead them to find the secret bookroom.

"It's what you're *not* telling us that has me worried," he said. "If there's even a slight possibility that this secret you've been keeping from me could be related to Owen's death, you need to tell us how it's related. And you need to tell us now."

My face heated. "I . . . I . . ." I shook my head.

"Tru," Jace said, his voice still soft. Safe. "You can trust me."

I found myself nodding. Yes, I could trust him. And yes, perhaps it was time to tell the police what was happening in the library's basement. If I stayed silent, others might get hurt or worse. I couldn't live with that on my conscience.

I opened my mouth to tell him about the secret bookroom and about the vandals. "I knew I was breaking the rules." My voice cracked. "It's just that the books—"

Someone started pounding on the door.

"Miss Tru!" a voice shouted. The pounding grew louder. "Miss Tru! You have to let me in!"

Detective Ellerbe and Jace exchanged concerned looks before Ellerbe opened the door.

Hubert, with a strength I wouldn't have guessed the older man possessed, pushed his way past the detective and ran over to me. His hair was disheveled. He was gasping for breath. There was a rip in the knee of his tweed pants.

"What happened?" I jumped up from my chair. "Are you okay?"

He shook his head. "I was mugged. Someone took it. All of it."

Jace steadied poor Hubert. "Took what?"

"My research about the poltergeist!"

"The poltergeist?" Jace turned to me and asked.

"In the library basement," I said. It was time. I needed to tell them. But before I could explain any further, Hubert launched into a protracted lecture about the history of the library, beginning with its cornerstone being laid and taking us through to the time of his grandmother and how she'd been warned to stay away because of the poltergeist.

"Enough!" Ellerbe barked. "That's enough."

"But you don't understand," Hubert said. "The poltergeist—"

"I don't want to hear another word about ghosts or another history lesson." I'd never heard Ellerbe's voice sound so sharp. "Owen Maynard was killed by a flesh-and-blood person, not a phantom. And, presumably, this same person hit Ms. Becket over the head this afternoon because she'd been asking far more questions about Owen's murder than anyone would consider wise. And now you've been attacked for the same reason. Y'all have to understand that amateur hour needs to stop."

"No!" Hubert shouted. "You have to listen to me." He whirled toward me. "Miss Tru, you have to listen. You have to!"

Ellerbe shook his head. "Out you go." He ushered Hubert to the door. "I'll be along in a moment to take your statement regarding the mugging." After he closed the door, Ellerbe rounded on me. "And you, Trudell Becket, need to stop playing detective and getting yourself hurt. I've been hearing around town how you think you're some kind of modern-day Agatha Christie just because you've read all of her books."

"I think you mean Miss Marple," I corrected. "Agatha Christie was a novelist. She never solved crimes. Miss Marple and Inspector Poirot were her most famous fictional sleuths."

Ellerbe growled. "Just—just stop. If I hear that you're interfering with my investigation again, I'll have you arrested. I'll do it for your own safety and for the safety of those around you." He gave Jace a nod and tossed open the front door. "That means you'd better keep your nose clean. Got it?"

Before I could answer, he marched out the door and slammed it so hard behind him it made the books on my shelves jump.

I winced.

Dewey, who'd been hiding this entire time, poked his head out from around a corner and meowed.

"Hey, little guy." Jace crouched down and held out his hand. Dewey rushed over and butted his head against Jace's knuckle. "I bet you're hungry."

I glanced at the mantel clock. "It is his dinnertime," I said.

"Why don't you go lie down for a bit while I feed him? You're starting to look like something Dewey would drag in."

"Thanks. That's what every woman likes to hear."

"You know I didn't mean—"

"I know," I said. And since my head was still pounding and the pain pill that I'd been given at the hospital was making my eyelids feel like lead weights, I nodded and took myself off to bed.

I didn't stop to consider that I'd left an inquisitive police detective unattended in my home or that I'd left a stack of library books on the dining room table along with my "sleuth's" notebook filled with all manner of speculations about who was breaking into the secret bookroom—which, of course, in the general public's mind, should not even exist.

Mama Eddy had been right all along. I should have never invited those detectives into my home.

Chapter Twenty-Four

———— · ————

Jace dropped me off at the library the next morning (a stormy Monday morning). He then refused to leave my side. Even after he'd secured my promise that I wouldn't go traipsing around town unguarded, he followed me around as I brewed a pot of coffee and prepared for the day.

Dewey wiggled in his tote bag. I wanted to take him down to the secret bookroom so he could get settled in, but by the way Jace was acting—glued to my side and all—I knew I couldn't go anywhere without my shadow coming along.

I had considered leaving Dewey at home today. But a late-September tropical storm had veered onto land last night. Bands of strong winds and heavy thunderstorms were going to batter our community all day. The safest place for Dewey was to be close by in the library's basement.

"I appreciate what you're doing, but you don't have to stay here. I am an adult, you know," I reminded Jace. "I've successfully lived on my own for more years than a good Southern woman cares to admit, thank you very much."

"I know you're capable," he said. "That's one of the things I like best about you. You're not always waiting for a man to do this or that. But, Tru, there is a killer out there." He thrust a finger toward the library's front door. "This is the same killer who sent you to the hospital yesterday, don't forget."

I rubbed the bump on the back of my head. "I promise you, that's something I don't think I'll ever forget. But—"

"Listen to me. I'm worried, not because I don't think you can handle yourself. I'm worried because I like you. I like you maybe too much. You don't take yourself too seriously. You wear the coziest-looking outfits, not caring if they're fashionable or not. You—"

"Are you trying to insult me?" I propped my fists on my hips. A loud boom of thunder punctuated my question.

"Insult you? No! Never. What I'm trying to say—and bungling—is that you're comfortable in your own skin. You have a passion that drives you. Those are the most attractive things I've ever seen in a woman. Heck, I really like the librarian look you have going on. It's like crazy sexy, and you won't go out with me, and it's driving me crazy. What I'm trying to say is that I love everything about you."

Wait. (Record scratch.) Love?

"I especially enjoy these adorable sweater sets you always have on. They make you look so soft and cuddly. And I want to—"

"Tru!" Frank Calhoun came bursting through the front doors carrying an oversized golf umbrella. Mrs. Farnsworth had just unlocked the doors, opening up the library for the day.

"Shh!" Mrs. Farnsworth shushed him. "And there's no running in the library, young man. And kindly leave that thing"—she pointed at his dripping umbrella—"by the door."

"Yes, ma'am." Frank did as she asked and returned to the front entrance. He slid the soggy umbrella into an umbrella stand. Jace and I watched as he came bounding like a leashed puppy toward us.

"Tru," Frank repeated, his voice whisper soft. He came to a skidding stop next to us. "Tru, Hubert told me what happened yesterday." He pointed to the back of his own head. "I nearly lost my mind worrying. No wonder you stood me up for our date last night."

"Date?" Jace demanded.

"Date?" I echoed.

Dewey meowed. (Thankfully, softly.)

"I know. I know. We hadn't set up the particulars. But you had left that message on my cell saying that you wanted to go out on Sunday."

"You did?" Jace asked, his eyes growing wide. He took a step away from me.

"I . . . um . . . it's not . . ." I stammered. Thunder crashed again.

"When you didn't answer my texts when I tried to set up where and when we should meet, I thought maybe you were away from your phone," Frank plowed on, not noticing the minidrama unfolding right in front of him. "But then I heard you were at the hospital because someone had tried to kill you. That's—that's awful."

"I . . . um . . ." I stammered again. "I don't think whoever hit me wanted me dead. I mean, I'm not dead, and I was unconscious after getting hit from behind like that, and the killer could have easily done me in. But here I am."

"Yes, here you are." Jace gave me a puzzled look as his gaze bounced between Frank and me.

"Jace, I—" I started.

"Tru, I don't mean to interrupt whatever it is that's going on here, but you really need to hear what Hubert uncovered," Frank said at the same time.

"About the poltergeist?" Was he serious?

"Yes, about the poltergeist. This is serious," Frank answered as if he could read my thoughts. "If you'll excuse us, Detective . . ." He placed his hand on my arm. "Tru will want to hear what I have to say."

"Is this about Owen's murder?" Jace asked.

I looked to Frank.

Frank looked over at me before shaking his head. "No. It's library business."

"I'll let you get to work, then." Jace gave me a tight nod. "Tru." He turned and headed toward the front doors.

My feet wanted to go running after him. Who was I kidding? My entire body wanted to run after him, not just my feet.

Frank still had his hand on my arm, though. "We really need to talk," he said.

"About the date," I blurted as I walked with him toward the book-room. Frank's wet shoes squeaked on the slick terrazzo floor with every step. "I changed my mind." I only hoped Jace hadn't changed his mind about *me*.

Frank drew in a long breath before saying, "I kind of figured that by the way that detective was looking at you and the way you were looking at him. Well, you can't blame a guy for trying. You don't, right? Blame me, I mean."

"You really wanted to go out with me?" the teenager in me with the crushed heart had to ask.

Frank stopped and turned toward me. "Why wouldn't I? Ever since you caught the last murderer, you've been the talk of the town. That's exciting. I'm sure there are at least a dozen other men out there who also want to be where your detective is right now."

"He's not my—" I started to say. But maybe he *was* my detective? Yes, maybe he was.

I smiled at that thought.

"Thank you for saying that," I said.

Frank shrugged. "Let's get down to the basement. Hubert said he'd be along soon. Apparently, he had an errand to run first."

Frank and I were the first to enter the bookroom. I let Dewey out of his tote bag while Frank turned on the lights. Thankfully, our vandal had taken the night off. The room looked like a library should look—neat and orderly. The sweet smell of leather and paper welcomed us.

"Did you hear that someone had stolen Hubert's research?" Frank asked as he wandered toward the back of the room where the local documents were kept.

"I do remember . . ." My head had been aching at the time. But now that he had mentioned it, I did remember Hubert bursting through my front door and reporting the crime. Detective Ellerbe had rushed off to help him. I was ashamed to realize that I hadn't been more concerned about Hubert. "I think it happened outside my house. Was he hurt?"

Frank shook his head. "No. It was a snatch and run. And, luckily, most of what was in his folder were copies of documents that are stored here." He tapped the top of the filing cabinet containing the bookroom's unbound papers. "And this is what Hubert is anxious for you to see." He opened a drawer and thumbed through the folders until he found what he was searching for. He pulled out an old newspaper clipping. He scanned it, gave a nod of satisfaction, and then handed it over to me.

My brows wrinkled with confusion as I read the date on the top of the newspaper page. "May tenth, 1935?"

"Read the headline," Frank said.

"'Local Speakeasy Closes Its Doors,'" I read aloud. I looked up at Frank. "Speakeasy?"

"Our poltergeist," Frank said just as the doors to the bookroom opened.

"Our poltergeist," Hubert echoed as he hurried through the doors. "I see you found the newspaper article."

"I don't understand," I said. The article went on to talk about how two years after the repeal of Prohibition, South Carolina finally began to allow liquor sales in the state. And as a result, the town's illegal bar, called "The Bookroom," closed its doors for the last time. "What does this have to do with the library?"

"It *is* the library," Frank said.

"And my maw-maw's poltergeist," Hubert added.

And just like that, the pieces seemed to click together. "The strange noises your grandmother used to hear in the basement when she worked at the library in the 1920s."

Hubert nodded with excitement. "The other librarians had warned Maw-maw to stay away from the basement in a creative way. Maw-maw had been a teen at the time. Going down into the basement where the town operated an illegal bar might have been dangerous for a young, pretty, underaged girl. So, they concocted the tale about a noisy poltergeist."

"We're guessing that the bar was in here." Frank gestured to the room at large. "It's big enough."

Hubert agreed and launched into a lecture about the types of alcohol the speakeasy served, where they were distilled, and how they were transported to the town by mobsters whose names I recognized from period movies.

While he spoke, I followed Dewey as my lanky kitty returned to the spot on the wall where our vandal had made a series of scratches.

"What did you just say?" I asked as I ran my finger along one of the deeper grooves.

"I said . . ." Hubert cleared his throat. "I said a fellow by the name of McKnight had a large operation over in Hell Hole Swamp. They distilled Hell Hole white corn whiskey and shipped boxcars of the moonshine all over the country. It was quite the operation. McKnight was one of Al Capone's main suppliers."

"But what does that have to do with what's happening today? That's the question, isn't it?" Frank said.

I nodded, still studying the grooves in the wall. Dewey had stretched up on his hind legs to look along with me. He turned toward me. His bright green eyes flashed with intelligence as he meowed.

"I think you're right," I said to him. "This is what you've been trying to tell us all along," I murmured.

"What's that?" Hubert asked.

"In your research, did you run across the building plans for this library?" I asked. "I don't remember ever seeing one."

"You wouldn't," Hubert said. "The plans were lost when town hall caught fire back in 1953. Faulty wiring was to blame. We lost a tragic amount of source material that day. A black, black day for Cypress, it was."

We were all silent for a moment.

"Well, that gives us something to think about." I started to leave. I had work to do upstairs and I needed some space to put my thoughts together.

"But what does it mean?" Frank followed along with me. "What does some bootlegger's speakeasy from the 1930s have to do with anything that's happening today?"

"That's the question, isn't it?" I said. There were still plenty more questions that needed to be answered before I could definitively say why someone kept wrecking the bookroom. "Did you ever figure out how your library book could have ended up with Owen's body?" I asked him.

He closed his eyes and drew a long breath. "I wasn't in town that night," he said.

"Yes, Jace told me. But that book was there."

He shook his head. "I thought it was at my house. But how could someone get inside my house to take it? I must have left it on my desk at the dealership."

"And anyone could have taken it, right?" Still more questions to be answered. But at least, thanks to Hubert, we finally knew where to look for answers. I was grateful for that.

Chapter Twenty-Five

W hat happened?" Flossie demanded as I emerged from the basement. Thunder rumbled in the distance. My friend rolled toward me with startling speed. Her lips were tightly pressed together in a way that reminded me of an unhappy Mrs. Farnsworth.

It took all my willpower not to turn on my heel and dash back down to the basement.

Instead I propped my fists on my hips. "What do you mean, 'What happened?'" What hasn't happened, would have been a more appropriate question. "What happened to you last night?" I demanded right back at her.

Flossie had promised to bring me take-out dinner.

She had promised to come and tell me what Hennie was doing at that hospital.

I had needed her to help keep an eye on Jace while I slept.

I'd slept all Sunday afternoon and Sunday night, only waking up when Jace came in and shook me every few hours to make sure I hadn't fallen into a coma. He admitted in the morning that waking me wasn't something the doctor had told him to do but something he felt he needed to do because he kept worrying about me and the damage the attempt on my life must have done to my head.

When I woke up and saw the sun shining and Jace sitting in the chair beside my bed, I had jerked out of bed and sent Flossie a series of frantic texts. She hadn't come to the house when she said she would. Something must have happened to her. "I pictured you lying in a ditch somewhere, dead at the hands of a vengeful Hennie," I told her. "I texted."

And she'd failed to answer any of them. In her defense, Flossie was often slow in responding to her texts. Unlike Tori (or myself), our older friend didn't keep her cell phone glued to her side. When at home, she often left it in her purse by the door.

Crazy, I know. But that was Flossie for you.

And yes, I did realize that my reliance on my cell phone was a contradiction of what we were doing with the secret bookroom, where we used actual card catalogs and rubber stamps to mark the due dates on book slips. It wasn't that I was against technology—although I was sure Anne would tell a different story. My passion was the books, the printed books. Walking through the stacks with a canyon of books towering on either side of me knowing that at any moment I could stumble upon a new discovery or run across an old favorite was like magic to me. Tiptoeing my fingers across a keyboard didn't have the same power or offer the same opportunity for finding unexpected treasures.

Flossie pulled her phone from her purse and squinted at it. "Oh look, you did send a text." She scrolled. "And another text. And another text. And another text. Gracious, there must be more than twenty here. What in the world were you doing sending that many texts so early in the morning? Isn't there an etiquette about this sort of thing? Or does your generation no longer believe in rules of etiquette?"

"I was worried out of my head about you. I thought you might be dead. I sent Tori over to your place to make sure you hadn't shuffled off this mortal coil."

"I must have left before Tori arrived. And as you can see"—Flossie twirled her wheelchair around in a circle—"I'm still alive and kicking," she announced. Loudly.

"Shh!" Mrs. Farnsworth sent us a quelling look.

I snapped my mouth closed. Flossie merely waved at her old classmate before turning back to me. "Honey, I don't know why you would be all riled up worrying about me."

I glanced over at Mrs. Farnsworth, who was still watching us, before whispering, "You're the one who rolled off in hot pursuit of Hennie. And then you didn't show up with dinner last night. You didn't text. You didn't call. And the killer was busy yesterday. Hubert was attacked last night. All his poltergeist research was stolen. Right in front of my house. It happened while two detectives were inside my house." I dragged in a long, slow breath with the hopes that it would calm my thumping heart. "I think the killer did it to stop us from finding whatever it is he wants to find in the library. And when I didn't hear from you, and you didn't answer any of your texts, I thought maybe . . . maybe . . ."

"Oh, Tru." Flossie got all serious. She reached over to me and gave me a hug. "Tru, I'm sorry you were so worried that you felt like you needed to send Tori banging down my front door. But, sugar, I did stop by last night with takeout in hand. And I brought a bottle of Coke with me, because neither you nor Tori ever keeps Cokes in your houses. I was there, ready to do whatever you needed me to do, but Jace stopped me at the door. He told me you were sleeping and sent me away."

"He did?" But he had to have known how anxious I'd been to find out what Hennie had been doing at the hospital. "He had no right to do that. He must have understood that I wanted to talk to you to find out what Hennie had to say. He must have known that."

"The boy was trying to dote on you. I saw him stalking around outside the library's entrance when I came in just now. He was looking quite nervous and upset. You scared him, Tru. You could see it in the way that he kept looking at you at the hospital, as if he couldn't believe his eyes that you were okay."

"I'm sure that's not right," I scoffed, even though he'd already admitted as much.

"Tru, his hands were shaking yesterday. After all those years he spent on the New York police force, I doubt that happens often."

"Frank showed up this morning when I was talking with Jace," I whispered. "He asked me why I stood him up for our date last night."

"Oh dear." Flossie pressed a finger to her lips. "I can't imagine Jace took that too well. You have been constantly turning that poor boy down every time he's asked you out."

"Only because the entire town is talking about the two of us incessantly. It's embarrassing."

Flossie tilted her head to one side. "Is that the only reason?"

No, it wasn't. Jace had hurt me when we were both in high school. I had harbored an oversized crush on him. I was the school geek, and he was the captain of the football team. Of course my heart had gotten crushed. But that was ages ago. We were adults now. So why was it that I never seemed to act like an adult when I was around him?

"Were you able to talk to Hennie?" I asked Flossie, changing the subject. I briefly wondered if I needed to be worried about my mental health when talking about murder felt safer than talking about my feelings. "Did Hennie tell you anything useful?" I had no idea how Hennie and Landry Goodloe fit into our poltergeist puzzle. Neither of them drank liquor. Besides which, the library speakeasy had been closed for decades now.

"It took some effort to chase Hennie down in the parking lot. She didn't want to talk to me at first. She kept yelling at me that I was harassing her. Like I'd harass anyone." Flossie blew out an irritated breath. "I tell you what, I was tempted to show her what being harassed looked like. But I cracked a smile and got her to settle down."

"Did she talk to you?"

Flossie nodded, looking pleased with herself. "Hennie explained everything. Well, everything she wanted to tell me. She told me that she was at the hospital because Gracie Mae had suffered a bad fall, real similar to what happened to you, and had to be rushed to the nearest emergency room."

"Really?" That sounded like too much of a coincidence. "Do you think the killer attacked Gracie Mae too? That would be three attacks in one day . . . that we know of!"

She squinted at me. "Hennie simply said Gracie Mae had fallen, but I've read enough Agatha Christie plots to know not to believe her. Once I caught up to her, I could tell she wasn't running away from me. She was running from the police detectives that were with us. She acted jumpy, like she was afraid to talk with the police, and when I pressed her on it, she admitted that she didn't believe that Gracie Mae had actually fallen. She was afraid that something else had happened, that some*one* had hurt Gracie Mae."

"The killer?" I asked.

Flossie nodded.

"And this happened around the same time someone had attacked me?" I pressed. "Where was Gracie Mae when this happened?"

"She was walking home from Sunday services at the Church of the Guiding Light. Not to her home, mind you. The young widow was heading to the Goodloes' home. She reached Hennie's front yard. Hennie says Gracie Mae can't remember what happened next."

I couldn't remember my attack either.

"Hennie's front yard is only a few blocks from the park where the killer hit me." My heart started beating faster.

Flossie nodded. "Hennie said she had started home with her brood of children not long after Gracie Mae left. Landry had stayed at the church to lock up the storefront. When Hennie arrived, she found Gracie Mae bleeding on the ground, but nobody was around."

"I wonder why Gracie Mae wouldn't want to report this to the po-

lice. She's the victim in all this. It's not as if she has anything to hide."
Or does she?

"I pressed Hennie about that. She didn't want to tell me, but I persuaded her to admit what she thought. She said Gracie Mae is scared."

"Scared? Scared of what?" I asked.

"That the killer is coming after her now."

"That doesn't make a lick of sense . . . unless she was involved with whatever Owen was doing that had gotten him killed." I chewed my bottom lip as I mentally tried to force the pieces of this puzzle together. It suddenly felt as if I was working from two different puzzle boxes.

"We need to find out what Candice is investigating." Flossie thumped the arm of her wheelchair.

"I agree. She's the one who found me in the park. She's the one who is stirring up a hornet's nest of a crime ring. I could go talk to her about my attack and see if she'll tell me about her investigation."

"I doubt she'll talk to us, but she might talk to a fellow officer of the law. You know, like a sexy detective who's all sweet on you?"

I blushed. "I don't know if he's talking to me after hearing that I agreed to go out with Frank."

"Oh pish, there's nothing wrong with playing a little hard to get. It makes the men in our lives only want us more."

"You sound like Tori," I said, surprised she would say something like that.

"That girl has more sense than most give her credit for," Flossie pointed out.

"Thank you," Tori said as she breezed into the library. She held up a plain paper bag. "I've got the goods."

"The goods?" Flossie scoffed. "You sound like a mob moll."

"A mob moll? Who even talks like that?" Tori shot back.

"You mean the security camera?" I asked.

"That's right. Our poltergeist won't be able to get past us with this—"

"Shh!" Flossie hissed. "Someone is coming."

We all stopped talking.

It was Doris. She came around the corner and seemed surprised to see us. As she eyed me up and down, I thought I saw her face go pale. I chewed my bottom lip and worried about her reaction for several moments before it hit me. We'd been all talking furiously until she came upon us. Then, as she approached, we clammed up. That had to look suspicious.

"Oh, it's just you, dear," Flossie said.

"We were talking about the poltergeist," I said at the same time. *Not you, we weren't talking about you*, I left unsaid.

"Not that we think the poltergeist exists." Tori excitedly held up the bag. "I purchased a camera. We're going to get a video of whoever is breaking into the bookroom."

"Oh." Doris smiled, but it looked a little forced. "That makes sense. Um, Tru, did you enjoy the apple pie I made for you?"

"Uh . . . uh . . . yes, it tasted lovely," I lied. I didn't have the heart to tell her that Mama Eddy, being Mama Eddy, had dumped the pie into the trash. "Are you going to enter the baking competition?"

"No, that's not my thing. If you'll excuse me, I have to look up something on the computer."

She hurried on past us.

"She looks tired," Tori said. "I hear children can do that to you."

"It's not the kids," Flossie countered. "She's got money trouble. All those jobs of hers pay next to nothing. If you ask me, I'd say she looked more worried than tired."

I disagreed with both of my friends. Doris didn't look worried or tired. She looked scared. And I couldn't help but wonder why. Was her fear somehow related to Gracie Mae's "accident" yesterday? She'd been working for Hennie. Perhaps she knew more about what was going on in that home than she was willing to admit.

"I thought librarians weren't allowed to help patrons with their apple pies," Edith Frampton said as she stepped in front of me and wagged her finger under my nose.

I jumped. How was the older woman able to sneak up on us like that?

"Ma'am?" I said. "I don't understand. I'm not helping anyone with their pie recipes."

"Then what was that?" She stabbed her finger in the direction Doris had gone. "You were tasting Doris's pies? You gave Cora a recipe book? That sounds like helping to me. Yes, yes, it does. What do you have to say for yourself, missy? Should I go report you to Mrs. Farnsworth?"

"I . . . um . . ." Her anger took me completely by surprise. Edith Frampton had always been one of the sweetest ladies to come into the library.

"Now, Edith, you need to simmer down." Flossie rushed to my rescue. "What our Tru does when she's not at work isn't anyone's business but her own. If she wants to loan out books or talk to neighbors about their pies when she's away from the library, isn't that just a benefit to everyone? Do you want to be known around town as the one who stopped her from helping others? Because that's what will happen if you go airing your displeasure to Mrs. Farnsworth, isn't it? Is that what you want?"

Edith opened her mouth and closed it a few times before saying, "Of course not. But I aim to win this year's apple pie contest. And all I want is what she's giving everyone else." She leaned toward me and whispered. "Everyone knows how you are in on your aunt Sal's secret recipe, and lately everyone is saying how you're sharing that secret with a select few."

"I'm not—!" I protested.

"Don't lie to me, missy. I've been watching you with my own eyes." She stalked off, muttering to herself.

Tori whistled a low note. "That woman has a screw loose."

"She's yelling at the wrong person. Other than handing out a recipe book, I don't have anything useful for anyone. I rarely bake, and I don't know the first thing about how to win a baking contest." I rubbed the sore bump on the back of my head. "But, I wonder . . ."

"What do you wonder, dear?" Flossie asked when I didn't finish my thought.

"Um . . . it's probably nothing." I turned to Tori. "Just to be on the safe side, though, Tori, can you help me get in touch with Charlie's ex?"

Tori grimaced, but she agreed to ask Charlie for Candice's contact information.

I still needed to tell my friends about the basement speakeasy and my weakly formed thoughts about how it might be related to Owen's death, but before I had a chance, Mrs. Farnsworth called me over to the front desk. She needed me to take over for her for a while so she could go straighten out things with the new town manager about Anne's tai chi classes.

"Town hall might be able to tell me that the library has to sell all kinds of lattes and sugary-sweet pastries, but they have no right in dictating the kind of programs we bring to the community. A little exercise never hurt anyone. That's what I'm going to tell those folks at town hall, and they are just going to have to live with it."

Chapter Twenty-Six

Candice Newcastle, looking every inch an FBI agent dressed in a long black raincoat, rushed through the front doors. She paused just inside the door to tuck her small black umbrella into a carrying bag and the bag into an inside pocket of her raincoat. Storm conditions had worsened all morning. The heavy rain seemed to be coming down sideways. It sounded as if someone were directing a hose at the windows. Candice glanced over her shoulder at the awful weather before heading over to the front desk where I was working. She rapped her knuckle on the desktop in a friendly manner. "Word on the street is that you've been looking for me."

"Knowing Cypress like I do, I wouldn't be surprised if everyone in town knew I wanted to talk to you," I said. "But I'm guessing Charlie called you?"

"He did." Her brow furrowed as she looked at me closely. "How's your head feeling today?"

"It's only a bit sore." Thinking about it only made it ache more. I rubbed the back of my neck. "Thanks again for yesterday's rescue."

She nodded. "It's what anyone would do. What do you need now?"

"As I know you've heard, I'm a bit of a sleuth," I said.

"The untrained kind that is in over her head."

I chose to ignore her assessment of my abilities. "I've been thinking about yesterday and something you said." I rose from my chair.

"Yes?" She sounded wary. "You know I can't tell you about—"

"I know. I know. I'm not asking you to give away why you're in town. I mean, not unless you want to tell me?"

She shook her head.

"That's what I thought." I walked around to the front of the desk. "This is about what you saw in the park when you found me. You said there were a few older members of our community either walking toward one of the churches or away from them. If you saw one of them again, do you think you could identify her?"

Candice backed up from me as if she thought I'd lost my mind and that perhaps she needed to keep her distance. "I don't see how this could—"

"Just humor me, please. If I pointed out someone to you, could you tell me if you saw her in the park yesterday?"

Candice closed her eyes and thought for a few seconds. When she opened her eyes again, she nodded. "I believe I could."

"Good." I started to walk toward the bank of computers at the heart of the library. "Follow me."

She gave me a quizzical look but followed anyhow.

The first person we saw was Doris. She was tapping away on the computer. She glanced up and gave me a sour look before returning to her work.

A few computer terminals away, I spotted Edith Frampton. The older woman was staring at the computer screen. Her nose was scrunched up. Her lips were pursed. And she was tapping on the keyboard. Not typing, just lightly tapping with the tip of her highly polished nails.

"Do you recognize anyone here?" I whispered to Candice.

"Yes, but I still don't—"

"Humor me. Do you see someone here who was also in the park yesterday when you found me?"

"That woman." Candice nodded over at Edith. "What is she doing? Is she trying to talk into that mouse?"

Edith had picked up the mouse and was holding it to her ear like it was a cell phone.

With a sigh, I walked over to Edith. It took considerable effort to keep my voice soft and steady as I asked her, "Why did you hit me over the head yesterday?"

The mouse in Edith's hand dropped with a loud *clank*.

I expected her to tell me that I was crazy, that I had no right accusing her of such a horrible act. Who was I to accuse such a sweet lady of attacking me over a pie recipe?

Edith turned toward me. The look of malice in her eyes nearly made me run for cover.

Candice put her hand on my shoulder. "Tru?" she said. "What's going on?"

Before I could answer her, Edith demanded in a harsh whisper, "What did you do with the cookbook? It wasn't in your bag. I saw Cora return it to you at church. But when I searched that tote bag of yours, it wasn't there. How did you manage to hide it from me?"

"You could have asked me for it," I said.

"I did come in and ask you for help, and Mrs. Farnsworth told me that I had to do it on my own, that librarians weren't allowed to help with the baking contest." Tears swam in the older woman's eyes. "I've never been in front of one of these contraptions in my life. I don't know what to do. It's so unfair. You're helping everyone *but me*." The last part she wailed.

"While it's true that I'm barred from helping anyone with their apple pie recipes at the library, there's no rule that I cannot talk with you after work hours. And if you need help learning how to use a computer, Anne is more than capable of showing you the basics. Plus, she teaches several classes on computers every week. I'm not playing favorites. No one is. You didn't have to hit me."

"She's the one who hit you?" Doris screeched. She jumped up from her chair. "But, Mrs. Frampton, you're nice to everyone."

"I've been entering that apple pie contest for the past thirty years. By rights I should have been the one to win after Prissy passed. Everyone has told me for years that I had the second-best pie in the county. But then your aunt Sal surprised everyone. Who would have guessed that the one thing she could cook would have been apple pies? That woman once brought charred peanut-butter-and-jelly sandwiches to a church picnic. Who messes up peanut-butter-and-jelly sandwiches? Why were they charred? You're not even supposed to cook peanut-butter-and-jelly sandwiches, for goodness' sake."

"I remember that." At Mama Eddy's urging to be polite, I'd actually eaten one of those blackened sandwiches. Just thinking about it brought an ashy taste to my mouth. I shuddered.

"Ma'am, nasty sandwiches aside, are you admitting to a crime?" Candice asked Mrs. Frampton.

"Crime?" Edith said with a gasp. She turned to me with a look of confusion.

I pointed to the back of my head.

"Oh. That?" Edith's shoulders drooped. "I suppose that was wrong of me."

"What did you hit me with anyhow?" I wanted to know. Had she filled a bag with bricks?

"Just my purse."

"What in the world do you keep in there?"

"I don't know. Purse stuff."

I would have asked more, but Candice's grip on my shoulder tightened as if in warning. She stood straighter. Her gaze sharpened. She kept her hands at the ready. "We need to call in the local police," she said.

"Do we really need to bother them?" Edith asked. "I mean, they're so busy with the murder investigation. I hate to disturb them over a little misunderstanding."

"Ma'am, you sent this woman to the hospital."

Edith shrugged. "She looks okay to me. You are okay, aren't you, Trudell?"

"I am," I said, because that was simply the polite way to answer such a query.

"See! She's fine," Edith crowed. "There's no need to get all official about it."

Doris shot me a look before heading for the exit. I didn't blame her. If I could slip away from this drama, I would too.

As she fled, Doris accidentally dropped several pamphlets for her essential oils. I scooped them up and tapped the corners until they made a neat stack. Candice took a pamphlet from me and stared at it a moment before saying to Edith, "There's no need to get upset, ma'am."

"Upset?" Edith's voice grew louder. "Who are you to tell me not to be upset? I don't even know who you are!"

"I'm Tru's friend," Candice said, which I thought was interesting. Why didn't she want to reveal that she was with the FBI? "I'm sure the local police will want to hear your side of the story. That way they'll stop wasting their time searching for the person who attacked Tru. Don't you agree that's a good idea?" Candice slowly pulled her phone from her pocket. She was acting as if Edith was dangerous, which was kind of laughable. The older woman's arms were about as thick as twigs.

"Edith, were you the one who sent me those two notes? The notes that told me that I needed to stop talking to people?" I asked.

"I did. Fat lot of good it did. But you were going around helping everyone else. I'll have no hope of winning if you keep telling everyone your aunt's secrets. Everyone but me!"

"I am sorry about that," I said, meaning it. I was sorry that Edith had felt as if she was being excluded. I'd spent most of my life feeling like I was being left out. I knew how much it stung. "If it makes you feel any better, I wasn't sharing any of my aunt's secrets. I promise."

"I'm not sure I believe you."

"Cross my heart," I said as I traced an X on my chest.

"Well . . ." Edith hitched her purse strap onto her shoulder, the same purse that was filled with rocklike "purse stuff."

"I'm curious, Edith. Did you also hit Gracie Mae over the head with that purse of yours yesterday?" I asked, keeping my voice gentle. I didn't want to upset the poor woman any more than we already had. "Were you worried that she might have a recipe that would match yours?"

"That woman?" Edith laughed. She was starting to sound more than a little mad. "Why would I worry about what she was doing? Her crusts are always so overcooked, you need a steak knife to cut them. It was her husband, Owen, who knew how to bake a pie."

"Wait," Candice said. "Let me get this straight. You weren't the only one this woman attacked yesterday?"

"I didn't attack no one. It's all a misunderstanding." Edith jumped up from her chair. "Get out of my way." She pushed past us. "I don't have to sit here and take this abuse."

Candice moved to chase after the poor woman. I grabbed the FBI agent's arm. "Let her go," I said.

"But she's—" Candice started to protest.

"We all know where she lives and what kind of car she drives. And ever since she skidded off the road when trying to get onto Interstate 95 three years ago, she has refused to drive outside of town limits whenever it rains. Let me call Jace and let him know what happened."

"No, not Jace. I need to call the police chief and explain I let a murder suspect get away just because she looked like a harmless old lady." Her finger stabbed her phone angrily as she muttered to herself about how much she disliked small towns.

"Murder suspect?" What was Candice talking about?

"And why didn't I hear about this second attack? Why didn't anyone share the police report with me?"

"There wasn't a police report. Do you really think Edith Frampton is capable of killing . . . well, anyone?"

"If she'd hit you even a little bit harder yesterday, we wouldn't be having this conversation right now. You get that?"

Oh. That wasn't something I needed to hear.

"And if she could hit you over the head because she was angry about something you did or didn't do, is it really that big of a leap to think she could have also hit Owen Maynard over the head? Perhaps he did or said something about her apple pies that made her angry enough to knock him dead."

I supposed that could be true. Aunt Sal had said that Owen could bake a pie worthy of winning the contest. But . . .

But darn it, none of this felt right. Edith didn't know about the secret bookroom, so she couldn't be the vandal. The more I thought about recent events, the more I (regretfully) believed that Owen's death and the basement break-ins had to be related. Why kill him behind the library otherwise?

Candice was no longer listening to me. She was now speaking rapidly into her phone, talking to Police Chief Fisher, by the sounds of it. She was laying out how she believed Edith Frampton was a murderess and perhaps even a crazy woman. Candice kept mentioning the apple pie contest. And she wasn't keeping her voice low.

I glanced up and noticed that we'd attracted quite an audience.

Oh, Mama Eddy was not going to like hearing that I was in the middle of something like this. But really, this time it couldn't be helped.

Chapter Twenty-Seven

———·———

Mrs. Frampton? *Edith* Frampton? I can't believe it. She's
like the sweetest woman in town," Tori cried when I found her and
Flossie in the secret bookroom to tell them what had happened. Tori
had an electric drill in her hand and was standing on a stepladder as
she installed the bracket that held the security camera.

Flossie, who was holding the small camera on her lap, smiled and
nodded as if what I was saying didn't come as a complete surprise to her.

"No." Tori wagged the drill at Flossie. "No, I will not let you tell me
that you suspected her all along, because I won't believe it. I simply
won't believe it."

"It's always the nice ones that you have to worry about," Flossie said
with a wink in my direction. "It's simple human nature, isn't it? People
can't go around being nice all the time. Look at you and me, Tori. We
both have nasty streaks, don't we? And we're not going around knock-
ing people over their heads, nor would we ever."

"What's that supposed to mean? I would never—" I started to
protest.

But Tori didn't let me finish. "By that line of thinking, Flossie, we should never turn our back on Tru, since she's the nicest person in town!" She swung the drill in my direction. I had to duck to keep from getting whapped by it in the face.

Flossie's smile only grew wider. "I do keep a close eye on her . . . and so should you."

"What?" I cried.

"She's pulling your leg," Tori said.

"I'm not." Flossie crossed her arms over her chest. "It's the nice ones who are always the first to snap."

"You're crazy." Tori turned back to the wall and drilled a hole. "Everyone knows that Tru is as trustworthy as the police chief's old hound dog," she shouted over the whir of the drill.

"Thanks tons." I loved being compared to a dog.

"All I'm saying is that you can't make assumptions about what's going on in someone else's head. Tru might be quiet and kind, but she's got a devious mind. If she didn't, she would never have been able to figure out that Edith had attacked her. She figured it out faster than even the trained professionals on the police force. Plus, she did steal all these books in order to open this bookroom."

"I saved the books," I corrected.

"You might have a point there." Tori, done with her drilling, turned and looked at me in a way she'd never looked at me before. "There is something devious going on in that head of yours, Tru. You are able to put yourself in a criminal's mind with surprising ease."

"Um . . . thank you?"

Frank and Hubert left their table near the local documents section to come stand next to Flossie.

"This was all about apple pie, you say?" Frank said, and chuckled.

"But what about the poltergeist? And the——?" Hubert mimed drinking a bottle of liquor.

"I don't know," I said. "I suppose that's something the police will find out." Those loose ends bothered me too.

And the break-ins to the bookroom, they'd started long before I'd loaned that apple cookbook to Cora. Why would Edith break in and tear the books off the wall? How would she even know the bookroom existed?

It was possible that someone had told her about it. But even if someone had, why would she come here and wreak havoc? It wasn't done in search of an apple pie recipe. The vandal had left the nonfiction section, where the recipe books were stored, alone.

"Well, I'm going to sleep better knowing that Edith is locked up," Doris said as she emerged from the mystery section. She plunked down a pile of books on the circulation desk.

"Oh, I didn't realize you were down here," I said, and moved to check out the books. She had several classic cozy mysteries, a Regency romance, and a nonfiction book on writing a winning résumé. "You seemed upset earlier. Is everything okay?"

She blinked several times before saying, "Peachy."

Now, anyone with a drop of Southern blood in them knows that there's more than one way to interpret that word depending on the speaker's inflection. It can mean "the world is my oyster" if said with a bubbly lilt. But that wasn't how Doris had said it. The flat, slightly sarcastic way she spat the word could only mean one thing. Her life was anything *but* peachy.

Once I was finished checking out the books, Doris scooped them up and dropped them into her oversized purse. "Hey, Frank," she said with that same flat tone. "I have some new openings on my schedule. How about I start coming over every Wednesday? You know you need me."

"I . . . um . . ." Frank pulled a hand through his hair. "I suppose that would be okay."

She winked at him and then, looking much happier than she had looked all morning, hurried out of the bookroom as if she was afraid that if she lingered he might change his mind.

"What in the world was that about?" Hubert demanded.

"Ever since I sold her that old car," Frank said with a sigh, "she's been coming over every other week to clean my house. I hired her to help her make ends meet. She cleans several houses in town. She does a decent job of it. And she's not wrong. I'm not the best housekeeper. My house would benefit from her coming more often."

"Gracious," I said. "Who else does she clean house for?"

"Oh, you know Doris. She's always somewhere, doing something for someone. It's hard to keep tabs on the girl."

"She looked after Fenwick's house," Hubert said. "He was usually so lost in his research projects that he'd forget to cook. She'd come over to fix his meals, pick up after him, and wash his clothes."

"His passing had to be a huge loss of income for the poor girl," Flossie said. "She's had so many bad breaks in life. I do feel bad for her."

Tori looked unimpressed. "I've said it before, and I'll say it again. Doris needs to slow down. Yes, she works hard. But she works for peanuts and never gets ahead."

"It seems like she's always chasing the next moneymaking scheme too," I said as a thought tickled at the back of my mind. "What was old Fenwick researching again?" I asked Hubert.

"Well, that's an interesting question. He'd been immersed in the history of Hell Hole Swamp." Hubert started to lecture us on the background of the tiny swamp community.

"Was there anything about his research—a hidden treasure or some source of profit—that might catch someone's interest?" I asked, cutting off his lecture before he could really get going.

"I can't imagine there could be anything of value in his papers," Hubert said. "Not to say the research wasn't without value. I mean, to old historians like us, that kind of primary-source information is priceless. I still hate to think his work might be lost forever."

"I understand. Those resources are priceless to librarians as well," I said.

"What are you thinking, Tru?" Flossie rolled closer.

"That bump on my head must have knocked a few wires loose," I said with a shrug. "I keep thinking I know what direction to take this investigation, but then I end up in the middle of nowhere."

"It is a shock to find out someone you trusted wanted to hurt you," Frank said kindly.

"A terrible shock," Flossie agreed.

I didn't realize I'd started hugging myself until Tori wrapped me in her arms. "It's a shock for us all."

"But why on earth would Edith kill Owen?" Frank wondered aloud.

None of us could come up with any good ideas besides the apple-pie-contest connection. Was Edith going around killing off the pie-making competition?

"That could be the connection," I reluctantly agreed, "but none of the other bakers in town have even suffered a splinter."

Tori slapped her hands together. "You suspected Anne," she said to me.

"I . . . um . . . just for a moment," I said, feeling my cheeks heat. "And not without good reason. She had come in the morning we found Owen saying she was mad enough to kill him because of what he'd done to her car."

"Plus, you have a chip on your shoulder when it comes to her," Tori reminded me.

"I do not." At least, I was trying not to *let it show*. I attended all her classes, tried to understand all that technobabble she liked to speak in, and (mostly) ignored her jabs disparaging my age or my love of books.

"Ri-ight." Tori rolled her eyes. She was a master of the eye roll. "I mean, you don't have to be embarrassed. Your suspicions when it comes to Anne might help us figure out this mystery."

"Do you think Anne and Edith were plotting together?" Even as I said it, I knew that it couldn't be right. "Forget I said that."

While Flossie and Tori laughed, both Frank and Hubert looked confused.

"Anne was angry at Owen, because he was supposed to fix her car," I told the men. "But he bungled the repair job and then dragged his feet when she demanded he fix it properly. She insisted he use new parts instead of the faulty old parts he used the first time he'd 'fixed' it."

Frank nodded. "I heard he would pull that trick on some of his customers."

"And I'm thinking he might have done that to Edith," Tori said.

"She drives an ancient Oldsmobile that she absolutely refuses to trade in for a newer model," Frank said. And he should know.

"Do you know if it has been in the repair shop?" I asked.

"When is that rust bucket not in the repair shop?" he answered.

"Well, that could be it. I've said all along that people naturally yearn to kill their auto mechanics," Flossie said. "It's a dangerous business."

Hubert, Frank, and Tori all seemed to agree.

But I didn't.

That reason seemed too easy and left too many threads unraveled, such as Fenwick's untimely death, Candice's mysterious crime ring, and the repeated break-ins to the secret bookroom.

There had to be another explanation.

Chapter Twenty-Eight

———•———

Sure, questions still nagged at me about the whos and hows surrounding Edith Frampton's guilt when it came to Owen's death. But everyone else seemed convinced that she'd killed him in the same way that she had tried to kill me. I confess that I felt a sense of relief knowing the police were more than capable of finding her and collecting the necessary evidence needed to explain her actions. I wasn't going to have to reveal the work we'd been doing in the basement. (Thank goodness!) As long as the break-ins were in no way related to Owen's death, the future of the secret bookroom would be safe.

For now.

We still had to catch the midnight vandal.

Tori and Flossie finished setting up the camera. I returned upstairs to prepare for the afternoon children's program. Despite the tropical storm raging outside, the children's room slowly filled up with tots along with their mothers or grandmothers. I was setting out art supplies on the tables when Hennie came in. She hurried up to me with her baby in her arms and her older boys running around with their hair un-combed.

"I hated to do it, but I had no choice," Hennie said in a burst.

"Do what?" I prompted when she continued to follow me around.

"I had to let Doris go this morning." Thunder rattled the windows. A few of the kids squealed with fear and excitement.

"Let her go?" I asked as I laid out washable markers in a rainbow of colors on each table.

"Noah, stop poking your brother," Hennie scolded her son before turning back to me. "Terminated her services. Having her in my home was going to upset Gracie Mae far too much. And what I'd just learned about Gracie Mae . . . well." Hennie shrugged. "She's going to be staying on at our house for much longer than I'd expected."

"Oh." I supposed that explained Doris's prickly mood this morning. "What did you learn about Gracie Mae?"

"She's not telling anyone officially yet, but the doctors at the hospital discovered that Gracie Mae fell and hit her head because she is"—Hennie lowered her voice—"in a delicate condition."

Gracie Mae was pregnant? That came as a surprise. "I thought she and Owen couldn't have—?"

"That's what we all thought. She's happy and scared. She can't handle this alone. Not on what she makes at the diner. So, you understand why I had no other choice, and Landry and I do love the thought of having another baby in the house. We had already been talking about opening our home to unwed mothers as a way to help out those in need. You wouldn't happen to know anyone else in the community who might be looking for a nanny, would you? I hated leaving Doris in the lurch like that. She's already been struggling to make ends meet. Noah! I said stop."

"I'll ask around and let you know," I said as I headed toward the front of the room. The program was scheduled to start in about five minutes. A larger crowd than I'd expected had already showed up, meaning I'd need to gather more art supplies. After reading the children a story about how a picture-book author draws her books, I planned to lead the kids in making books to take home with them. Real, live, hold-in-your-hands paperback books. What a concept.

A poster of a scary purple monster that was like the monster in the picture book rippled where it was hanging from an easel at the front of the room as the air conditioner started to blow. A few of the younger kids looked away. Because of the storm, everyone's nerves already seemed to be jumpy. I tried to make a joke out of it by posing next to the poster as if I was the monster. But then the lights flickered.

A little boy sitting in the front near the poster hugged his knees to his chest and started to cry. I crouched down beside him.

"The lights do that sometimes when it storms." The lights flickered again and then dimmed. "Don't worry. There's a generator in the basement. I can go turn it on. Why don't y'all play with the clay I have out on the tables while you wait?"

I jogged from the children's room. Hennie followed.

"She blames you," Hennie said as she chased after me.

"What? Who?" I asked.

Mrs. Farnsworth emerged from her office to frown.

"I'm on it," I called to her without slowing my stride.

"Shh," the head librarian answered.

Anne stomped out of her office. "These brownouts could ruin the equipment. I need to shut things down."

"You do that. I'm heading down to turn on the backup generator."

Anne smiled. She actually smiled at me. Had we finally found a way to work as a team? I hoped so. I also hoped her tai chi classes continued. I did enjoy the first one.

"Doris," Hennie said as she jogged alongside me. "She blames you for losing her position."

"Why?" I asked. I paused at the door leading down to the basement.

"She thinks you poisoned me against her." Hennie hugged her baby to her chest. The lights flickered again.

"I need to get that generator running." But I didn't open the door. Instead I turned toward Hennie. "Why would Doris think I did anything against her?"

"Because after I fired her, she raged that this was your fault. She thinks you came over to my house the other night to tell lies about her. She then swore up and down that she hadn't been talking behind my back about me or Landry."

I shook my head. "I don't understand."

"I tried to explain to her that you hadn't told me anything." Hennie glanced at my not-so-thin stomach. "But at the same time, I couldn't tell her the real reason why you came over."

"I'm not pregnant!" I said a little too loudly and a little too forcefully.

"I know, dear, I know," Hennie soothed. "Your secret is safe with me. That's why I couldn't tell Doris that she was mistaken. Well, I did try to tell her that she was wrong, but she wouldn't believe me because I had no good explanation for why you dropped by the other night when you've never come by before."

"I . . . um . . ." She was right. I didn't have a good reason for stopping by her house. Not a good reason I was willing to share. I certainly wasn't going to tell Hennie the truth—that I went to her house only because I suspected her to be guilty of murder.

"I knew it! I knew you were expecting." Cora, who just happened to be coming out of the café at that moment, slapped her hand on her thigh. "That's why you and Jace are planning that quickie wedding."

"I'm not—!" I called after her as she ran toward the front.

"Shh!" Mrs. Farnsworth admonished.

"Oh dear." Hennie pressed her hands to her mouth. "I *am* sorry."

"Hopefully, everyone will be so caught up talking about Edith's arrest that they won't spare too much time thinking about me."

"I still want to help you." She put her hand on my arm (which wasn't easy considering that she was still holding a newborn). "I truly do."

If she wanted to help, I supposed she could clear up a few of those unanswered questions that wouldn't leave me alone. "Where do you and Landry go when you stay out all night?" I asked her.

Her cheeks colored. "Why would you—?"

"Doris mentioned being tired after babysitting for you all night. She looked beat. And I know you don't drink or dance, so I'm wondering, what do you do?"

"What does that have to do with—?"

Again, I didn't let her finish. "It doesn't have to do with anything. But it's been bugging me."

Hennie, who I'd never thought was too clever, surprised me when she said, "Oh my goodness! You suspected Landry and me of killing Owen, didn't you? That's why you came over, isn't it? Everyone talks about how you're some super amateur detective, but I didn't think twice when you came to the door. You brought cinnamon rolls, for Pete's sake. I had welcomed you into my home. I wanted to help you. And you were there hoping to prove I was some kind of homicidal maniac?"

When she put it that way, it did sound kind of . . . wrong.

"You're not even pregnant, are you?" she whispered.

"Good gracious, no. That was all a misunderstanding. I've tried and tried to tell you that I'm not."

Her baby started fussing. Hennie rocked gently from side to side as she made some soothing sounds. Amazingly, the baby settled right down.

"I heard Owen owed you money." That was just a guess on my part. I *had* heard someone in church say that Owen was on the verge of paying someone back. Add to that, the other rumor that Owen and Landry had recently had a falling-out. When Hennie gave me a funny look, I quickly amended my guess. "I mean, he owed Landry's church money."

She drew several sharp breaths before nodding. "He embezzled. The fool was always up to his ears in debt. He drank too much, gambled too much, and did heaven knows what else with his money. Because of my friendship with Gracie Mae, Landry had taken Owen under his wing hoping to reform him. He gave him responsibilities in the church, hoping that would help keep him too busy to get into trouble." She shook her head. "He acted like he wanted to reform, even attended AA meetings. But then at night, he was wilder than ever."

"Poor Gracie Mae," I said.

"She wanted to leave him, but Landry counseled her to stay, to give Landry more time to try and change Owen's straying ways."

"Was that before or after Owen stole the money?" I asked.

"Owen kept promising that he had some big windfall coming in, that he'd be able to pay Landry back and make a big donation to the church as well."

"Do you think he was doing something illegal?"

Hennie only sighed. "I'd better get back and see what trouble my boys are getting into now." She started to head back toward the children's room.

"Hennie?" I said, my curiosity still eating at me. "Where do you and Landry go all night?"

"Oh, you're not going to let that one go, are you? If you must know, we check into one of those hotels along Interstate 95."

"A hotel?" No wonder they had so many children.

"It's not what you think." Hennie blushed a deep red. "You saw how tired Doris was after one night with my boys? I live that every night. Every once in a while I need to get away so I can get a full night's sleep."

"Oh, that makes sense." So much for imagining that Hennie and Landry were selling babies or involved in some kind of sinister crime ring that had caught the FBI's attention.

As Hennie hurried back to the children's room, I jerked open the door leading down to the basement. Thunder boomed and the lights flickered again. I needed to get that generator going.

It took only a few minutes to get the old generator up and running. It rumbled happily and the lights brightened to full power. With that done, I headed down the basement hallway. There were kids waiting in the children's room for the program to start.

A moist breeze tickled my cheek. I stopped. I was next to the door that led outside. But it was closed. So, where was the cold air coming from?

The poltergeist?

And if you believed that, let me sell you Aunt Sal's apple pie recipe.

I looked up. Maybe there was a vent I'd never noticed before.

No.

I held out my hand and spun in a circle, trying to locate where the airflow was coming from.

The door.

But it was closed.

I walked over to it and gave it a gentle push.

It opened.

If the latch had been engaged, a push on the door shouldn't have opened it.

As it swung open, a small pebble clattered to the ground. I picked it up, placed it back into the doorframe, and held it there as the door closed again.

Sure enough, the door appeared closed. And when it was closed, it automatically locked from the outside. Oh my goodness, this was how our vandal was getting into the library without a key! They were rigging the door so it looked locked when it really was not.

I pushed the door open again and let the pebble fall to the ground. I then pulled the door closed and checked that the latch clicked.

I may not have caught a ghost, but I did stop a phantom.

And earlier that morning I had even caught a killer.

I was on a roll. Nothing, and I mean *nothing*, could ruin this day.

Nothing.

Looking back now, I wished I hadn't jinxed myself by thinking that.

Chapter Twenty-Nine

The children's program was a smashing success. The kids wrote and illustrated the most creative books I'd ever seen. My heart swelled when two of the girls traded their books. The younger of the two hugged her friend's book tightly to her chest and declared that it was her most prized possession.

Moments like these were why I felt so passionate about my job here at the library. Books had served as a refuge and had saved me during my parents' divorce. And from what I'd seen time and again, the written word had to be the most powerful tool man had ever created.

I felt as if I floated out of the children's room after the program ended.

Anne walked by. She bit her bottom lip when she saw me and started to walk faster. Had the storm damaged her equipment? I hoped not.

Delanie and Hubert were near the front desk, chatting. When I walked up, they stopped talking and frowned at me.

Did I have part of one of the kids' art projects stuck to me? I looked down at my sweater set and tan slacks.

Nothing looked out of place.

I had left the blond highlights in my hair from my weekend make-over. But they shouldn't be causing this much attention. No one had seemed to notice my hair when I came in this morning. And further-more, Anne had a full rainbow shooting through her hair and no one ever acted shocked by how she looked.

"Ms. Becket," Mrs. Farnsworth called out to me in that whispery voice that no one ever had any trouble hearing. "Please come over here."

She had returned from her meeting with the town manager. By the stark look on her face, the meeting hadn't gone well.

"What's going on?" I asked after crossing the room to meet her at her office door. "Is everything okay?"

"No," she said. "Everything is definitely not okay. You have some explaining you need to do."

Oh no. My face started to heat up.

Doris walked out of Mrs. Farnsworth's office. "I had to tell them," she said to me.

Jace followed Doris from the office as well. He looked at me and frowned.

"Tell them what?" I asked, trying to sound innocent, but I couldn't keep the tremble from my voice. My stomach clenched.

They knew.

"Doris has been telling us that you've knowingly withheld informa-tion regarding Owen Maynard's murder investigation," Jace said.

"But Edith confessed to hitting me." I pointed to the back of my head, which had suddenly started to throb again. "She's the one who killed Owen. Didn't Candice tell you? Didn't Chief Fisher arrest her?"

"We picked her up," Jace said. "She's admitted to attacking you in the park."

"She said she hit Tru because she's been giving other patrons help with their apple pie recipes," Doris added cruelly.

"Ms. Becket, we have an express rule at this library not to get involved with the apple pie contest for precisely this reason." Mrs. Farnsworth bit off the words in a way that sent a shiver down my spine.

"Yes, ma'am." I studied my comfortable shoes. "I only loaned out a cookbook to a few of my neighbors. I didn't do anything during work—"

"Tell them where the cookbook came from," Doris interrupted. "This is why we're here. This is why Owen is dead, isn't it? This is why the police cannot find his murderer. It's because you're keeping secrets from them."

"But Owen's death has nothing to do with the library." Surely, that was right. "Edith killed him because she was mad about how he fixed her car or something like that. I don't know. That's for the police to find out."

Mrs. Farnsworth turned to Jace. Her brows rose up toward her hairline. "Is this true?"

"Edith told us that she and her husband were at a fish fry on the night Owen was killed. Police Chief Fisher is personally checking out her alibi now."

Mrs. Farnsworth nodded.

"Let's not forget that Tru has been keeping a whopper of a secret from all of us," Doris said.

Delanie, who had walked closer, sucked in a sharp breath. She tried to send a message to me with her eyes, but for the life of me, I had no idea what that message might have been.

"And what is this grand secret?" Mrs. Farnsworth said, stepping in front of Delanie. "I hope this isn't a trick to try and sell us your snake oil again. Because if it is—"

"It's in the basement," Doris blurted. "I already told Detective Bailey all about it."

"She did," Jace confirmed.

"I still don't see how anything down in my basement could have anything to do with a police investigation," Mrs. Farnsworth said. "A murder investigation at that. If anything, this would be an internal matter, not a police matter."

I stood a little taller. "Thank you," I whispered under my breath.

Mrs. Farnsworth might be stern and (quite frankly) scarier than a Stephen King novel, but she fiercely protected the library and those who worked for her.

"I am sorry." Jace looked at me as he apologized. "Doris insists that there is a secret library in the basement, and that there are documents in that basement library that the police need to see regarding Owen's death. The documents might explain a motive. Which is, unfortunately, a police matter. If I need to get a warrant, I will."

Mrs. Farnsworth jerked her head back. She turned to me. "Ms. Becket? What do you have to say for yourself?"

My shoulders dropped. I closed my eyes, prepared to admit defeat.

"Lida," Delanie said to her friend, "why don't we go downstairs and see for ourselves?"

"If this is a crime scene, I'd prefer we didn't have a crowd." Jace sounded quite miserable about this. A large crowd had gathered around us. I searched the faces for Flossie and Tori. Neither was there. Were they still downstairs? Were they about to get ensnared in what should be solely my problem?

I pulled my cell phone from my pocket and sent a quick text to them.

Get out of the library.

Tori texted back almost immediately. We're both at Perks.

Good. I was glad they were out of the way, glad they wouldn't find themselves in trouble with the police because I couldn't let go of the idea that a library had to have printed books.

"Are you suggesting that you go downstairs by yourself?" Mrs. Farnsworth asked Jace in a disapproving tone.

"No, of course not, ma'am. I would like you to accompany me. And

Ms. Becket, of course, since Doris has indicated that Ms. Becket is responsible for creating what she's calling a secret bookroom."

Mrs. Farnsworth sniffed.

We all took it to mean that she agreed.

"I should come too." Doris pushed her way to the front. "I can make sure Tru doesn't try to hide any vital evidence. After all, she's in serious trouble, isn't she? She's been obstructing justice or something?"

Jace rubbed his temples as if trying to ward off a headache. "I can handle it, Doris. You'll need to stay here."

"Of course he can handle it," Mrs. Farnsworth said. "Let's get this over with. I have other pressing matters that require my attention."

I dutifully followed Mrs. Farnsworth. The crowd parted around us like the Red Sea. The three of us silently crossed to the back of the library, headed down the back stairs, and stopped in front of the heavy double doors of what used to be the town's official bomb shelter.

"Is it locked?" Mrs. Farnsworth asked me.

"No, ma'am. It should be open," I said.

She gave a quick nod and pushed open one of the doors. After a moment's hesitation, she stepped inside.

I hadn't looked at Jace once since we started this walk to my doom, and I was determined to avoid looking at him now. I felt both angry and embarrassed. In a way, I always knew it would come to this. I always knew that breaking the rules would end disastrously.

"I haven't been holding back any important information," I said in my defense before following Mrs. Farnsworth into the secret bookroom.

"I hope not," Jace said behind me.

When I crossed the threshold into the room, I couldn't believe what I saw.

The books?

Where were they?

How . . . how did this happen?

Chapter Thirty

———•———

Where were my books? Not *my* books of course, the library's. But I was their custodian. I felt responsible for them.

We had to be in a different storage room. That had to be the answer. The basement was a warren of storage rooms. Perhaps Mrs. Farnsworth had taken a wrong turn. Perhaps I'd been so nervous about what was about to happen that I hadn't noticed her mistake.

I stepped out of the room. No, those were the vault's double doors.

I stepped back into the room. The old circulation desk was still there. The bookshelves were all there. The filing cabinets were in the back of the room, their drawers sitting open. Empty.

I spotted the security camera Tori had installed. Its red light warned that it was recording.

I wandered around the room, looking at everything as if I'd never seen any of it before.

"Ms. Becket told me that she had directed some of the workers to take several of the bookshelves and old library furniture to the basement. This must be where she had them store it. If that's all, Detective, I think we all have work that needs to be done."

Jace held up a hand. "Just give me a moment."

He stared hard at the security camera and its damning red light before moving on to look at the empty shelves.

Doris, who had obviously ignored the detective's order to wait for us upstairs, burst into the room. "What?! What?!" she shrieked. "This isn't what the room looked like this morning. There were books in here. There were patrons checking out books. Ask Hubert Crawford. Ask Frank Calhoun. They were here this morning. They were pulling out documents while discussing Owen's murder."

"Shh," Mrs. Farnsworth admonished. "We might be in the basement, but this is still a library."

"Not anymore," Doris snapped. "Someone stripped it." Her finger shot out toward me. "She must have stripped it." She lurched toward me. "What did you do? What are you covering up?"

Jace took Doris's arms and directed her toward the double doors. "Please wait upstairs."

"But someone must have warned her," Doris complained. "She must have emptied the room before we could get here."

"Wait upstairs," Jace repeated. He deposited her on the other side of the double doors and pulled them closed with a loud *clank*.

He turned back to where I was standing and crossed his arms over his chest. "I know you have friends at the police department. Did someone call and warn you? Did you spend the afternoon cleaning out this room?"

"I'm surprised you would ask such a thing, young man. Ms. Becket was busy leading a children's program all afternoon." Mrs. Farnsworth came to my defense before I had a chance to utter a sound.

"Just as I thought." The smile Jace gave us made my knees feel funny. "I do apologize if I offended either of you. But, ma'am, I have to do my job. I have to ask these questions, especially if someone is going around making accusations."

I had some questions of my own that desperately needed to be answered. Where was Dewey? Where were the books? But I couldn't ask any of them. Not until after Mrs. Farnsworth and Jace left. Thankfully, after just a bit more poking around Jace agreed with Mrs. Farnsworth's assessment that the room was being used for nothing more than storage.

"I don't understand why Doris would make such an accusation," Mrs. Farnsworth wondered as we returned upstairs. "She's a pain when it comes to those crazy things she's always trying to sell us, but she's never gone out of her way to cause trouble like that."

"I think I have an idea what it might be about," I said. "Hennie told me this morning that she fired Doris. She'd been working as a part-time nanny for Hennie's five boys for some time and relied on the income. For some reason, Doris got it into her mind that I was the reason Hennie had fired her, which isn't true." I was quick to add that last part. "But Doris is convinced that I repeated to Hennie some of the criticisms Doris had made about the Goodloes over the past few days. I didn't say anything to Hennie, mind you."

"Of course you wouldn't," Mrs. Farnsworth said sharply.

"Thank you." I felt unaccountably pleased by her trust in my character.

"Now that that bit of unpleasantness is over, I need to go have a chat with Ms. Lowery about her tai chi classes. We're not canceling them, even though several members of the town council are pressuring me to do just that. But I will need Ms. Lowery to write some articles and create a pamphlet explaining what it is she is teaching. There seems to be some confusion about the nature of the exercise classes."

"Is there anything I can do to help?" I asked.

"Just keep out of trouble," Mrs. Farnsworth advised.

Keep out of trouble? Lately, that seemed like a tall order.

• • •

My heart pounded like a drum. I wanted to rip out my phone and text like crazy to Tori and Flossie. What in blazes could have happened to those books?

Was this the work of our mysterious vandal? Had he finally taken his ultimate revenge and stolen the books?

Were they gone for good?

My hand was on my cell phone as I parted ways with Mrs. Farnsworth. But I didn't get a chance to send that text. There was a line of patrons at the circulation desk waiting to be helped.

It took nearly an hour to help everyone. When I returned to the desk after showing a teen how to use one of the new recording studios, I found Jace waiting for me. He had a funny look on his face, a cross between an amused smirk and an irritated frown.

"Didn't your mama ever tell you that you shouldn't make faces like that for fear your face might get stuck that way?" I teased, hoping to distract him from asking me about whatever he saw in the basement that was putting that look on his face.

"You're lucky your face didn't get stuck with the look you were making a little while ago. The obvious shock frozen on it made you look like some kind of crazed mannequin as we walked around that old vault." He tapped his square chin. "I wonder why that was. What did you expect to see in—?"

"I already told you. Doris was just trying to make trouble for me."

"Yes, yes. Because she thinks you got her fired. But that doesn't explain why you looked so surprised when you walked into the storage room, a room that you had set up."

"It's an old bomb shelter," I explained, taking a page from Hubert's playbook. I started to tell Jace everything I knew about the space. "It was built back in—"

"Nor does it explain," Jace said, not letting me distract him, "why

Doris would think to make such an accusation. Telling us that you're keeping a secret in the basement seems so . . . so random, don't you agree? Also, it's obvious that the old *bomb shelter* is being actively used. The chairs are placed not for storage, but in cozy corners. My mom recently redecorated her living room and it looks just about the same as your 'storage area.' Plus, the desks look as if they're set up for readers to do research. What's been happening down there that's been worrying you?"

"It's that silly cat of hers," Anne said as she came up to the desk. She flipped her rainbow-colored hair.

"I beg your pardon?" Jace asked.

"Her cat. Most days she brings him in with her. The patrons who know about him go down there to spend time with him. They call him the library's new mascot or something." She squinted at me. "I've warned you more than once that someone was going to report you. You're lucky that cat of yours wasn't down there."

"Um . . . yes, my cat." I silently thanked Anne for butting into our conversation.

"That's Dewey's room?" Jace asked me, his voice taking on a slow, careful cadence that I imagined he used when questioning difficult suspects.

"He likes it there," I said.

"Hmm," was all he said.

I bit my tongue to keep from filling the silence with some kind of nonsense that would cause him to think there was more to the story.

Anne smiled at him.

"But he wasn't in the bomb shelter." Jace seemed unwilling to let the matter drop. "You brought him with you to work this morning. Where is he?"

"He's not roaming around out here again, is he?" Anne demanded, her eyes darting around the room. "I already warned you that if I caught him chewing on my wires, I was going to have to report him."

"Flossie must have taken him with her when she went to lunch. She does that sometimes," I said. "But she also usually tells me that she's going to take him. I was about to text her and ask her about it when I didn't see him in the room, but things have been so busy here at the desk, I haven't had a chance to hit send."

"You should go ahead and send that text," Jace said. "I'll wait in case Dewey did get out and you need help finding the little guy."

I turned my back to him before frantically sending out a text to both Flossie and Tori. Is Dewey with you? What happened to the books?

A moment later my phone pinged. It was a message from Tori. Dewey is in the small maintenance room. All is safe. Are you okay?

I think so, I texted back. She didn't answer my question about the books.

"Well?" Jace asked.

"Um . . ." Where could the books be? "Dewey is with them. I mean with Flossie. And Tori. They're together. With Dewey."

"O . . . kay." Jace was looking at me as if he was trying to figure out what I wasn't telling him. But really, I couldn't tell him the truth. "Are you feeling okay, Tru? You look pale."

"I'm feeling jumpy. But why wouldn't I? How would you feel if someone had just accused you of helping a murderer get away with murder? Plus, my nerves are still in shock from yesterday's attack."

"Oh right. That must explain it." He didn't look convinced. "I need to get back to the station. But, Tru, be careful around those crazed bakers. You never know who else out there is dead set on winning the pie contest."

"Don't have to tell me twice." I rubbed the back of my (still) sore head.

As soon as he left the building, I let out a long sigh and slumped down into the desk chair.

"You owe me," Anne hissed.

"What?" I looked up to find her hovering inches from my face.

"You owe me and Delanie and Hubert. We all pitched in and saved your—"

"You emptied the bookroom?" I whispered. "You?"

"Got to work on clearing out the books as soon as I overheard that spiteful Doris going on and on about how she was going to get you fired. What did you do to her?"

"You knew about the bookroom?" I asked, feeling as if I'd suddenly dropped into an alternative bizarro universe.

"Please. I've known about it ever since the day before the library's grand reopening." She rolled her eyes as if this should have been obvious.

"You did?" I still felt like I'd been dropped into a world where up was down and right was left.

Anne made a "duh" noise. "I had to check on some fiber-optic wires that were run across the ceiling in the bomb shelter. All those books in the room are kind of hard to miss."

"And you didn't report me to Mrs. Farnsworth?" Perhaps the knock on my head had caused more damage than anyone suspected. Perhaps this was a hallucination. I wondered if I should pinch myself. Or did that only work for dreams?

"Why would I tattle?" Anne asked. "What you're doing down there is none of my business."

I opened my mouth and then closed it again. This had to be a hallucination. Was I in a coma? Anne would never go out of her way to be nice to me.

"Sheesh. This is the place where you say 'thank you,'" Anne said.

"Thank you," I parroted back. "I mean it. Thank you. I'm . . . I couldn't be more grateful. You didn't have to do any of that."

"I know," she said, and pranced off toward her computers.

Chapter Thirty-One

"They let her go," Tori announced that evening. With an elaborate twist of her wrist, she snapped her fingers. "Just like that."

"They didn't let her go," Flossie countered. Dewey had jumped up onto her lap and was enjoying riding around my living room as Flossie paced. He'd perched with his front paws on the wheelchair's arms, his head held stiff as he gazed out like a captain on the deck of a ship.

I'd called together an emergency book club meeting at my house so we could pool what we knew and try to solve Owen's murder. The tropical storm, thankfully, had moved north, taking the rain and wind with it.

"They did so let her go." Tori pointed to my front door. "I saw Edith walking down the street on my way over with my own two eyes."

"It's redundant to say 'with your own two eyes' if you already said you saw her," Flossie muttered. She then said louder, "Edith might be walking around town, but that doesn't mean she's a free woman. She's out on bail."

"Anne saved the bookroom," I pointed out both to change the subject and because I still could not believe it. "She heard Doris telling people how she was going to get me fired. Anne didn't hesitate. She went straight to work on getting the books out. There were hundreds of books in that room. It couldn't have been easy."

"That's what I've been trying to tell you," Delanie said gently. "My niece is a good kid. The *best*, really."

Delanie was the last of the original members of the book club to arrive. She'd brought her funeral cake, which I thought was an interesting choice.

Flossie had taken one look at the dessert and asked, "Who the heck died now?"

"We're talking about Owen's death," Delanie answered with a smug smile that looked very much like Anne's smirk. "I thought the cake was appropriate."

"Don't complain. Chocolate with chocolate icing and pecans? This isn't just cake, it's a masterpiece of culinary art," Tori said as she took the cake from Delanie and carried it off to the kitchen. I could hear plates being taken out of my cabinet.

"At least it's not apple pie," I said as I rushed off to help her.

"Didn't Doris bring an apple pie by for you last night?" Delanie asked once we were all sitting around the living room with plates of cake balanced on our legs. "How was it?"

"I didn't get a chance to taste it." Which was a shame too. I would have enjoyed eating a piece for breakfast this morning.

"Let me guess. Mama Eddy?" Tori asked right before taking a big bite of the cake. She reeled back and moaned as if she'd entered nirvana.

The rest of us laughed.

Tori opened her eyes. "What's so funny?" she asked, which only made us laugh that much harder.

We ate cake and chatted about the books we'd been reading and gossiped a bit before getting around to talking about the real reason we'd gotten together.

"I suppose it's time to put on our Miss Marple hats," I said as I started gathering up the plates.

"Not that woman's old dowdy hats," Tori groaned.

"They have to be cuter than donning Detective Poirot's waxed mustaches. I pluck every morning to make sure I don't start looking like that fussy little Belgian, thank you very much," Flossie put in.

Dewey meowed and rubbed his muzzle on Flossie's leg as if agreeing with her about not wanting a mustache. He really loved it when I had people over. He'd spent the past half hour going from person to person, poking his nose in their purses and taking an active part in the conversation with little growls, sharp meows, and loud purrs.

"This isn't about hats," I said. "I don't even have any hats for y'all." I pulled out my notebook and flipped open to a blank page. "We really need to organize what we know and look for patterns. I feel like we've been going around and around in circles and not getting anywhere. We need to start thinking like detectives again."

"Can I pick a different detective?" Tori asked. "Surely there's a sexy one I could be."

"In that case, I want to be Amelia Peabody," Flossie said.

"Is she sexy?" Tori asked.

"Not really. But she's a tough-as-nails Egyptologist. She wields her umbrella like a sword."

"If we're picking our own sleuths, I want to be Miss Fisher," Delanie said. "I love her sassy style and the clothes she wears."

"I'll be a grown-up Nancy Drew," Tori decided. "Didn't they make a movie about that?"

"Don't get me started about how they've ruined poor Nancy whenever they put her in a movie," Flossie said. "You can be Modesty Blaise. Read the books, don't bother with the movie. It's unwatchable. Delanie, you'll be Miss Fisher, and Tru, you can be Nancy Drew, since I know how much you idolize her."

"Why does Tru get to be Nancy Drew? And why do I have to be someone no one has ever heard of?" Tori complained.

"Let's just be ourselves, but smarter versions of ourselves, okay?" I asked, regretting having mentioned Miss Marple.

"But I like role-playing," Tori said.

Flossie sighed. "We don't want to hear about your love life."

"I do," I said. "Perhaps afterward?"

I wrote Owen's name on the top of the page. "What do we know—*really* know—about poor Owen?"

"Didn't Aunt Sal mention that Owen's family was from Hell Hole Swamp?" Tori asked. "Maybe his ancestors were moonshiners?"

"Isn't everyone from the swamp related to a moonshiner?" Delanie asked.

"Sure seems that way," Flossie said. "You can still find good hooch out there if you know where to look. But why would anyone kill him because of that?"

"I don't know. Tru asked what we knew about Owen. I told her," Tori explained.

"We are brainstorming," I reminded everyone. "I suppose it wouldn't hurt to research more about Owen's family tree." I wrote down *The Maynards' family history*, in the notebook with Aunt Sal's name next to it.

"Owen was in debt and had stolen money from the Church of the Guiding Light," Flossie said. "That sounds more like a motive than some distant relation."

"Still brainstorming," I warned. I wrote in the notebook: *He was expecting a windfall*. And then added: *From where?* next to it.

"He gave Doris a hard time, flirting with her." Tori wrinkled her nose as she said it.

"Gracie Mae claims Doris was flirting with Owen," Delanie countered.

"So, we have conflicting stories." I tapped my pen on the page. "Who do we believe, the scorned wife or the young, pretty nanny?"

"Clearly, Doris is telling the truth," Tori said. "There's no way she'd initiate things with Owen. He was too old for her and too gross."

I agreed with her, but put the interaction between Owen and Doris into the notebook with a question beside it: *Which one made trouble for the other?*

We filled the page with notes, including the fact that Owen was interested in Hell Hole Swamp, that he might have stolen research from Fenwick on the swamp, and that he had purchased a book on antiques and their value from Charlie's bookstore.

As I wrote that last bit, I looked up at Tori. "Where is Charlie tonight? Didn't you invite him?"

"He has one of his book club meetings," she said. "They tend to run late."

"I hear they're really popular with the young, single ladies in town," Delanie said.

"That's because he serves wine," Tori said.

"Yeah, it's the wine that's drawing them in." Delanie laughed.

"They're all after your hunky ma-an," Flossie sang. We all laughed again, especially after Tori started to turn pink.

"He *is* a catch, isn't he?" She blushed even harder. I'd never seen Tori fall this hard for a guy.

"He's the best kind of guy," I assured her. "The kind who is crazy about you for you."

I turned the page and wrote *Suspects* in bold print at the top of this new page.

"I spoke with Hennie this morning," I said. "She saw through our ruse to get information from her, by the way."

"Owen took advantage of that family," Flossie said as she stroked behind Dewey's ears. "They tried to help him. They tried to get him to stop drinking. And what did he do? Stole their money so he could drink and gamble even more. If I were writing this plot, they would make the perfect justified villains of the story. They have this too-good-to-be-true religious veneer and more than ample reason for being furious with him."

"They do have plenty of motive," I agreed, "but after talking with Hennie, I don't think either one of them hit Owen over the head with a liquor bottle."

"Even the murder weapon is poetic justice for him," Flossie said. "Killed by his drinking."

Instead of writing Hennie's and Landry's names down, I wrote, *The bottle? Where did it come from? Was it his?* Probably.

"What about Edith?" Tori asked. "Do we really believe that her alibi for Owen's murder checks out? She could have gone to the party and then killed him after leaving. Dinner parties like the one she says she attended rarely last past nine o'clock. That leaves her with plenty of nighttime hours to meet up with Owen and knock him into the afterlife."

"Jace told me that her husband claims he took her home and put her to bed. She snored loudly until morning. Apparently, she enjoyed the muscadine wine that was being served a little too much that night," I said.

Instead of writing down Edith's name, I wrote *Angry customer?* which triggered a memory. "Hubert had been angry that Owen had taken Fenwick's research," I said. "And someone stole Hubert's research right out of his hands."

"Do you think Hubert killed Owen in an attempt to recover the research?" Flossie started to pace again. Dewey stood up on the chair's arm and struck his captain-at-the-helm pose.

"Hubert did turn curiously silent when he heard we'd found Owen's body outside the library," I remembered. "But the research is still missing, isn't it? And who took Hubert's research? And why?"

Instead of writing Hubert's name on the page, I wrote, *Missing Hell Hole Swamp research* and *Fenwick Harrington's death.*

"What about the vandals?" Delanie asked. Dewey jumped from Flossie's wheelchair to Delanie's lap and meowed as if he agreed that we needed to talk about those monsters who'd been wrecking the library books. "Do you think Owen spotted the people who've been breaking into the library and was killed because of what he saw?"

"No," Flossie said before anyone else could utter a sound. "No. His death can't be connected to our work in the basement."

I understood her passion. She wanted to protect the bookroom as much as I did.

"How can you possibly know this?" Tori demanded. "Besides, we're brainstorming. Every clue needs to be examined."

"She's right," I said. "We can't eliminate anything until we know more. Which reminds me: I discovered how the vandals are getting in. They're coming down to the basement during the day and propping the back door open with a rock. I noticed it today because the strong tropical winds were leaking through the crack and into the hallway."

"So our vandal is someone we've seen downstairs, someone who has been invited to the bookroom?" Flossie sounded quite disheartened by that idea.

"I believe so." My heart beat a little faster.

"But . . . but none of our patrons are capable of murder," Flossie insisted. Both Tori and Delanie nodded in agreement.

"If that's true, it means we don't have to worry that we've been withholding information from the police." Tori turned to me. "*You* don't have to worry about it, Tru. People frequently park behind the library at night, remember? All sorts of shenanigans happen back there after dark. Anyone could be sneaking into the basement during the day and propping open the door without ever having been invited into the bookroom."

I wish I could share their conviction. The best I could do was, instead of writing *The vandals* on the suspects page, I wrote, *Break-in connection?* The question mark at the end of that note was probably wishful thinking on my part, but adding it did make me feel better.

"What about the apple pies?" Delanie asked. "Is it possible that the baking competition is still at the heart of all of this trouble? I mean, if one person in town has lost her mind in her quest to have her pie picked as 'the best,' it's reasonable to assume that there are others out there who have also gone pie crazy."

Again, instead of a specific suspect, I wrote, *Apple pie.*

"Who attacked Gracie Mae, if not Edith?" Tori asked. "How is that related to her husband's death? I bet she knows more than she's telling."

"No one attacked Gracie Mae," I said. I related to them what Hennie told me about Gracie Mae, how she was pregnant and had simply passed out. "I don't think she's involved."

"Of course she's involved," Tori said. "It's always the wife who did it."

"Only in a poorly crafted mystery," Flossie muttered.

For some reason, I didn't have the heart to add Gracie Mae's name to my suspect list. She'd suffered enough already. Instead I wrote, *How was the murderer related to Owen?*

I ran my finger down the page of suspects. Hmm . . . My page was filled with notes, but I hadn't written down even one name. Not. One. Name.

But—I scanned the page again—I hadn't needed to write down a name. All of these clues I'd jotted down created a pretty clear picture of what had happened and why Owen was killed that night.

Our murderer was someone who wanted to find something in the library, something that Owen knew about thanks to his connection to Hell Hole Swamp. The murderer and Owen must have had an argument. Owen needed money and quickly. Perhaps he had tried to cut his partner out of the deal and that was how he ended up dead.

I closed the notebook with a snap.

"I know what we need to do."

Chapter Thirty-Two

As I drove to the Cypress Local History Museum, I called Mama Eddy and thanked her for throwing out the apple pie. She was surprised (and pleased) I was finally accepting that I needed to eat healthier food. I neither agreed nor disagreed. But I did tell her that I loved her. She grumbled that I took after my father too much and told me to stop trying to charm her.

"I don't understand," Tori said after I hung up with my mom. My best friend was riding shotgun with me to the museum. Delanie and Flossie were following behind us in Flossie's pretty red Corvette. "Was there something wrong with the pie Doris had baked for you?"

"Maybe." I bit my lower lip. "I do know, though, that Doris is angry and blames me for her misfortune."

"Someone needs to give that girl a lesson in real-world economics. She works too hard and never has anything to show for it." She turned in her seat toward me. "But enough about her. You can tell me. Who do you think killed Owen?"

"I need to talk with Hubert about the library's history and its old basement speakeasy before I can be sure," I said.

Luckily, Cypress is tiny. It took only a few minutes to get to the museum, located in a small converted one-story brick home from the 1940s just a block off Main Street.

Hubert's brown Chevy was parked in front.

"What's the excitement, ladies?" he asked when the three of us joined him inside the museum's front foyer. There was a pair of printed boards that had been greeting visitors to the museum ever since I was in grade school. One celebrated the town's agricultural past. The other highlighted the history of the man-made Lake Marion, which formed the town's northern border. The photographs glued to the two boards had curled and yellowed over time. However, the buildings in the pictures looked pretty much how they look today. Update the cars and the fashions, and those photos could have been taken yesterday.

"We're interested in hearing more about the speakeasy in the library," I told Hubert.

"We are?" Flossie asked.

"The speakeasy is the bond that links the Hell Hole Swamp community to Cypress. And look at this." I pulled out of my purse the article that I'd been carrying around since Thursday. The headline read, "Local Kershaw Man Hits Jackpot with Hell Hole Swamp Bootlegger Bottles." When I first looked at it, it meant nothing. But now . . .

Hubert nudged his glasses up his nose as he read the article about how a man in the upstate made a fortune selling old bottles he'd found in his grandparents' basement.

He cleared his throat. "Of course. Of course. I have my papers over here."

"Weren't they stolen?" Tori asked.

"The research that I was gathering on Hell Hole Swamp was taken along with my notes for the old speakeasy, but I have the files from the library here."

He opened a long file drawer that held old maps and building plans. He pulled out the top papers. "I hid them in here," he explained as he lifted out a thick sheaf of papers that were clipped together.

"I like how you think." Flossie jotted down something in the notebook that she always carried with her. Had Hubert given her an idea for the novel she was working on? She wouldn't tell even if I did ask, so I didn't ask.

Hubert cleared his throat again and then started to lecture us on the history of Cypress's library. He showed us photographs of the building being constructed back in the early 1900s. He then showed us photographs of the building during the renovations that were made in the 1940s when the bomb shelter vault was built.

"Wait," I said, interrupting his monologue about the cost of food during that time. "What about the speakeasy? When was that put in?"

"Soon after Prohibition," he explained. "I daresay the day after the Eighteenth Amendment was ratified, the townspeople dragged in tables and started serving hard liquor in the library's basement. According to a diary I found in your bookroom, the mayor and head librarian were both in on the scheme. The librarian at the time was a fellow out of New York. He was also a tutor. His name was Theodore Books. Isn't that the perfect name for a librarian?"

As he talked about Theo Books and his secret "bookroom" in the basement, I ran my finger along the walls in one of the photos. Prior to the library's most recent renovation, the first floor looked exactly as it had in most of these old photographs. Now, with the modernization, those spaces were being used for technology centers, meeting rooms, and the café. But the basement in the photographs looked nothing like what was there now and had been there as long as I'd been coming to the library. The picture I was most drawn to showed that the basement had once been mainly one big open area with just a few storage closets, not the maze of rooms it was today.

"Why is it different?" I asked. I wished those old building plans hadn't been destroyed when the town hall had caught fire.

"What's that?" Hubert asked.

"Why is the basement so different today? Why was it changed?"

"Oh, that all happened in the thirties. According to what I'd read, it was all slapdash. They tossed up the walls to make space for food storage. The Depression had hit everyone hard. The farmers in our area were having trouble selling their crops because no one had money to buy the food. The churches and local governments bought what they could. They gave some away. Canned some. And shipped some to other towns where there was a need for food and some hope of selling the crops."

"And this happened after Prohibition ended and The Bookroom closed?" Delanie asked.

"That's right. The town had quite a bit of cash on hand, and so did many of its residents, thanks to the illegal liquor sales. The town officials also made a fortune from the payoffs they received from Hell Hole Swamp bootleggers in exchange for not turning them in to the feds," Hubert explained.

I ran my finger along one photograph in particular. It was one of the photos of the library basement that must have been taken during the 1930s renovation. I kept going back to this one picture. It was a photograph from before the bomb shelter had been built, which would have happened about ten years later. But the room I was looking at appeared to be the same area where the bomb shelter/bookroom was located today.

According to the photograph, what I thought was an outside wall in the basement couldn't be. The space in the photo looked as if it should be at least ten feet longer.

Why would that be?

And in the background, if I squinted, I thought I could see remnants of the old speakeasy. A bar spanned the length of the back wall with a broken mirror behind. I held the photograph under a bright light and peered at it quite closely. Were those old liquor bottles on the floor?

"What are you thinking?" Flossie asked.

"She definitely has an idea brewing," Tori said.

I looked up at them. They were both smiling. So was Delanie. Hubert cleared his throat, trying to get our attention back to what he'd been saying.

"I'm sorry, Hubert," I told him. "What you're telling us is interesting, but I need to go check something out. Delanie, didn't you say Anne has a key to the library now?" It pained me to include the young techie in our investigation, but there really was no reason not to. She already knew everything about my secret bookroom anyhow.

"She does. She promised Mrs. Farnsworth she'd use it only in an emergency."

"This is an emergency," I said.

"I can call her." Delanie stepped to one side and dialed her cell phone.

"Tell her that we need to hurry. I want to get there before the killer does." I pulled out my phone. "Tori, can you check the camera with your phone and tell me if it's still working?"

"I think so. But I don't understand what's going on."

I held up a finger. "Just a minute. I need to call Jace."

"He's not going to like this," Flossie warned.

"He should go down on his knees and thank our girl for solving this murder problem for the town," Tori said.

"Well, that's the truth," Flossie agreed. "He should be grateful. As long as you can bring him proof. You can, can't you?"

"I think we can get it tonight . . . right now, even." I hoped we could. I laid out the photographs I'd been studying. "Look here. The old speakeasy became one of the new storage rooms in the 1930s. But then, look here. The bomb shelter, with its metal walls, was built in a way that blocks the only door leading into the speakeasy, essentially shutting it off from the outside world forever."

"And our vandal, with Owen's help, has been trying to find the lost door to the speakeasy," Delanie said.

"That's right." The more I talked about it, the more certain I felt. "But it's never going to happen—our villain is never going to find his— or her—way into the speakeasy, because the steel walls are too thick to knock through."

"We need a plan." Flossie rolled toward me. "If there's a chance that we might meet up with a killer, we need to slow down and make a plan."

And she was right. We did need to think this carefully through. So we sat back down around the old scarred wooden table at the museum and, with Hubert's help, put together a plan for catching a killer.

Chapter Thirty-Three

About an hour later we all piled into our cars and steered toward the library. The choruses from several species of frogs filled the thick, humid post-storm air. Tree limbs littered the ground. And occasionally the wind rushed by to remind us that although the storm had passed, it wasn't too far away.

Flossie and I both parked a block away near Charlie's bookshop. Jace waited for us by Charlie's front door. Dressed all in black—black jeans and a black T-shirt—he looked as dangerous as ever. And while, unlike Tori, I preferred my men safe and tame as kittens, my silly mouth turned bone-dry at the sight of him. What was I supposed to do with my hands?

As we walked up, I struggled to come up with something to say to Jace that wouldn't sound weird or forced. I heaved a deep sigh of relief when Charlie emerged from the bookstore and locked the door behind him.

"Ladies," he said in place of a greeting, "I heard we are going on a hunting expedition." Like Jace, he'd dressed all in black. Only instead of black jeans, he was wearing neatly tailored black slacks with the kind of fitted sports shirt that runners often wore.

I glanced over at my girlfriends. None of us was dressed in black. None of us had even *thought* to dress as if we were trying to blend in with the shadows. Flossie wore various shades of red. Tori looked stunning in a pale green maxi dress. Delanie had on another one of her signature vintage dresses. This one was a pretty turquoise swing dress with cute cap sleeves. And I still had on the light pink sweater set with wide-legged tan slacks I'd worn to work that morning. We looked like we were trying to blend in with the town's showy flower beds. Should we go home and change? Was there even time?

"Sheesh, Tru. What did you do? Invite half the town?" Jace asked.

"There's safety in numbers." I smiled as I said it. At least I hoped it was a smile. I felt so awkward, I had no clue what my facial muscles were doing.

Whatever expression I made, Jace didn't look amused. He crossed his arms over his chest. "There's also safety in staying home and letting the professionals handle matters."

"Edith didn't kill anyone," I blurted to show why we *couldn't* leave matters to the professionals.

"I know that." He'd said it as if I should have already known that he'd dismissed Edith as a suspect. "But we're letting her dangle as our number one suspect to give the real killer a false sense of security. Do you know Betty has snagged the front-page headline with her 'Apple Pie Killer' article?"

"She must be thrilled. Do you know who killed Owen?" I pressed.

"Do you?" he countered.

I nodded.

"Who?" he asked.

"You go first."

"Y'all could count to three and say the name at the same time," Flossie said.

"Or write the names on a piece of paper and tuck it into an envelope only to be read after our villain has been caught," Charlie suggested.

I recognized both of those suggestions as having been lifted from different (but equally famous) mystery series.

"Or you could all go home and let the one person here who has actually been trained to handle an investigation handle it," Jace said, not at all amused by our help.

"Believe it or not, I would much rather be home," I said. Why shouldn't I agree with him? "But now that I know what I think I know, I have to be here. If you don't like it, *you* don't have to stay."

His expression hardened even further. "When is your car salesman getting here?"

"He's not my . . ." Tired of this game, I huffed out a breath. "Before Frank showed up this morning, I was on the verge of suggesting that we go out sometime. You know, as in you and me. I mean, after this is over."

"Finally!" Tori cheered. So did Flossie. Delanie clapped.

Jace's expression didn't soften. His gaze narrowed as he stared at me. He didn't even flick a glance at my celebrating friends. If I could have, I'd have jumped right out of my own skin to escape from the increasing amount of tension between us.

"Forget I said that," I said.

"*Never.*" His voice was low and quiet, seductive. His hand brushed against mine.

"How about I forget it, then? It was stupid." I felt stupid. And jittery. And did I mention stupid? "Blame it on the head injury. I don't know what I'm saying." I needed to shut my mouth already.

With a wry smile that gave away very little, Jace shook his head. He then asked in his detective's just-the-facts tone, "So, what do you expect to happen at the library tonight?"

"If we're lucky, we're going to find a treasure."

Jace seemed to perk up at the mention of a treasure. "Then you're not planning to confront a killer and nearly get yourself killed like last time?" he muttered under his breath.

"Like a real treasure, Tru?" Charlie rubbed his hands together.

"Like a real treasure," I said.

A little while later, Anne met us at the library's entrance. "What are you up to?" she demanded of me. "Did you forget to bring that cat of yours home?"

"I'll explain it later," Delanie answered for me. "It's all very exciting."

For any history buff, what we were doing *was* exciting. While at the museum plotting our plan, we had researched why someone might be interested in the remnants of an old speakeasy hidden behind a wall.

The old photographs of the library's basement in Hubert's collection showed empty bottles and an old, battered homemade bar.

"See here." Hubert's voice had been filled with excitement as he provided another lecture about the library's past. "The speakeasy was run by members of Cypress's community. Families like yours, Tori, and yours, Tru . . . they were the ones who would have been involved either as customers or employees."

"My family is from Charleston," Delanie volunteered.

"Yes, well." Hubert cleared his throat. "Owen's parents moved out of the swamp in the hopes of finding work to help put food on their table. While families still operate the old stills out in the swamp, there's not much money in it anymore, not unless you decide to go legit and wholesale the hooch to major retailers. But that takes money, money most families don't have."

We all nodded.

It seemed like meaningless information. After a moment of contemplation, I groaned. "Hell Hole Swamp." Of course, of course. "I bet Owen grew up listening to stories of moonshine, revenuers, and secret pubs."

"Yes? But that still doesn't explain why someone would be so determined to get inside the walled-up room," Tori complained.

"Not yet. But remember what Charlie told Jace the other day. Owen wanted to purchase a book on the history of Hell Hole Swamp. Plus, he did purchase a book on the value of antiques."

Tori looked at the photograph lying on the table in front of us and shook her head. "What I see is just a bunch of worthless junk on the ground."

"Half the stuff you can find in Doris's online vintage shop looks like junk," Delanie pointed out. "But much of it is worth a pretty penny to the right collector."

"There's only one way to find out if we're right," Tori said as we all sat around the table and stared at the dusty bottles littering the floor in the photograph.

"We'll need to tear down the wall." Delanie pantomimed swinging a sledgehammer as she said it.

I cringed at the thought, but my friends weren't wrong. The vandals were only wrecking the areas around the edge of the secret bookroom. And then there were the scratches on the wall that Dewey had found. Someone had been trying to get through the walls. But the secret bookroom was located in an old bomb shelter. The interior walls were made from six layers of corrugated metal sheets that had been bolted together. (Thanks to Hubert's research, I now knew this.) The vandals wouldn't have been able to break through, and apparently from the haphazard nature of their attacks, they also didn't know where to break through the wall. *Perhaps Owen had known?*

If we wanted to find the treasure behind the wall, we were going to have to go at it from another angle. Or at least from another wall. After studying Hubert's old photographs for several minutes, I thought I had found the perfect place where we could go through the wall without having to try to bust through an impenetrable bomb shelter.

Which was why we all crowded inside the basement maintenance closet that was located right next to the secret bookroom.

"This should be the wall." I started to remove cleaners and other chemicals that were neatly organized on the maintenance room shelves. Everyone else joined in.

"If we're going to take down the shelves, we'll need tools," Charlie said.

Tori reached into her oversized purse and withdrew a small travel toolkit. "We came prepared."

It took about a half hour to clear the wall. I stared at the bare plaster we'd uncovered. Were we really going to do this? Were we really going to tear down a wall in the middle of the night? Was I going to get *fired* over this?

Flossie had been carrying the sledgehammer on her lap. For some reason (I hesitated to ask what it was) she kept one in her car's trunk. She handed it to me.

I looked at the wall and then at the sledgehammer. We'd come too far to back down now. I raised the heavy hammer.

Jace lifted it from my grip. "Let me."

"You don't have to . . ." Although I was glad he'd offered.

"If Mrs. Farnsworth complains, it'll be on me, not you. I'll tell her it had to be done as part of the official investigation into Owen's death, which is the truth. I've been wanting to find out what y'all have been hiding in this basement for a while now." The boyish smile he flashed me probably would have melted my heart if we weren't all smooshed in a closet and on the verge of destroying library property.

Instead of smiling back, I inhaled a shaky breath.

"Are you ready for me to do this?" he asked me, his smile fading.

"She's as ready as honeysuckle on a vine," Flossie answered for me.

"I don't know what that means, but yeah, what Flossie said," I said. I took another shuddering breath. "Let's get this done."

Jace swung the sledgehammer, smashing its wide head through the wall. Plaster flew everywhere.

"I'll be damned," he said as he peered through the hole he'd just made. He stepped aside so the rest of us could take a look. The others allowed me to be the first one to step up and shine a flashlight through the hole. I felt like Howard Carter staring into King Tut's tomb for the first time. My heart raced as the light bounced from one dusty item to another. There was no mistaking what had been plastered over.

"By gum," Delanie declared as she leaned over my shoulder to peer inside the hole. "It is the speakeasy. Just like in the pictures."

There were bottles lining the far wall with a long, wooden bar in front of it. This was the secret room Owen's killer (and perhaps also Owen) had been searching for.

"I still can't believe anyone would kill over this," I mused aloud.

"Collectors can be crazy," Flossie said. "I once knew someone who'd been robbed at gunpoint over an original Cabbage Patch doll."

"That's insane," Tori said.

"That's collecting for you," Flossie said.

"I don't get it," Jace said. "Who would go through all this trouble to find a forgotten room that holds nothing but garbage?"

Before I had a chance to answer, the lights in the library went out, plunging us all into darkness.

No one moved. The only light in the room was from the flashlight in my hand.

"Turn that off," Jace whispered.

I hesitated for just a moment before flipping the switch. We all stood silent in the darkness.

"Do you think she's out there?" I whispered to Jace.

But he didn't answer. I reached out my hand to where he was standing and found that he was gone.

Chapter Thirty-Four

After what felt like a tense hundred years, the lights flickered and then came back on. We all breathed out a collective sigh of relief. Well, not Jace. He was gone.

"Where did that boy go?" Flossie asked.

"I bet he thinks the killer is stalking us. And here we are stuck like sardines in a tiny closet. It'll be like shooting fish in a barrel," Delanie said as she plastered herself against a wall.

"I've always wondered about that saying," Flossie said, not sounding the least bit nervous. Perhaps, thanks to her world travels, she'd developed nerves of steel. "Shooting fish in a barrel, indeed. Who in their right mind would shoot fish? It's dangerous to shoot a bullet into the water. Anyone with good sense knows that. It could ricochet right back at you."

"What are you yammering on about?" Tori demanded.

I laughed. "Flossie is distracting us from our nerves. And doing a good job of it too. Do you think we should go look for Jace? Or should

I go turn on the backup generator in case there's another power outage?"

"No," Charlie said. He had maneuvered himself so he was now standing between us and the door. "Jace knows what he's doing. Let's stay here and stay together."

"The power has been dodgy all evening thanks to that storm," Jace said a few moments later when he returned to the storeroom. He tucked his gun back into its holster. "There's no one out there."

"Should I go start the generator?" I asked.

Jace gave a curt nod and followed along as I cranked up the generator, which was only a few rooms away. It rumbled loudly in the hallway.

"Let's get to those bottles, then," Tori said when we got back.

"I still don't understand." Jace peered through the hole he'd made again. "What's so special about a bunch of old bottles?"

"They're from the Prohibition period," Flossie said, as if that should mean everything.

Jace stared at us.

"You couldn't legally buy liquor during that time," Delanie said gently.

"I know that," Jace scoffed. "But they're just old bottles. They can't really be worth that much money, can they?"

I had nudged Jace aside and peered into the room again. "Fifteen, sixteen, seventeen," I counted. "That's how many bottles I see. Who knows how many more are on the floor behind that massive bar? It could be twice as many."

"And . . . ?" Jace prompted.

"And while many old bottles are worth a few dollars, according to our research, some Prohibition-era liquor bottles could fetch as much as a thousand dollars apiece," I explained. "I mean, if those are Hell Hole Swamp bottles, which we all suspect they are. They are in high demand among collectors right now."

"Seventeen thousand." Jace frowned at that. "That's not a fortune, by anyone's measure."

"I think you've lived too long in New York. To some around here, that's quite a treasure," Delanie corrected.

"It is," I agreed. If I could get my hands on that kind of money, I would be able to get my retirement fund back into good shape. "Don't forget how Owen was going around telling people that he expected to come into a windfall soon."

"I heard that he'd been saying that." Jace lifted the sledgehammer and moved to finish demolishing the wall. "He'd stolen money from Landry Goodloe. We brought in a financial forensics team to comb through his accounts to try and find out what happened to the money, which they easily did. He drank it. But they still haven't been able to find where this supposed windfall was going to come from."

"Here." I pointed to the hole he'd just enlarged. "He knew about the bottles from his family history. Fenwick Harrington dies, and Owen sees a chance to turn his life around. He volunteers to take over Fenwick's position as vice president of the museum board, a position that anyone associated with the museum knows is a thankless job and miserable, thanks to Hubert's constant demands."

"Don't forget how he was bothering Doris for information," Tori said.

"I haven't forgotten." The memory kept nagging at me. Doris said that Owen had been obsessed with the fact that Doris's family was one of Cypress's founding families. He had grilled her about her family history. It was one of those things that stuck out like a puzzle piece smashed into the wrong spot.

"When I asked Gracie Mae about Owen's relationship with Doris," Jace said, proving that his investigation and ours had led us in the same direction, "she came at me with such rage that I feared for my safety." He slammed the sledgehammer into the wall again, creating a hole nearly big enough for us to crawl through. "What I don't understand is what led you to suspect that they were after something down in this basement. My investigation hit a wall when I couldn't figure out what Owen had been searching for. How in the world were you able to break through it?"

What could we say? We all silently looked at each other.

"I bet Frank knows the answer to that question." Jace leveled his "detective" glare at me, and my cheeks instantly started to burn. "That's what I thought," he said under his breath.

"I . . . I . . ." I stammered.

"But what about Frank's mystery novel that was found on Owen's body?" Charlie asked in a valiant effort to break the tension.

Jace, who'd kept his gaze locked with mine, raised a brow when that poor abused library book was mentioned. "Yes, what about it?" he asked.

"If Frank has an alibi for the time of Owen's murder, how did the book get there?" Charlie asked.

"The killer put it there," I said. I'd been thinking about that book quite a bit lately. And that was the only explanation that made sense. "The killer planted it to throw suspicion on Frank, who had a motive for killing Owen. That means the killer also has to have access to Frank's belongings."

"Hey, I was going to say that!" Jace exclaimed.

"So this wasn't a crime where Owen was sleeping it off behind the library and accidentally saw someone he shouldn't have seen?" Tori asked.

"Not if I'm right about how things happened." I didn't think I was wrong, but it felt too much like bragging to say that out loud. "I don't think Owen was always involved in the scheme to find and sell these bottles. But I'm sure he was involved at the end." I got down on my hands and knees to see if I could wedge myself through the hole. It looked like it might be a tight squeeze. Maybe if I wiggled I'd be able to get through?

"We know this because of what Doris told us?" Tori asked.

"Partly." I stuck my arm through the wall and tried to reach one of the bottles.

"That still doesn't explain why you think this room and these bottles are the motive for Owen's murder. How did you connect those dots? Where did the idea come from?" Jace simply wouldn't let it drop.

"WWMMD?" Tori blurted, much to my surprise.

"What?" Jace made a face. "Was that even English?"

I stretched. The tips of my fingers brushed against a bottle. It rolled out of reach.

"WWMMD," Tori repeated slowly, as if she thought he was an idiot. "That means 'What Would Miss Marple Do.' Doesn't everyone know that?"

Flossie snorted.

"We've been using that line of thinking as our investigative guide. And that's how we figured everything out. You should try it."

I half squeezed into the hole in the wall and felt around on the concrete floor—praying I wouldn't run my hand over a dead mouse.

"Why do I get the feeling that you're pulling my leg?" Jace asked. "Tru? You've been unusually quiet. What do you have to say?"

"Quiet? I don't know what you mean. I'm a librarian. I adore silence." An overstatement. I wasn't a shusher like Mrs. Farnsworth. But then she was an old, old-school librarian. I reached even farther into the hole.

Jace started to say something else. But I didn't hear him, because at that very moment I wrapped my fingers around the neck of a bottle.

"Bingo!" I cheered.

"Did you know the origin of that word dates to back around the time The Bookroom speakeasy was in operation?" Flossie asked. "I'm not sure how it migrated from the winning of the game of the same name to something someone cheers when completing a task. That would be an interesting research project, don't you think?" I could hear her scratching her pen against her notebook.

It took some hard-core wiggling to squeeze back out of the hole in the wall. Like most things in life, it was harder getting out than it had been to wedge myself in. Finally, I was able to free the dusty, empty bottle from its tomb. Still lying half on my side on the ground, I held it aloft, like a hero returning victorious from some great quest out of one of those fat fantasy novels.

"Oh, you found one," Charlie said.

"Someone shine a light on this." Delanie crouched over me. "Let's see if it's one of the Hell Hole Swamp bottles that are really worth something."

I sat up and polished the bottle with the sleeve of my sweater, which was already ruined from running my arm along the filthy floor. I hadn't returned to my village with a magic elixir. But I had in my hand something better.

Hard evidence of a motive.

"That's a whiskey bottle. A fine one at that," Charlie said as he shone the light from his cell phone onto the bottle's face. There was a lounging unicorn stamped into the side of the semiflattened, amber-colored bottle. "Pre-Prohibition, perhaps. A shame the whiskey isn't still inside it. That's where the real value lies."

Tori had her phone out and was swiping like crazy. "Here it is," she finally said. "Oh. This isn't good. That bottle is worth only about fifty dollars."

"There are others in there," Delanie said. She was peering inside the hole in the wall now. "Perhaps those are the ones worth a fair bit of money?"

"Could be." I ran my finger over the lovely imprint of the unicorn on the bottle. "I imagine Hubert will want to display the bottles in the museum."

"I'm confused," Jace said. "This bottle isn't your treasure?"

"Depends on who is looking at it." Not everything has to have a big, shiny price tag to have value. Not every great historical find needed to be laden with gold, like what Howard Carter had found in King Tut's tomb. Just look at the books in the bookroom. I had taken them from boxes filled with books deemed old and worthless and that were headed for the landfill. But those books were priceless to the readers who checked them out. "The history associated with this find is what's important. It's the history that will enrich us all."

"I'd rather have the money," Delanie grumbled, which was funny considering how she was part of one of the richest families in town. Maybe that attitude was how they became so wealthy. "We need to make the hole bigger."

"I don't know," said Jace. "Your theories are interesting and all. And finding this room is . . . crazy. But I don't see hard evidence here that would provide a motive for Owen's murder. Or even evidence that anyone other than us has been searching for this room."

"Come on now. Don't be stubborn. Someone thought they were going to get rich. That's motive," Flossie argued. "And Tru knows who it is."

"She told us that if all goes according to plan," Tori added, "you'll have a reason to use those handcuffs of yours. And not in a fun way." She glanced over at Charlie, who winked at her in a way that made my best friend blush.

Jace moved to stand directly in front of me. The look on his face made me blush, but not in a good way like Tori. This kind of blush—born of embarrassment and worry—made a patchwork of unsightly red splotches all over my face that looked more like some kind of infectious rash than girly rosy cheeks.

"What have you done, Tru?" He lingered on the end sound of my name, making it sound like "Truuuuuu?"

"Nothing. We set out tonight to prove our point." I knew simply finding the bottles wouldn't provide enough evidence against the particular person I was now sure had committed the crime. "Our killer is growing all the more desperate for the money these bottles might bring."

"What have you done?" he repeated.

"I sent a text. And as we came in, I put the rock that was keeping the back door from being locked back into place." I held up my hand when he opened his mouth to (I was sure) argue with me. "I also sent you a text."

"You sent me a text? As if I'm freaking Rambo, prepared to take on ruthless murderers with no backup? That was your plan?"

"I—"

He didn't give me the chance to defend myself. "You set us up for an ambush."

"No, I didn't."

"You're going to get us all killed."

"But I have a plan."

"You have a—" He cut himself off and closed his eyes. He took a long, slow breath. "I'd better go have another look around." He gave Charlie a nod before leaving.

"Rude." Tori wrinkled her nose. "He didn't even want to hear your plan."

"And it's a mighty fine plan too," Flossie said.

Charlie put his arm over Tori's shoulder. "I think you should share this mighty fine plan with me."

So, we did.

Charlie nodded and smiled as he listened.

"I think that might work," he said once we'd finished.

"He's a keeper." Flossie winked at Tori and then handed the sledge-hammer over to Charlie. "Now, if you don't mind, let's make that hole a little bigger so we can get those bottles out."

Charlie had just started to smash through the wall again when . . .

"Did I miss anything?" a voice sang out.

Chapter Thirty-Five

Oh, it's just you," Delanie said with a great big smile of relief. "You scared us."

Doris wedged herself into the little closet and stood where she was blocking the door. "My goodness, that's a big ol' hole in the wall. Tru, did Mrs. Farnsworth approve of your renovation plans?"

She'd pulled her hair into pigtails, which made her look like a teenager. The smile she flashed was wide and innocent.

"How did you get in here?" Flossie demanded. She turned her wheelchair to confront her.

"Me? Oh." Doris pointed her thumb over her shoulder. "I was walking by and saw the back door sitting wide open. Seemed odd, so I stuck my head in. Called hello and everything. Didn't you hear me? No? Well, that's when I spotted Jace in the hallway. He told me where I could find you."

She sounded so sweet and young, but I suspected that underneath all that sugar was someone who could hit a man over the head with a bottle and feel no remorse for it. Also, I couldn't forget how just a few hours ago she'd tried to get me fired. And she'd done it by trying to expose the secret bookroom, which was worse.

"I feel the need to confess something to you, Doris. I lied to you this morning." I inched toward her.

She was dressed in loose overalls with large pockets that could hold any manner of weapons. She kept her hands hidden behind her back. "I already know what you did." She didn't sound nearly as sugary sweet as she had just a moment ago. "You blabbed to Hennie and got me fired."

"No, I didn't do that. I didn't tell Hennie anything. But I also *didn't* eat your apple pie. I lied when I'd said I had. Mama Eddy tossed it into the trash before I could even smell it."

"Oh, that is a shame. You didn't have to lie about it, though. I would have understood."

I felt a twinge of uncertainty. Had I made a mistake? Were my suspicions wrong about her? Did she really just want to become part of our group?

But then Doris added, "Everyone in town knows your mother is nuts."

Did she just insult my mother?

"Don't go disparaging Mama Eddy. She saved my life, and you know it. You knew the moment you saw me that I didn't eat your apple pie."

"Why are we talking about pies?" Delanie asked. "I thought we'd already dismissed the idea that Owen's death had anything to do with his superior apple-pie-baking skills."

"*We* had dismissed it, and so had the police," I said. "But Owen's killer hadn't known that when she brought a pie to my house. A poisoned pie."

"Doris! You didn't!" Delanie gasped.

"You can't prove—!" Doris shouted, that sweetness act gone quicker than I could have snapped my fingers.

"Oh yes I can. I dug that pie out of the trash and I'm going to hand it over to the police. And don't you try and deny giving it to me. Two police detectives saw you put that pie into my hands."

"But . . . but . . . I didn't bake it. Gracie Mae did. I took it from Hennie's house when I went to pick up some of the educational toys I'd left there. If it was poisoned, that was Gracie Mae's doing. Neither Gracie Mae nor Hennie was there, but Landry heard what happened to you in the park. He gave me the pie to bring to you. He's the one who told me that Gracie Mae had baked it. Perhaps she was trying to do Hennie and Landry in so she wouldn't have to pay back the money Owen took. I don't know. I don't know anything about it."

Again, my confidence faltered a bit.

Was she telling the truth?

Did I get someone else's poisoned pie? Was the pie even poisoned? Or had I convinced myself that it was weaponized to fit the story I was telling myself to explain why Owen had been murdered behind the library? I mean, it did sound awfully fanciful when I stopped to think about it. Doris and Owen both breaking into the secret bookroom to find a way into this old speakeasy so they could sell the bottles in here that in reality really weren't worth very much, indeed!

But then I looked at Doris again, really looked at her.

What was she hiding behind her back?

And where was Jace? He'd been gone an awfully long time.

"Jace!" I shouted, and immediately cringed at how loud my voice sounded. We were in a library, after all. "Jace?" I called again, not as loud.

"What do you have behind your back, Doris?" Charlie asked, talking very slowly.

"Nothing. Just . . . this is how I like to stand. I think y'all are crazy. I should go."

"What did you do to Jace?" I grabbed her arm. Was Jace dead? Was she hiding a bloodied murder weapon behind her back?

He hadn't answered when I'd shouted out to him. He should have answered. Good gracious, he was dead. I'd gotten him into this and now he was dead.

"Doris, do you mind showing us your hands?" Charlie, I noticed, no longer had his arm around Tori's shoulder. He had straightened. The sharp look in his eyes reminded me of how Dewey looked right before he would pounce.

With a violent jerk she dislodged my hand from her arm. That's when we got a chance to see what she was hiding behind her back. Because she shoved them directly at me.

Two enormous Clint Eastwood–sized handguns.

Charlie gave a shout and lunged toward her.

I tried to pull away from her while Flossie, with a crazed look in her eye, rolled toward her.

I appreciated both my friends' valiant efforts to save me. But it was too late. There was no way either of them could knock the guns from that woman's hands.

Not wanting to have to look death in the face, I started to close my eyes. That was when I saw a flash of movement behind Doris.

Jace! The side of his face was bloodied and starting to swell. He moved like a bull charging a matador. Or like a football team's star quarterback. I'd never seen a more welcome sight.

"Doris!" he shouted.

The fool! What was he trying to do? Draw her fire away from me? He was going to get himself shot.

Doris whirled around and shot twice in rapid succession in the same moment that I swung the bottle in my hand, smashing it against her shoulder with all my might.

She collapsed to the ground.

So, sickeningly, did Jace.

At about the same time, Charlie knocked me aside. He landed on Doris and tossed the guns away from her. He looked up at me with worried eyes.

"Tru?" Tori put her arm around me. "Tru? It's going to be okay."

"What did Doris think she was doing?" Flossie demanded. "She had to know that she couldn't take us all on. She couldn't kill us all. There's too many of us."

"I used to babysit her when her mama was working at the diner." Delanie frowned down at Doris. "Even as a tot, Doris had always been ambitious. But she's always made poor choices."

"You shot Jace," I forced through clenched teeth.

"It's your fault. All I wanted to do is take those bottles and start a new life away from this hateful town." Doris didn't sound at all like her sweet, innocent self anymore. She glared at me. "If there was anyone I wanted to shoot, it was you, not your lover boy. You're just like Owen, getting in my way." Her words came quick and forceful. She wiggled around as if trying to get out from under Charlie. "Owen thought he could get to the treasure first. The drunken fool wouldn't have known about how much the bottles were worth if I hadn't gone to him. Fenwick's research had too many holes to help me. But Owen's family had told the tale of running bottles of liquor to Cypress for as long as he could remember. And when he got drunk, he liked to recount those stories. I bought him drinks, and he'd talk. It worked out great until Gracie Mae heard about it and started acting all jealous. Her griping is what got Owen interested in following the trail I'd inadvertently laid for him. That's when he joined the museum board. He then started following me around and acting like he wanted to be my partner. But he needed the money too. I could tell he was going to steal it all out from under me, just like you're trying to do. That's when I knew he would have to be stopped. What's wrong with you? Aren't you going to say something? Are you going to try and deny that it's your greed and lies that just got your boyfriend killed? I am an innocent victim in all of this."

"Tru? Don't listen to her. Tru?" Tori started to rub her hands up and down my arms as if she thought I was going into shock.

I wasn't. I was fine. I wasn't the one who'd just been shot twice. Doris may have wanted to shoot me, but I was the one walking away unharmed.

Jace was lying on the ground. Why wasn't anyone taking care of him?

I tried to move toward him, but Charlie was still sprawled on top of Doris—who squirmed like a feral cat. The two of them completely blocked the doorway.

Even so, I pulled away from Tori. "Jace," I whispered. "I need to get to him."

"No, don't." Tori, tears filling her eyes, tried to grab my arms again. "She shot him at point-blank range. You don't want to see that."

On the other side of the door Candice (wearing an FBI vest) and Police Chief Fisher came bursting down the hall. Fisher took in the scene and uttered a colorful oath that involved backwoods raccoons and a fishing line. Candice glanced down at where Jace had fallen and grimaced. But she didn't stop to help him. She pushed Charlie out of the way, flipped Doris onto her back, and pinned the small woman to the ground.

"What are you doing here?" Charlie barked.

"You know me, Charlie dear. I always hate to miss a party."

Chapter Thirty-Six

Police Chief Fisher knelt down beside Jace. I still hadn't seen Jace's body, since he was on the other side of the doorway, which was still blocked by Doris, Charlie, and now Candice.

I was unable to stand it any longer. If he was dead, it was my fault. My folly had brought us to this. Why in the world did I think I could handle bringing a murderer to justice? Just because I'd read a few hundred (or more) books on the subject? I read fiction. Fiction, for goodness' sake. Well, I'd read a few true crimes and some procedural handbooks, but mainly I turned to fiction for my crime fix.

Justice. I'd been hungry for justice. Who wasn't in this world today?

But in single-minded pursuit of my goal, I'd forgotten about the people around me. I'd forgotten about their safety. And because of that, *this* happened.

"Get out of my way," I growled. I pushed aside Candice, who was slapping handcuffs onto Doris's wrists. Stepped over Doris, who tried to spit in my direction but only managed to get her chin wet. And fell to my knees beside Jace.

His face was covered in blood. His eyes were closed. And the police chief looked quite worried.

I bit back a sob.

"What the hell happened here?" Fisher leveled a hard look in my direction. "I'd ask my detective but . . ." He gestured toward his fallen colleague.

"I . . . I . . ." What did I tell him? Where did I start? "We found a secret room. It's the secret room Doris had been searching for. She simply didn't know the library well enough to know how to get into it."

"And?" Fisher made a rolling motion with his hands to indicate that he wanted me to get to the point of the story.

"And Doris showed up and—"

Jace moaned.

"Jace?" He wasn't dead?

"Stick with us, boy. EMS is on their way," Fisher said. He sounded truly worried.

Jace groaned again. His eyes opened and he turned his bloodied head toward me. His lips parted. Words came out, but they were too soft to hear.

I placed my hands lightly on his chest and leaned closer. His warm breath tickled my ear.

"*You saved me,*" he rasped.

"No, Jace. You saved me. She shot you. Twice."

He shook his head. "*Head. Wounds. Bleed.*" It sounded as if it took quite an effort for him to string the words together.

"No kidding." A bloody Olympic-sized swimming pool was forming on the concrete floor next to his right temple.

His lips pulled up into a weak smile. But then his eyes started to drift closed.

"Keep talking to him," Fisher urged. "Keep him awake. The ambulance is only a few minutes out."

I nodded. "Hey! Jace! Don't leave me. Don't you dare die on me, not after I agreed to go out on a date with you."

His eyes opened halfway. "Just—just grazed me. Not bleeding out."

"What?" What was he talking about?

"The bullet." He closed his eyes again.

"Hey! Where are you taking me on this date? I expect to be dazzled, you know."

"You knocked . . . Doris's arm . . . saved me . . . you know . . . I'll take you . . . nice place . . . Mama would kill me otherwise . . . you are carrying my child." His eyes slid closed again.

Fisher gasped. So did the two EMTs who had chosen that unfortunate moment to arrive.

I moved out of their way so they could get to work at saving Jace. And I prayed they could save him—so I could kill him with my bare hands. "He's kidding. He's kidding," I said. "It's not true. I swear."

"That's a long string of protests there," Candice said as she pulled Doris to her feet.

"What are you doing here?" I asked the FBI agent.

"I followed Ms. Heywood." She nodded toward Doris. "That pamphlet she dropped was the tip-off I'd been looking for."

"The one for her essential oils?" I asked.

"That's what she calls them," Candice said. "But that's not what's in them."

"Do you mean to say that Lida Farnsworth was right?" Flossie asked as she rolled out of the closet now that the door was no longer blocked. "Doris was selling snake oil after all?"

"They're essential oils," Doris shouted. "The best in the industry. I can prove it!"

"They're olive oil and a few kitchen spices and some nasty stuff that could be harmful," Candice said. "Ms. Heywood has been selling them online for nearly a year, making all kinds of claims of healing properties, shipping her counterfeit goods across state lines. We knew the packages were coming from Cypress, but we were unable to uncover who owned the website selling that awful stuff."

"Doris! I've been rubbing that stuff on me for the past three months," Delanie cried.

"It's the best-quality essential oils on the market," Doris insisted.

"Right. Right." Candice pushed Doris toward the library's back door. "And you also didn't just try and shoot that nice detective in the face?"

"I was defending myself. They were all attacking me! You saw it. That big oaf of a bookseller was on top of me when you rescued me. I'm going to sue. I'll sue all of you!"

Chapter Thirty-Seven

Two weeks had passed since Doris's arrest, and Cypress once again resembled the idyllic small town that we all knew and loved, especially this weekend. The weekend of the Fall Festival.

Banners with pictures of pumpkins and apples hung from every streetlight. Children wore red-and-green apple-shaped hats with a green stem and leaf coming out the top that the local women's club had knitted for a fundraiser. Main Street had been closed to traffic to allow vendors from all over the southeast to set up booths featuring artisans' crafts. I had my tote bag slung over one arm. But for once it wasn't filled with books. Instead, I'd filled it with my many purchases. I had apple butter, three kinds of apple jams, pumpkin and apple breads, and my favorite apple salsa.

"Have you seen Jace today?" Tori pulled away from Charlie and hooked her arm with mine. We walked over to a woodworker who'd carved wooden pumpkins with amazing human expressions. "You see that over there?" She nodded toward where Charlie—dressed as sharp as ever—was chatting with Police Chief Fisher. Charlie had five shopping bags looped over his arm. "I have lover boy carrying my shopping bags. You should find that detective of yours and put him to work."

"We haven't talked," I admitted. "Not since that night."

"What?" Tori shouted. People around us stopped their shopping and eating to stare.

"Shh. You're too loud." And I sounded like Mrs. Farnsworth.

"You didn't visit him when he was still in the hospital? You didn't welcome him home when he was discharged over a week ago?"

I didn't. It wasn't that I didn't care. The problem was that I cared too much. Thankfully, Detective Ellerbe had agreed to provide me with frequent updates on Jace's recovery. He and I had texted back and forth multiple times a day. Ellerbe had kept urging me to go to the hospital, because I had been driving him mad with all those texts. But I simply couldn't go. I was too embarrassed to face him.

"Coward," Tori scoffed, and nudged my shoulder. "I bet he's somewhere in the crowd today. You should look for him."

I shook my head. "I'm heading over to check in with Aunt Sal. Since she isn't entering the apple-pie-baking contest this year, they made her a judge. She's been cleansing her taste buds all week by only drinking water and eating bland foods."

"Coward," Tori repeated, but she followed along with me.

Over at the grandstand in the middle of the park, two tables were filled with apple pies waiting to be judged.

There we found Flossie chatting with Mama Eddy and Aunt Sal. Sal had a huge red, white, and blue ribbon attached to her dress. I wondered where she'd gotten it. None of the other judges were wearing ribbons.

"Unhealthy. All of it. You shouldn't agree to judge such a contest. You're putting yourself at risk." I heard Mama Eddy lecturing Aunt Sal as we approached. "I'm sure you've heard how I saved Tru's life by tossing an apple pie one of her friends had brought over for her."

"That's because there was rat poison in that particular pie," I said.

I kissed Mama Eddy on the cheek. "Plus, I wouldn't call Doris my friend. She tried to kill me, twice. That's not proper friendship behavior."

"My goodness. You're looking younger than ever, Mama Eddy," Tori said.

"Stop with your flattery, Victoria," Mama Eddy scolded, but she smiled as she said it.

Aunt Sal was beaming from ear to ear. "I should have given up baking pies years ago. This is the most fun I've had in ages." I accompanied her over to the tables where the pies were waiting to be tasted. She smacked her lips and made various faces as she tasted each one. Everyone watching laughed.

I briefly spoke to friends who were nervously waiting to see what the judges thought of their pies. I wished them all well. This year, any one of them could take home the prize.

A little while later, I spotted Hubert and Frank watching the festival from outside the Cypress Museum. When Hubert saw us, he raised a hand and waved us over.

"Have you finished cataloging the bottles we found at the library?" I asked him.

"We have." Hubert looked enormously pleased. "There were nearly twenty-five bottles in the old speakeasy. Some were cracked. But most were local and will make for a wonderful exhibit. It'll shoehorn nicely with the exhibit Fenny had been preparing on Hell Hole Swamp before his passing."

"Did you hear?" Flossie asked. "The police added Fenwick's murder to the list of charges against Doris. She cleaned his house too. They think he might have caught her trying to steal his research. His body is being exhumed. They expect to find that he was poisoned with the same rat poison that Doris used in her attempt against Tru's life."

"Poor Fenny." Hubert kicked a rock on the sidewalk. "He didn't deserve to go that way."

"What I don't understand is why now?" Frank asked. "Why did Doris get into her head now that those long-forgotten bottles were going to make her rich?"

"Probably from Fenny's own research. If Doris was reading his papers and trying to steal them, I bet that's where she got the idea to go looking for those bottles," Flossie said.

"Were any of the bottles worth anything?" Tori asked.

"They're priceless. Every last one of them," Hubert said with great solemnity.

"You might get a couple of thousand bucks for the lot," Frank said.

"You can't put a value on history," Hubert argued.

"Doris tried to," Tori said, shaking her head. "She's always worked too hard, never slowing down to think. As a result, she ended up with nothing. Less than nothing."

We were silent for a moment, thinking about poor Owen.

Crowds started converging on the bandstand. The judging for the apple pie contest was winding down.

"Are you coming?" Hubert asked us. "They're going to announce the winner."

"I . . ." This experience had violently knocked my love of apple pies clear out of me. If I never saw or tasted another apple pie again, it would be too soon. "I have to get to the library."

We had books to set up. Flossie, Tori, and Charlie accompanied me down the block to the library. Since over half of Cypress's population was at the apple pie festival, the library was practically deserted.

Mrs. Farnsworth was working the front desk. She had her hands full helping an older gentleman navigate the new computer system and didn't notice us come in. We rushed past the two of them and went straight to the basement.

I found a cart and loaded several boxes of books onto it from the storage room where Anne and my friends had hidden the books. I'd been so anxious to get the secret bookroom put back into order that my dreams were nothing more than an endless cataloging and shelving of books. We hadn't been able to bring more than a few books back into the bookroom before today. With the discovery of the speakeasy, the basement had been overrun with historians, reporters, politicians, and all manner of looky-loos. I could only work on setting the room up during the hour before the library opened in the morning.

But with the Fall Festival in full swing, we could finally put the bookroom back into order. With some hard work and a little luck, I hoped we'd finish the work before the library closed for the day.

We carried boxes of books and wheeled the cart over to the secret bookroom's double doors. When I opened them, Dewey came running out with a red crinkly ball in his mouth. He dropped it at my feet and meowed with pride.

"Where'd that come from?" I asked him.

"It came from me," Jace answered for my kitty.

Jace was standing inside the bookroom with his arms crossed over his chest. There were books on the shelves to his left that hadn't been there the last time he visited. Plus, we were all standing in the doorway with boxes of books in our arms and a cart filled with more boxes. It wouldn't take a detective to figure out what was going on.

The air in my lungs seized up.

"Jace," I choked out.

My friends stayed by my side. Dewey looked at me and back at Jace. He let out a loud, unhappy meow.

"What are you doing here?" Flossie asked.

"Visiting with Dewey." He pointed to the crinkly red ball. "I brought him a present. But the poor little guy seems to be missing his books."

"I . . . I don't understand," I stammered.

Jace tilted his head to one side. "Come on now, Tru. Certainly, you didn't think that I was too dense to guess at what was really going on in here."

"I had hoped that you hadn't taken the time to think about it too much." Though I'd lived with a nagging sense of dread ever since Doris had demanded Jace investigate the library's basement, I had hoped that the murder investigation would have kept him from wondering about what he'd seen.

Tori jumped in front of me. "You can't arrest her. I won't let you!"

"Arrest her?" Jace seemed taken aback by the thought.

"I knew taking the books was wrong," I admitted as I stepped out from behind my brave best friend. "They were supposed to go to the landfill, but I couldn't let that happen. I took them and carried them down here. I'd do it all over again, but I'm also willing to face the consequences."

"Consequences?" he echoed.

Was he really going to force me to spell it out for him? Fine. "The consequences for stealing the books."

He looked at me. He looked at the boxes of books. And then he looked down at Dewey. A smile loosened the corners of his mouth. "The way I see it is that you didn't steal anything. The library books are still here, in the library. Heck, they're still being loaned out to the public. What's the crime?"

"Really?"

He came over to me and lifted the heavy box of books from my arms. "Can we talk?" He looked at the crowd that was with me. "Alone?"

I followed him back to the storage room where Anne had hidden the books. We weren't alone in there. Dewey had followed us.

Jace still had a large bandage plastered over one temple. Purple bruises radiated out from under the white gauze. It pained me to look at him. It pained me to think that I'd caused that.

"I'm so sor—" I started to say.

"Are you angry with me?" he asked at the same time.

"Angry with you?" Why would he think that? "No." He was the one who should be angry with me. He'd almost died that horrible night.

"Then why didn't you come and visit me? Why didn't you call? Why don't you answer my texts?"

"I . . . um . . ."

"Is it because I teased you? Fisher told me what I'd said. I don't remember saying it . . . about you carrying my baby. But it does sound like the kind of stupid thing that comes out of my mouth when I like someone and I'm trying to be funny. I'm sorry. I didn't mean to hurt you."

"Hurt me? I didn't come around because of what I had done to you. I couldn't face you. It hurts me to be standing here right now." I pressed my hand to my chest. "It hurts me here knowing that you could have died because of me."

He lifted my hand from my chest and pressed it against his own. I could feel the thump, thump, thump of his heart underneath my palm. "Feel that? I'm fine. And you know what else?"

I shook my head.

He leaned in close and whispered. "If we'd written down our suspects for Owen's murder and put them in an envelope like Charlie had suggested, the name I would have written would have been the same one you wrote."

"Are you bragging?"

"No. I'm saying that I didn't go to the library clueless that night. You made mistakes. But I made some too." He took my hand and held it in his as if it were the world's most precious object. "I think the biggest mistake we made was failing to trust each other. If we had worked together, I doubt anyone would have gotten hurt that night. So, please, don't let what happened two weeks ago get in the way of you agreeing to go out with me. I do remember that you already said you would. You still want to, don't you?"

"Jace," I said. "Stop talking."

He opened his mouth to say something else. I don't think he could help himself. So I kissed him. I kissed him to let him know that yes, I'd go out with him. I kissed him to assure myself that he was alive and healthy. And I kissed him as a silent promise that if we ever faced another murder investigation, I wouldn't keep any secrets from him.

He seemed to understand.

Acknowledgments

Writing a book can be a lonely experience. Writing a book during a pandemic can turn that lonely experience on its head. I never had time alone. I had to work around a family who never left the house.

Never.

I missed that lonely experience.

But it wasn't all bad. I learned how to handle school from home for my amazing daughter and adopted a pandemic puppy that we aptly named Panda. And our morning walks did wonders for our overstressed minds.

I cannot thank my Berkley team enough for being so understanding and awesome. This book wouldn't exist without any of them, especially my editor, Michelle Vega, who has always been in my corner, cheering me on. For this book, I really, really needed that. And thanks to my agent, Jill Marsal, for always being in my corner.

Let me also thank my librarian friends, Leslie Koller, assistant branch manager, for inspiring me and being so generous with your time, and Frankie Lea Hannan, assistant branch manager at my local

Acknowledgments

library. I knew after taking the tai chi classes she taught in the library's meeting room that I'd have to use that in a book.

Thanks to my EMT friend, Lynn Roldan, for making sure I got that part of things right.

And, as always, I need to give a shout-out to my writing tribe. We stand on each other's shoulders in order to climb to new heights.